BUCKLED IN BARBWIRE

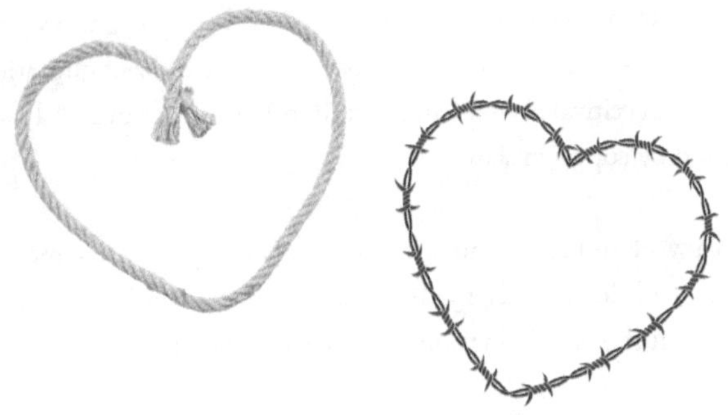

USA TODAY BESTSELLING AUTHOR

HARLOE RAE

NOVELS BY HARLOE RAE

Reclusive Standalones

Redefining Us

Forget You Not

#BitterSweetHeat Standalones

Gent

Miss

Lass

Silo Springs Standalones

Breaker

Keeper

Loner

Quad Pod Babe Squad Standalones

Leave Him Loved

Something Like Hate

There's Always Someday

Doing It Right

I'd Tap That (Knox Creek Standalones)

Wrong for You

Yours to Catch

Score on You

Headed for Home

Cloverleaf Meadows
Buckled in Barbwire

Complete Standalones
Watch Me Follow
Ask Me Why
Left for Wild
Lost in Him
Mine For Yours

Screwed Up (part of the Bayside Heroes standalones)

For my dad. You're gone, but not forgotten. Whenever the sun breaks through the clouds, I feel you shining down on me. I hope I'm making you proud.

And to the women who kick up a fuss to make sure they're cherished like the twinkly treasures they are. But that doesn't mean he can't be the boss when the mood strikes. (; Giddy up!

PLAYLIST

Worst Way | Riley Green
Colder Weather | Zac Brown Band
Fix What You Didn't Break | Nate Smith
LEYLA | Frankie Venter
Haven't Been Talking To You | Sawyer Utah
Pretty Liar | Ken Xox
Country Songs | George Birge
Cowgirl | Parmalee
Hopeless Love Song | Zoe Mellick
Upside Down | Rnla feat. Julia Alexa
This Is What A Broken Heart Looks Like | Marina Lin
Who's Afraid Of Little Old Me? | Taylor Swift
I Had Some Help | Post Palone feat. Morgan Wallen
She Hates Me | Dierks Bentley
Hang Tight Honey | Lainey Wilson
Cowboys Cry Too | Kelsey Ballerini feat. Noah Kahan
Love Is Where You Are | Kadesh

Listen to the *Buckled in Barbwire* playlist on Spotify

"Save the bronco and bang a Benson."
—Mama June Keaton

BUCKLED IN BARBWIRE

CHAPTER ONE

Brody

"**I**'M LEAVING."

Bianca's soft voice cuts into the silence, interrupting my glaring contest with the spreadsheet crumpled in my fist. A glance at my sister makes the profits from our recent livestock auction seem trivial. The tears in her eyes are a punch to the gut. I clench my jaw to avoid the emotion trying to climb up my throat.

"Since when do you tell me about your plans? Go do whatever it is you do all day. I'll be in this exact spot when you're done." My hand motions to the stacks of paperwork demanding my attention.

She fidgets before dropping the bomb. "Um, well… I've decided to take a trip."

"A trip?"

Her head bobs quickly. "To Europe. Alone. Kinda crazy, but it feels right. Germany seems like a good place to start. Not sure where I'll go from there. My flight leaves tomorrow."

I freeze halfway through her speech. Once she's done, a dry chuckle scrapes free from my grimace. "No."

Her watery eyes roll. "I wasn't asking permission."

"Doesn't matter. There's no chance in hell that you're traveling to a different country by yourself. It's way too dangerous. I forbid it."

"You can't stop me. I'm an adult." She lifts her chin at a haughty angle, appearing thirteen rather than twenty-three.

I pinch the bridge of my nose. "You're being reckless. Spend the weekend in Florida or something."

"No, I need an adventure. Somewhere unknown and far away."

"Too bad. We need you here," I counter.

Flames spark in her narrowed gaze. "You don't. As you just so eloquently stated, my contribution around here is meaningless."

"That's not what I said."

Bianca huffs. "Doesn't matter. I'm going."

"You might want to reconsider."

"Why would I do that?"

The ten years that separate us are mocking me. I don't have the luxury of hopping on a plane to abandon the grief. My sister is a fucking princess and has the freedom to do whatever she wants. But it's our fault for allowing this behavior to continue.

My molars are dangerously close to becoming dust at the rate I'm grinding them. "Think about your horses. You don't expect me to just let them stand around and get fat off expensive hay. What's to stop me from selling the spoiled lot at the next auction?"

Am I proud of threatening her? Not really. But these

are tough times. She doesn't get to skip town while I'm stuck in the trenches.

Fresh tears glisten in her eyes. "You wouldn't dare."

"Try me."

"Mom would be pissed at you right now," Bianca rants. "Losing her was painful enough. Don't be such an asshole."

Air expels from my pressed lips in a hiss. She's right, of course. Mother wouldn't condone my behavior. But she's gone. It's my responsibility to keep the rest of our family together. I clench my hand into a tight fist under the desk and resist the urge to punch the wall.

"You have to stay," I command. "Think about Dad. You can't just leave while he's suffering."

She sniffs and drops her gaze. "Don't use him as an excuse."

"Fine. How about me? Consider the position you're putting me in. There's already too much shit on my plate. Dealing with your pampered herd is the last thing I need."

Tension coils tightly between my shoulders as I consider the mountain of demands that require my attention. Overseeing the productivity of our multiple businesses is a full-time job, but that's just the tip of my obligations. Between reviewing weekly output reports and increasing profitability across the deficits, my patience is stretched thinner than foreskin. And that's just the agenda for this afternoon. My head hangs for a very brief reprieve.

I didn't realize how much my mother did for Benson Farmstead until she was gone. With my father out of commission and Bianca choosing to flee the scene, the weight of our empire falls heavily on my shoulders. It's become my responsibility to ensure we remain afloat.

My sister smiles, although the edges wobble. "Lucky for you, I found someone to care for those precious babies in my absence."

The restless energy brewing in my veins sparks as if preparing for battle. "Who?"

"My friend."

"Oh, that narrows it down."

"Paisley."

My expression wipes into a blank slate. "Am I supposed to recognize that name?"

Bianca's grin spreads ever so slightly. "You know who she is."

"Can't say that I do," I drawl.

My sister crosses her arms, staring down at me like I'm a stubborn toddler. "She's the bubbly bundle of sunshine usually at my side. You can't miss her."

And that's the truth. Not that I'll ever admit it. Paisley Keaton might as well be an infected pimple on my ass for how much she annoys me. The pure joy she emits grates on every nerve until I'm rubbed raw. I find it inconceivable that a person can be filled with sheer glee and compassion at every turn. She really outdid herself at the funeral. That reminder flexes my muscles as heat rushes through me.

"Not happening," I grit. "She's not a suitable candidate for the job."

"Oh, puh-lease. Paisley has more cowgirl experience than me."

But I'm not hearing it. "I'll find someone else to handle the horses and barn chores."

My sister scoffs. "Sucks for you, big brother. Paisley

already accepted the position. She started yesterday, gainfully employed by Benson Farmstead."

"Under whose authority? I didn't approve of hiring her." Especially not for the astronomical amount I'm certain Bianca offered to pay her friend.

"Talk to Teresa if you have an issue with her payroll process. My work here is done." She begins backing away.

Family is a soft spot for me, one of my only weaknesses. Bianca is too aware of this and uses it to her advantage. She knows I won't deny her. I'll let her leave and pick up the slack, not that she's expecting me to. Nope. My thoughtful sister hired Paisley to do the honors. Little does Bianca realize, I'd rather wrap my dick in barbwire than grant that woman easy access to my property.

I launch to my feet, crashing the chair into the wall. "Wait a damn minute."

"For what? It's clear you won't wish me well on my journey."

"Fuck." I rake through my hair. "I'm not trying to be an asshole. This isn't what I expected when you stepped into the office."

Bianca nods. "It's been a rough adjustment, which is why I can't be here. Just… give me time. I'll be back."

"When?"

She shrugs. "I can't say for sure. But I won't be gone for good."

My mind spins in too many directions. "Why doesn't Paisley go to Europe with you? Then you won't be alone."

"Nope. I need to do this for myself. Soul searching," she says.

This evasive maneuver shouldn't come as a surprise.

We've been coping in our own separate ways since my mother passed two months ago. Her death shattered our family at its core, testing our strength. Dad was the first to crumble. He's a shell of his former self. If I went searching, I'd find him sitting alone with only a bottle of scotch for company.

I flatten a palm on my abandoned paperwork. "Did you tell Dad?"

"Tried. He's in a sour mood." Which is a polite term for his benders.

My exhale is choppy. "Well, make sure you say goodbye before you go."

"You're giving me permission?"

I almost laugh. "Thought you didn't need it?"

She fidgets with the hem of her shirt. "I don't, but I'd still like your approval."

My boots scuff on the hardwood as I round the desk, resting my ass on the edge. "Promise to be careful?"

"Yes, I promise." Bianca squeaks, dashing across the room to wrap me in a hug. "Thanks, big bro."

I pat her back. "There's one condition."

My sister straightens, suspicion tightening her features. "What?"

"Colton is going with you."

"Absolutely not." Her arm slices through the air.

"Just to keep you safe," I continue.

Bianca is shaking her head. "I don't need a babysitter."

"Think of him more as a bodyguard."

"No."

"Yes," I spit. "This isn't a negotiation. If you leave without anyone watching out for you, I'll follow and drag you back home myself."

She draws in a slow breath. "Fine, but you have to do me a favor in return."

I grunt. "Not sure you're in a position to ask for anything."

"Don't give Paisley too much crap, okay?"

"No guarantees."

"I figured you'd say that," she quips. "Good thing I offered her a hefty salary to make it worth her while. And if she's forced to deal with your surly attitude, she gets a bonus!"

"You must be joking."

"Not even a little bit. Just stay out of her way and you won't bleed money." My little sister winks and retreats to the door. "Good luck."

Those parting words sit heavy on my chest. For whatever reason, I feel like I'll need all the luck I can get.

CHAPTER TWO

Paisley

IDLE CHATTER MIXES WITH THE SWANKY COUNTRY song streaming from the overhead speakers. I scan the familiar faces gathered at our local watering hole. As someone raised halfway between here and Knox Creek, I have several options within close range. But my loyalty falls on this side of the fence. Cloverleaf Meadows is home.

It's a typical crowd for a Wednesday night as we attempt to take the edge off after the daily grind. The Paddock grants us a reprieve from our troubles in the form of cheap booze and good company. That's what keeps us coming back for more.

Coffee beans get lost in foam when I take a sip of my espresso martini. This Western-themed dive bar—or old-fashioned saloon, if I'm being generous—might resemble the interior of a barn, but their cocktails can rival any upscale city joint. And at a fraction of the price.

Movement from my left pulls me from those random thoughts. I swivel on my stool to face my best friend as she props her elbow on the wood counter. Bianca has been unusually quiet since we arrived thirty minutes ago. My focus doesn't waver while she twirls a dark strand of hair around her finger, appearing lost in thought.

"Hey," I murmur. "Will you be okay?"

Her responding laugh borders on shrill. "You're asking me?"

"Um, yeah?"

She waves me off. "I'm worried about how you'll manage without me."

"It'll be a real struggle," I admit. "But I'm glad you decided to go."

"Really?"

"Absolutely. You're chasing what your heart desires. That's a dream come true. An adventure of a lifetime." I flick my wrist for theatrical flair. "Not many people get to fly across the ocean to visit a foreign country for as long as their heart desires."

She gnaws on her bottom lip. "Seems pretty crazy, huh?"

"It's incredible." Not that I'd ever be brave enough to follow in her cowboy boots.

Her lashes flutter as moisture collects in her eyes. "You don't think I'm running away?"

"No." My voice clangs with conviction. "There's nothing wrong with leaving your struggles by the door while you kick your feet in a beautiful fairytale cottage."

Bianca exhales, slumping lower in her seat. "Mhmm, sounds like paradise."

"Definitely."

Her nod is resolute. "This is exactly what I need."

I rub her back, my palm moving in soothing circles. "You'll be able to breathe easier over there."

"Gosh, I hope so." A small smile touches her lips. "And I hope she'd be proud of me for taking the leap."

"Very much so. It was practically her idea, right? She'll be watching over you every step of the way."

"I'll find her in the sunrise."

"And in your heart," I add.

A single tear rolls down her cheek. "I can't believe she's gone."

An ache spreads through my chest. That hollow throb hasn't ceased in the months since Marion Benson's life was snatched in an instant. I was there when she collapsed. It's a moment that haunts me.

My nose stings and I sniff. "She will never be forgotten, Bee. Her spirit lives in your memories. That's how you keep her with you forever. Just think about her and then she's there."

Bianca rests her head on my shoulder when I loop an arm around hers. "That's a beautiful sentiment. I'm sure she's smiling at us right now, surrounded by peace and love."

"Along with Mimi," I whisper. My grandmother passed years ago but her loss still feels like a fresh wound on certain days.

"They're probably riding Secretariat and Seattle Slew as we speak."

"Yeah." I reach for my drink to chase off the tightness in my throat. "What a race that would be."

Bianca straightens and wipes at her face. "Whew, okay. Enough of that. I swore to myself that I wouldn't cry all over you tonight."

My lips wobble as I smile. "You know I don't mind."

She shakes her head. "I'm already taking advantage of your kindness."

"Hardly," I scoff. "That champion herd of yours is better stocked than a fantasy team."

"But you have your own to worry about. My horses are very demanding. They'll test your patience on the daily."

"Challenge accepted," I boast.

"What if your parents need you at the store?"

"Just on the weekends when the market is open. Gemma and Ryder are still home from college for a few more weeks. They can take extra shifts," I tell her. "Quit stressing. There's nothing to worry about. You're doing me a favor by keeping me busy. How else will I pass the time while you're gone?"

Bianca purses her lips. "Go on a date. Get laid. Maybe find a handsome fella to claim as your boyfriend. You're gonna get lonely without me."

"Not possible. I'll be surrounded by your most prized possessions. There won't be a dull moment." I grin while envisioning the extra hours I'll soon be spending in the saddle.

"You should bring Ritzy and Maverick to the ranch."

My smile spreads at the mention of my two horses. "That's not necessary. I can go back and forth."

She flicks off the suggestion. "There are empty stalls and an extra corral for them. Plenty of pasture too. Why waste time and energy?"

"Are you sure?"

"Absolutely."

"Shouldn't you ask—?"

"Nope," she cuts in. "This is my decision. You're going

out of your way for me. The least I can do is pave the road for you."

I laugh at her choice in phrasing. "It would make my life easier."

"Consider it done." She brushes her palms together. "Feel free to haul any of mine to jackpots and rodeos while you're at it. Don't let them get lazy. It's tough to get them conditioned."

"Uh-huh, whatever. Those natural athletes could get a year off and still be in competitive shape."

"That type of attitude will lead slackers to the trough." Bianca wags a finger at me.

"Okay, fine. I won't let them stray from the circuit." An exaggerated exhale sends my hair flying. "This is a dream gig, Bee. Not sure why you insist on paying me. It should be the other way around."

My bestie giggles into her cocktail. "As if. Can you imagine? It's the least I can do for abandoning you. Besides, how else will you keep The Paddock in business while I'm away?"

"That's a fair point." My concentration drifts across wagon wheels and whiskey barrels, leading to the far corner where Bucky rests. Fire singes my cheeks while a very specific memory involving that mechanical bull floats to the surface. I square my shoulders while gathering courage to ask my next question. "How did Brody take the news?"

"Better than expected." But her grumbled tone suggests otherwise. "He tried bossing me around, but soon realized that I wasn't backing down."

Just thinking about Brody Benson's grumpy demeanor elevates my temperature. I swallow another swig of espresso martini for liquid courage. "Did you tell him that I'll be in charge of your barn?"

Her nod synchronizes to the upbeat song telling us to *shake it off.* "I strongly advised him to stay away from you."

The boozy concoction gets stuck in my throat and I choke. "What? Why?"

"You don't need his broody brand of assholery blocking your path. He'll just drag you down and cause problems." Bianca tosses a glare over her shoulder at the shadowed figure darkening the corner. "Like that pain in my plans. He's starting his guard duty early. Freaking loser."

My gaze joins hers to scrutinize how Colton is failing at blending into the background. "Could be worse. At least he's nice to look at."

"But his personality is more abrasive than a brick wall."

"That's probably why your brother assigned him to this task. You'd have any other guy eating out of your palm before landing overseas."

Bianca offers a noncommittal *hmph* in response. "Don't give Brody any credit. Not one inch. He'll use it against you. That's how you end up looking weak and stuck with security detail."

Laughter bursts from me to tease her sour expression. "He's just watching out for you, Bee."

"That's a nice way of putting it, which he doesn't deserve." A gentle smile betrays her grumbling. "I shouldn't be too hard on him. He's doing so much for our family and the business. I'd crack under the responsibilities he had to accept practically overnight. But he's different too. Colder. Maybe that's how he manages to keep himself together."

A painful sting spreads across my upper body and I flinch. "That sounds… really rough. Is he okay?"

She's quiet for a moment, heavily chewing on contemplation. "He's probably fine. The man acts like a machine. I think the constant workload helps him cope. He needs purpose. That driving force."

"Are you sure?"

"No."

I pause before asking, "Have you talked to him about your mom?"

"A little." She crosses her arms and avoids my questioning stare. "He's ignored the subject whenever I've asked."

I bob my head, recalling how Brody reacted when I broached the topic of his feelings at their mother's funeral. "Grief is…"

"A real bitch," Bianca finishes for me and hitches her shoulders. "Don't worry about Brody. He's got a support system to lean on if he chooses. Our dogs and horses are great listeners. The rest of the animals aren't too bad either."

"Not to mention the horde of women ready to soothe his aches and pains," I mumble under my breath.

"Gross." My friend shudders and pretends to retch. "Don't talk about my brother and *women*. As if I need that visual stamped in my brain. How traumatic."

"Whoops," I laugh. "Figured it was common knowledge."

"Puh-lease," she drawls. "Brody might be a virgin for all I know. He's never brought a girl home to meet us."

That stops me short. "Interesting."

"Not really. Why are we still discussing my brother's dating habits?" Her eyes narrow on me. "Are you interested in him?"

"What? No," I sputter. "I don't even know him. We're practically strangers, which is odd since you're my best friend. It's almost like he pretends I don't exist."

Bianca swats at that comment, gaining the bartender's attention. She graciously accepts the opportunity to order another round of drinks from Sal. "Brody's a busy guy. Don't take it personally."

"I don't."

Her watchful stare is still glued to my face, prepared to spot a slip. "You'll rarely see him in the barn, but he's never far if you need help. He's reliable like that. I'll put his number in your phone just in case."

My focus is riveted to her fingers tapping on my screen. "Seems fair enough."

"Glad that's settled," she chirps. "I don't want to spend my last night in the States gushing about my brother."

"Me neither." Our fresh martinis arrive, and I drift my fingers along the delicate stem. "I'm gonna miss you, Bee."

"So very much, Lee." Bianca plops a noisy smooch on my cheek. "I'll be back before you know it."

That's when I notice our fellow patrons throwing sympathetic looks at Bianca. "Our public display is gathering attention. We've got rubberneckers."

My friend glances at those nearby. "They're waiting for me to crumble."

"But you won't."

"Just might if I stay in town. I have to escape this"—she motions wildly around the room—"before I turn into a hermit and never leave the house."

I nudge her with my elbow. "As if I'd ever let that happen."

"Putting thousands of miles and the Atlantic Ocean between me and Cloverleaf Meadows should help. Tomorrow can't come soon enough. Cheers." Bianca raises her glass.

Nerves bubble in my stomach as I lift mine to clink against hers. "Here's to finding exactly what you need where you least expect it."

CHAPTER THREE

Brody

MY MEASURED STRIDE KICKS UP DUST ON THE TRAIL that leads to the north pasture gate. "Good to see you out and about for a change."

Dad doesn't turn as I approach, continuing to stare at the grassy field straight ahead. "Shouldn't you be working?"

I chuckle and scrub over the stubble on my jaw. "Could ask you the same question."

"You've got it under control."

The confidence he's dumped on me isn't misplaced, but some active involvement in the company would be appreciated. Especially with certain conflicts.

"Uncle Jimmy is breathing down my neck," I mutter.

My father's posture goes rigid at the mention of his brother. He straightens off the fence post, turning slightly to meet my stare. "About what?"

"He wants to sit at the head of the table. Believes he's more fit for the leadership role considering your current…

lack of interest." I won't go into specifics about our most recent conversation, but it gave me an idea.

Which might pay off if the steely glint in my father's gaze is any indication. "Don't let that greedy bastard bully you. He should be grateful I let him run the auction barn. Maybe I'll demote him to trailer sales. That'll give him something to complain about."

A dry chuckle escapes me. "I wouldn't be opposed."

Dad's hand clenches into a fist as if he's aiming for his brother's inflated ego. "We're mourning and he tries to take ownership of the whole company? Nope. But good on him for trying."

"And this isn't his first attempt to restructure," I remind.

"That asshole better back off or we'll remind him of his place."

"How might we do that?" I'm practically salivating at the possibilities.

Dad goes quiet, his glare softening at the edges. "Just tell him to stay in his lane."

"Call him yourself then, and pass along the message." I brought up my uncle's treachery in an attempt to light a fire under Dad's ass. The momentary spark is already dwindling, but it's not snuffed yet.

At least until the fight bleeds from him and he slumps against the fence again. "Nah, Jimmy's a little shit, but he's right about me. I'm not in a state to be calling the shots. My mind isn't sound."

I appraise Dad's disheveled appearance from under the straw brim of my cowboy hat. This man lost the better half of his soul. There's no real recovery after such a devastating hit. That doesn't mean I'll quit trying to drag him out of the fog.

"But you can't let him keep pushing us like this," I urge.

"No, *you* can't." He tosses me an empty look that squeezes my lungs. "That's why I've put you in charge, Brody."

I scoff. "Just until you get back on your feet."

Dad waves at the summer air. "Consider the promotion permanent."

My brows fling to the clouds. "Are you going to make an official announcement?"

"When you're ready," he evades. "It's just a title. You're already the boss where it counts."

"Depends who you ask." A certain pain in my ass would disagree. Uncle Jimmy's nose is shoved so far into my business that he might as well be giving me a prostate exam. If he's not careful, I'll let one rip and forever taint his sense of smell.

Dad's vacant stare roams over me like icy fingers probing at personal territory. "Am I putting too much pressure on you?"

"No."

His haunted focus doesn't relent. "Would it be easier to share more of the responsibilities with your uncle?"

Frustration bubbles to the surface and I swallow a bellow. I've poured myself into this job. Our legacy. The nonstop demands keep me occupied, not allowing me to dwell on pain and sorrow. Business is easier to manage than emotions.

"I've got us covered, Dad. You can count on me."

"That's my boy. You're the one meant to continue our success. Don't let anyone assume otherwise."

"I won't." My spine straightens into a titanium rod. "You have nothing to worry about."

"Other than miss my wife with every beat of my broken heart. I can mourn her in peace knowing you're at the helm of our company," he mumbles.

Air whistles between my teeth from that sucker punch. "Fuck."

"Make me proud. For your mom's sake." Dad grips my shoulder, stronger than I would've given him credit for. "And if you don't mind, I'd like to be left alone now."

A retort is perched on my tongue like a sharpened blade, ready to annihilate his despondence. But then a car door slams and our attention swivels toward the sound. Paisley struts across our property as if she owns the place. Sunlight bathes her hair, spinning the strands into pure gold. Her athletic tank top is fit for the August heat, but the snug style molds to her breasts very *unprofessionally*. Especially for her first day on the job.

Not that it matters what she wears. I couldn't care less, which reminds me where my concentration belongs.

"Better get back to the office," I grumble while backing away from this disaster waiting to happen.

My father's eyes are narrowed in the blonde's direction. "Is that the oldest Keaton kid?"

My retreat halts and I snort. "More commonly known as Bianca's best friend."

"What's she doing here?"

I rip my gaze off our new employee to gape at the man

who rules this roost. "Your daughter didn't tell you before she left?"

"Why, yes. Of course. This is the expected response from somebody in the loop." His sarcastic retort almost makes me smile.

"Bianca hired her to manage the barn while she's gone. We also gained two more horses in the process."

"Interesting," Dad muses.

"Not really. I tried to talk her out of it."

"And why would you do that?" There's no missing the conniving lift in his tone.

My eyes stray to where Paisley is petting my sister's favorite gelding. I become captivated by her even strokes along the palomino's neck. She doesn't notice us or chooses to ignore our presence. Most likely the latter.

"We don't need her help," I grind out.

"Are you planning to keep those horses in shape? How about mucking out the stalls?"

I grunt at the suggestion that my sister does dirty work. "Bianca hasn't touched a pitchfork since she dressed as a devil for Halloween in third grade."

"No matter. It gets done on her watch." Dad's attention slides toward the corral. "Decent stock."

I send him a curious look. "Bianca won't settle for less than the best bloodlines."

"Not talking about the horse." If I didn't know better, I'd think amusement colors his tone.

"She's not a broodmare."

"Could've fooled me with the way you're ogling her hindquarters."

I cut my gaze off Paisley, taking a sudden interest in the dirt. "Don't be ridiculous."

"Holy shit," my father hoots. "Are you blushing?"

My eyes snap to his laughing face. This is what it takes to get a rise out of him? Fuck, I'll sacrifice my dignity to prolong his boost in mood. It's not like anyone else is around to witness my unconventional methods. A sideways glance proves that Paisley is still ignoring our existence.

"She's a walking distraction," I mutter. "A liability waiting to happen."

He pats me on the back. "Might as well be a marriage proposal."

"Fuck that." And forget putting on a show for his benefit.

Dad's chuckle threatens to thaw my frozen heart. "Happens before you realize you're too far gone. You're completely in control one minute, living your best bachelor life. The next, a pretty filly prances across your path to rearrange your priorities."

"Not gonna happen to me."

A disturbing twinkle flashes in his stare. "Don't act like it's a hobble on your freedom. Couldn't be further from the truth. The day I convinced your mother to spend her life at my side was the best thing that ever happened to me."

"That was different."

But for some inexplicable reason, my focus strays to where the blonde is bent over to give me a peek at her cleavage. I tug at the collar of my western shirt that's suddenly too suffocating. Unlike Paisley's casual outfit, the straw hat on my head is the only proof that I relent to the heat. From the neck down, I'm dressed in my standard button-down and Wranglers combo. I wouldn't be caught in fiery hell wearing less. That's when I notice my jaw is clenched hard enough to slice through wire. A long exhale loosens the strain but it's too late.

My dad's attention is taking a leisurely loop from the hired help to me. His thoughts are loud enough to be audible, but he still voices them. "She'll be good for morale."

"Maybe where you're concerned." I'm willing to admit that woman has scared off Dad's demons for a few precious moments. Meanwhile, mine remain securely locked away and heavily guarded.

"Mhmm, already chasing off the gloom." He flicks his fingers to where Paisley has her face tipped to the sky. "We can use a dose of sunshine. You especially."

I don't appreciate the direction of his scheming. "That's my cue to get gone."

"Not so fast." His hand on my arm stills my retreat. "Go welcome Ms. Keaton to our farmstead. I'm gonna call my brother and silence his complaints or I'll give him something to actually bitch about."

That gives me pause. My mouth works silently for a moment. I'd rather get fucked by a thistle than confront Paisley, but my father is willing to do something other than drown his sorrows in whiskey. My earlier conviction resurfaces. Dad's revival is worth the annoyance of introducing myself to our new barn manager.

I'll give Paisley the treatment she deserves, just like every other weed that dares to pollute my path. She'll have her head bowed and spirit broken before lunch.

CHAPTER FOUR

Paisley

I ANGLE MY SCREEN HIGHER, BUT BANDIT'S LARGE HEAD is still cut off. The palomino stands patiently while I attempt to fit us in the frame for a picture. No such luck. As it turns out, I haven't perfected the skill of snapping a selfie with a horse. Bianca will appreciate an update regardless.

"You're off to a productive start. Why am I not surprised?"

A gasp rips from me as I whirl to confront the gruff voice. My phone almost drops into a pile of manure from the abrupt motion, but I barely notice the bobble. Not while Brody Benson is leaning on the paddock gate, glaring at me. I gulp at the sudden dryness in my throat.

"Um, hi. I didn't see you there."

"Wonder why," he deadpans. "Is this what I can expect from your work ethic?"

I blink at the snark in his tone. "Is everything okay?"

"You tell me."

"I'm fine. You're the one…" I trail off and gesture at his surly expression.

Brody's scowl deepens into a sharp point that punctures my confidence. "This is what you get for slacking off while on the clock."

I'm shocked silent by his obvious irritation. "Slacking off?"

"What would you call it?"

"I'm doing my job."

"You're not getting paid to be a photographer."

The smile I give him is honey slathered on a thorn bush. "It won't break the bank if I take a quick pic. Bianca approves of my methods. You can trust me too."

"I'd rather eat horseshit."

In a fluid motion, he hops the fence and lands in the dirt. The loss of the barrier between us feels detrimental. I'm an open target as he stalks toward me. Brody's stride is a lethal prowl, like a predator hunting the stench of weakness. Nerves punch my stomach the closer he gets. We've only been alone on one other occasion and that didn't end well.

But that previous stumble doesn't register in this moment. I'm too preoccupied by his steady approach, and the fantasy he represents. It's no secret I've always been attracted to cowboys. Brody turns that general interest into a specific point.

The shade from his straw hat does little to conceal his devastating features. I almost choke on my tongue. My ovaries are singing hallelujah and ready to spit out eggs like a firing squad, which is wrong on so many levels.

But damn, he's sexy. Such a manly man. The complete opposite of those sorry excuses for masculinity who parade around rodeo chutes after just sprouting their first chest hair. Don't even get me started on his Wranglers. Brody is distinguished and chiseled and striking and… I'm staring. He notices my blatant ogling, which sets fire to my cheeks.

"Aren't you hot?" I blurt.

His eyes smolder into green flames. "Excuse me?"

"I'm hot just looking at you."

"And now you're hitting on me," he mutters under his breath. "This just keeps getting better."

"What? No." My cackle is shrill. "You're wearing long sleeves and it's almost ninety degrees. I'd be sweltering in that shirt."

"My clothes aren't your business, but your poor work ethic is mine."

I recoil from the hostile barb. "Are you upset about something?"

His penetrating glare is beginning to give me a complex. "What was your first clue?"

"Your sister assured me that we"—I point from his chest to mine—"won't have any problems."

"She isn't here to keep that promise. You let her run off."

Static crackles in the air, raising the hair on my arms. "I didn't *let* her do anything. Bianca is in control of her own destiny. I just offered to help so the decision to leave wouldn't weigh on her."

He snorts. "Must be nice."

"Maybe you're the one who needs a vacation," I hint.

Which is the wrong suggestion to offer. There's blistering fury in Brody's stare, ready to be unleashed. "Listen, Twinkles—"

"Twinkles?"

"You're so"—he waves a hand at my rhinestone belt and bling jeans—"sparkly."

"Should I take that as a compliment?"

"Absolutely not. You're too much."

I blink at the attitude he's flinging my way. "Too much?"

"Are you going to question everything I say?"

"Can you blame me when you're making ridiculous statements that I don't comprehend? I'm beginning to feel like this is an interrogation."

He grins but the expression is cold and detached. "Glad we're finally on the same page."

My mind gallops to uncover the reason why his anger targeted me. Our only other interaction was when I tried to offer him comfort and he swiftly dismissed my attempt. Considering the circumstances, I shrugged off his cruel words easily enough. It seems like grace might still need to be granted. That's reasonable to a certain extent.

Silence stretches and expands while I study the fury curling off Brody like wisps of smoke. This guy recently lost his mother. Marion Benson was the center stone that kept everyone else settled. Since she passed, her family has been scattered about and forced to reassemble. This new normal is badly broken but trying to mend. There's more strength in that than they give themselves credit for.

I'm not a therapist or an expert in grief, but it's obvious that Brody is struggling. Maybe this is how he copes. He lashes out when the pain demands a release. I just so happen to be conveniently located, and I'm willing to handle his temper for a few rounds. But I don't dare voice that offer aloud.

The main reason being that his attack feels personal.

More than suppressed mourning. I'm not volunteering to be his doormat.

Bandit nudges my arm and knocks me from the spiral. I drift my palm down the slope of his head, taking comfort in the familiar motion. The palomino's gentle shove reminds me that he's at my side and I'm not alone. It also gives me the courage to stand taller.

"I think we've gotten off on the wrong hoof," I joke. "Regardless of what you believe, I'm not trying to overstep. Your sister hired me to do a job, and I plan to do it well. There's nothing for us to fight about."

Brody bends until our faces are level and the brim of his hat almost thumps my forehead. At this distance, I get a tantalizing whiff of crisp pine and mayhem. It's too tempting. My concentration buzzes and blurs at the edges. His clean scent has me picturing him fresh from the shower, only a towel wrapped around his waist. The visual of stray droplets trickling along his muscles doesn't pass the current vibe check. I scold myself and decide to take Bianca's advice about going on a date.

That resolve gains momentum when Brody's glare narrows into sharpened blades. "This is a family matter, and you're not family. You don't belong here."

I suck in a sharp breath. That statement is similar to the one he spat at his mother's funeral. Heat stings my eyes, but I refuse to cry. He'd probably rejoice in my tears. Forget that. I can handle his wrath and beat him with sweetness. He'll look like an ass, at least to me. What I won't recover from is letting him see how his words hurt me.

It's a small victory that my voice doesn't tremble when I ask, "Are you planning to fire me?"

Veins bulge in his neck as he seems to fight with himself to take the bait. "Nah, you'll choose to leave on your own. I'm just showing you the fastest exit."

The urge to flee almost quakes my knees, but I won't let him intimidate me. "How considerate."

His eyes blaze when I add more fuel to the fire. Brody crosses his arms and widens his stance, towering over me like a thunder cloud. "Is this how you speak to your boss?"

"Not usually, but I'll let you know after I talk to her later."

Steam very well might be spewing from his ears. "You're being insubordinate. That's grounds for termination."

"Do you have the power to make that decision?" I paste on a demure grin that's suitable for chapping his ass. "Besides, you said I'd be the one to quit."

His jaw clenches until a joint twerks in his cheek. "Might not be fast enough if you keep testing my patience."

"Well, too bad. I'm not going anywhere. Your sister is relying on me and I won't let her down. Until she returns, you're stuck with me."

"I won't make it easy on you."

Just to prove my lady balls are swinging for the challenge, I give Brody a slow once-over. "Fine by me."

CHAPTER FIVE

MY SHRILL WHISTLE ALERTS THE DOGS TO GO after a lone calf skipping away from the herd. Almost immediately, another one trails off in the opposite direction. Frustration bubbles to the surface as I steer my horse toward the straggler. What a clusterfuck. This interruption puts me behind schedule, and I can't afford to waste a second.

My glare whips across the pasture as the cattle finally begin backtracking on their escape attempt. Somebody forgot to close the south gate. All signs point to Paisley. I wouldn't put it past her after I deleted her access code for the driveway entrance. It didn't delay her for more than a minute. That flashy cowgirl rang the bell incessantly until Dad came to her rescue. But this hassle is next level.

I'd love nothing more than to send her packing. Too bad Bianca refuses to consider the idea, or my opinion on the matter. My sister only makes the situation worse—insisting I stay out of Paisley's path. As if it's that simple.

The twinkly bundle of sunshine appears everywhere I go, whether she's directly in front of me or plaguing my memories. Bianca has been friends with Paisley for years but suddenly I can't escape her. If I didn't know better, I'd assume the universe was conspiring against me and shoving us together. That nonsense gets my blood boiling hotter.

"C'mon," I beckon to the livestock version of a traffic jam. "Hurry up."

"I'm coming, I'm coming. Keep your chaps on."

My ass swivels in the saddle to watch Paisley's uninvited entrance. Her blonde hair is mostly hidden under a baseball cap, but she still manages to glow. She smiles at me like we're friends. That couldn't be further from the truth. We've been flinging shit at each other since she started her job a week ago. Although, her insults tend to be dipped in sugar and sprinkles, which is even more aggravating. She makes me feel like the bad guy.

If I'm being honest, she makes me feel a lot more than that. I've managed to keep a lid on my bottled emotions until she showed up to shatter my composure. I'm not capable of smothering my temper when she's nearby. There's something deeply unsettling about that woman. She rattles me to the core.

And right now is no different. She rides my mother's favorite buckskin mare like the horse now belongs to her. The pair moves fluidly as one, approaching at a leisurely lope. Paisley's tits sway to the beat of the smooth gait. Whoever designed her sports bra should be fired. That gentle jiggle is obscene, and I can't quit looking.

I tip the brim of my hat at her. "Twinkles."

"Boss." She flutters her lashes.

My jaw ticks but I swallow the barbed retort ready to spank her. "To what do I owe this pleasure?"

"Your dad sent me. He figured you could use a hand corralling the cows."

"Did he now?" I almost smile.

What can I say? The notion is comical. Last I saw, my father was holed up in his den and having an intimate chat with Johnny Walker. He shouldn't know about the cattle getting loose. I didn't want to burden him, which means he found out from someone else or this debacle is a different sort of mess entirely. Maybe Paisley deserves more credit. Not that I'll willingly give it to her.

Paisley is staring at me like I've sprouted horns. "Is that funny?"

"Hilarious," I rasp. The start of a headache throbs at my temples. "Thanks for the offer, but I don't need your help."

"Ohh-kayyyy," she exhales. "Well, I'm already out here."

"Good for you. Feel free to show yourself back to the barn."

"After I'm done securing the herd." She nudges her horse forward, easing into a trot that bounces her breasts again.

I gnaw on a curse and follow after her. "Do you ever listen?"

"When someone says something worth hearing."

That sassy mouth could be put to better use. Paisley's posture stiffens as if I voiced that suggestion aloud. When she glances over at me, her blue eyes gleam in warning. An ache spreads through my chest. The pain and suffering are just waiting to be purged. If I'm not careful, she'll conquer my darkest secrets. Talk about a trap.

Instead of creating more trouble for myself, I decide to stew in silence. We round up the cows easily enough and push them ahead where they belong. I'll never admit it but the task is completed much faster thanks to her.

Once the gate is locked, Paisley rides off without a backward glance. Fine by me… except I'm stuck watching her go. She sits deep in the saddle but I still get a decent view. That curvy ass hugged in denim and bling does wild things to my imagination. Fuck.

I scrub a palm down my face. "Enough of that."

My horse snorts to call bullshit. The sound of his betrayal echoes across the lush acres surrounding us. Responsibility rests heavy on my shoulders as I signal for him to move us along. There's a fresh pile of contracts demanding my attention in the office.

But those demands will have to wait a bit longer when I catch sight of Dad at the chicken coop. He kicks at the door, which is hanging crooked from one hinge. Paisley is standing right there beside him as if her sparkling personality will solve this issue.

I tug on the reins, pulling my horse to a stop next to them. "How did that happen?"

My father shrugs. "Beats me. I was taking a stroll, minding my own business, when I spotted the cock racing outta the henhouse. Assumed he got himself in hot water until I saw the busted door gave him a clean break."

The exhale that breezes from me is weary. "I don't have time for this."

"Too bad, kid. Gotta take care of this before the chickens become fox food."

"I'm aware." My knees creak as I swing off the saddle and squat to check the damage. I find the missing hinge on the ground. "You've got to be kidding me. The damn thing is bent in half."

"Huh." My father purses his lips. "That's odd."

"Sure is," I drawl. "First the cows and now the coop. What's next?"

Paisley blanches. "You shouldn't ask that."

Dad pats her shoulder. "No need to fret. It's just a strange coincidence. Might be a sign to take it easy for a change and smell the clover."

I pinch the bridge of my nose. "That's not an option for me."

My dad scoffs. "You're the boss. Take the day off and get stuff done around the farm."

"I have to keep our multiple businesses afloat or we'll lose the farm," I grumble. But the door needs to be repaired. "Maybe I have a spare hinge in the shop. If not, I'll make a trip to town."

"There's the solution we need. I can always count on you to get the job done." Dad begins backing away.

"Where do you think you're going?"

He huffs and puffs and damn near blows the entire structure down. "What do you want me to do? I sure as shit can't fix it."

"Maybe I can," Paisley chirps.

"Not by yourself," I growl. "The wood is too heavy."

My dad nudges her. "Told you he woke up on the wrong side of the stable this morning."

She giggles. "He isn't always this grumpy?"

"Nah, my son is a true delight. Don't let his recent behavior fool you."

"I'm beginning to think he doesn't like me," Paisley murmurs.

"What's not to like? You've been extremely helpful since Bianca left. I can't thank you enough for reviving the flowerbeds. My Marion would be giddy at the sight."

Her grin is sweet enough to rot my teeth. "That's very kind of you to say, Dennis."

"Only speaking the truth. I'm happy you're part of the team. You've become like a second daughter to me."

"Oh, my." Paisley clutches her chest. "Keep this up and I'll be crying on your shoulder."

"Feel free to let it out. I'm a great listener."

The two continue flapping their chaps like we're on vacation with nothing better to do. I wasn't aware that our recent hire had clawed her way into my father's good graces. Once again, I'm struck by her tenacity. She's determined to push me to my limits. And by the looks of it, she has Dad's support. How predictable. It wasn't enough for her to ruin my reliable routine. This woman is turning my own father against me.

They keep talking while I grab a halter and tie my horse to the nearest hitching post. Paisley tells Dad a cheesy joke. Her lyrical laughter grates on my nerves. She's too much, which I tell her at every available opportunity. My father doesn't seem to mind. Their exchange is effortless, a continuous stream that flows evenly between them. I'm the odd fuck out in this scene. Annoyance bubbles in my gut, and I have the sudden urge to intervene.

Dad is in a fragile state. She's going to drive him to drink more. But the longer I watch them, I recognize a difference about him. He seems… lighter. The gloom that's been hovering over him since Mom died has lifted slightly. I'm almost jealous that Paisley has this impact on him. Fuck, maybe she is good for morale. At least for everyone but me.

"Brody?" Dad waves a hand in front of my face. "Did we lose you?"

I blink from the fog. "Been here the entire time."

A telltale gleam flickers in his gaze. "What do you think?"

My mind goes blank. The last thing I want to do is admit weakness or defeat. I glance at Paisley, then refocus on my dad. Silence isn't an acceptable answer.

"It's doable," I mutter.

His expression brightens and he claps. "That's my boy. Knew you'd see it our way."

I get the feeling I've just stepped into a trap. "Since you two have the coop handled, I'll unsaddle my horse and get back to the office."

"Very funny," he chuckles. "Maybe you didn't hear me correctly."

"Message received. You're doing it your way." I swat at the conspiring duo. "Have at it. The door won't fix itself."

"Oh, I know. Which is why Paisley volunteered to help you." Dad's grin is more smug than a pig rolling in mud.

"That's not necessary," I counter.

He wags a finger at me. "It's a two-person job. She'll

take good care of you. And now, if you'll excuse me, I'm due for a nap."

My hands curl into tight fists as Dad casually strolls to the house. It feels like every tendon in my body is about to snap. I turn to unleash a snarl on the only available target. "What the hell was that?"

Paisley doesn't balk, greeting my malicious bite with a blinding smile. "You're stuck with me, boss."

CHAPTER SIX

Paisley

"Your brother is such a jerk." The words are out of my mouth the instant Bianca answers my FaceTime call.

Her wince fills the screen. "What did he do now?"

"What didn't he do? It's been two weeks of torment. Yesterday he decided to hide the halters. Every. Single. One. That put me in quite a pickle. How can I do my job if I can't take the horses out? I'm clearly incompetent and deserve to get fired." My bubbly tone is saturated in sarcasm.

Bianca laughs. "Um, wow. Did you retaliate?"

"Pfffft, heck no. Why get revenge when proving myself is more rewarding? Rather than surrender or return fire, I used twine to fashion very chic rope halters. It's all about the knot placement. You should've seen his face after I put my innovative creation on Ritzy and led her out of the barn. He thought he bested me, but victory is mine! It was beyond satisfying." My chef's kiss has extra pizzazz.

She releases a low whistle in appreciation. "My brother has finally met his match."

"Damn straight," I spout. "That man doesn't know who he's messing with."

Her eyes narrow. "I'm not used to seeing you so... vengeful. It's kinda hot, babes."

"Thank you, thank you." I bend into a slight bow.

"This is an unfamiliar side of Brody too. He's normally very disciplined and collected. Controlled. Deliberate. Rarely strays from his strict routine. The opposite of how he's been lately," she muses.

"What can I say? We bring out the worst in each other."

"Is there more to it?" There's no missing the suspicious quirk in her question.

"Only if you're referring to Brody constantly crossing my path. I thought he never steps foot in the barn, hmm?" Not that I mind seeing him. It's only an issue once his mouth opens.

"He rarely does. Or did. To be honest, Brody isn't acting like himself. Maybe he's finally losing his grip after Mom..." Bianca's voice drifts off, but her meaning is clear. She sniffs and pastes on a smile. "Either way, he's damn determined to take control of your employment status. Don't worry, Lee. That's not happening."

"It'd be nice if he got back to locking himself in the office or wherever he counts his billions. Running such a valuable company should keep him busy."

She snaps her fingers. "That's it! He needs a new challenge after reaching that financial tier."

"And he chose me as entertainment? How sweet." I inspect my chipped manicure as another thought occurs to me. "But that doesn't explain all the random incidents cropping up all over the ranch. I assumed it was Brody messing with me, but that wouldn't make sense. He's the one who has to fix everything. Unless he enjoys manual labor."

"Not when it comes to repairs. From the bit I've gathered, he's extremely frustrated about wasting precious time. It just might bother him more than your delightful presence." Bianca winks.

"Uh-huh, the feeling is mutual. And we're forced to fix stuff together. Did you know an entire section of the paddock fence was cut straight down the middle? All three rows. It's like the wires were sliced with a sword. How does that happen?"

"No idea. Wow. What does my dad have to say?"

I shrug. "Dennis just does his own thing. He doesn't get too worked up about much."

"That sounds about right," she mutters. "For what it's worth, I doubt those damages are done on purpose. The pranks are another story."

"Such a mess. It's safe to conclude the place is falling apart without you. When are you coming home to end the chaos?"

For once, her laughter isn't bogged down by gloom. "It can't be that bad."

"You're right. It's worse." My grin is a crooked slant. "He calls me Twinkles."

"To be fair, you have a lot of sparkle. Inside and out."

"But you mean it as a compliment. Your brother is a condescending ass." Steam is probably spewing from my nostrils.

Bianca twists her lips. "Should I cut my trip short?"

"No," I huff. "I'm just venting and hogging the conversation. Tell me the latest on your end. Still in Germany?"

She nods. "We arrived in Essen on Monday. It's this adorable little town where my grandmother grew up."

"Are you living the dream?"

Bianca's smile could chase off the threat of rain. "Better than I imagined. I feel like this is where I'm meant to be. It's beautiful here. The architecture alone is stunning. Everything takes my breath away. Their culture and customs are really interesting. There's so much history to be found. A sense of peace too. Does that make sense?"

Tears prick my eyes as I listen to her describe the trip she was desperate to take. "Definitely. Just what you needed."

"Yeah." More pain sheds from her with a heavy sigh.

"And how's Colton?"

Her carefree expression folds into a frown. "Urgh, he's awful. The man is always hovering. I barely get enough personal space to pee without him stuck to me. Don't even ask about what happened when he caught me in bed with my favorite toy."

Air gets trapped in my throat and I choke on that unwanted visual. "I'm not even sure how to respond to that."

"Terrible, right? It's his mission to ruin this vacation for me." A hint of her previous smile returns. "But it's not all bad. Despite his stalkerish efforts, I've managed to find fun people to hang around. A group of them took us out to a club last night. I met this guy who was crazy sexy. My pussy purred when we locked eyes. He had a smolder that could've brought me to my knees. I was seconds away from—"

"La-la-lahhhh! Too much information," I cut in while glancing at my very public surroundings.

It doesn't faze Bianca. "Unfortunately, a certain bodyguard stepped in before I had the chance. Colton totally blocked me from the cock."

"Good grief." My palm meets my forehead as several gasps claim offense.

"Where are you?"

"The farmer's market," I mumble.

My friend cringes. "Yikes. You should've censored me several sentences ago."

"It's fine. Most of them have heard worse."

Bianca nods knowingly. "What are you doing at the store? I thought Gemma and Ryder were still in town."

"They are, but I decided to stop by… just because."

"Since when would you rather be anywhere other than the barn?"

A huff sends stray hairs off my forehead. "Ask your brother. He's the one determined to be enemies."

"You're avoiding him?"

"Hardly," I scoff again. "This is just a quick reprieve."

"Are you sure about that?"

My brave face slips. "Not really. This might be above my pay grade, Bee. The constant tension is maddening. I've considered moving my horses back to Crooked Tree."

Her jaw unhinges on a gasp. "Sounds like you're admitting defeat."

"Which will only encourage him."

"We can't allow that. Brody might be predicable, but he's also stubborn and competitive. If he gains even the tiniest sliver, he'll want to command the entire board. He's ruthless like that."

A shiver trickles along my spine as an explicit memory

rushes forward to captivate me. I recall how furious green eyes glared at the mess in the hayloft. The bales that had been neatly stacked were now strewn about. Just one more calamity to add to the growing list.

Large hands gripped the twine and muscles flexed while each square was tossed back into formation. How would it feel to be hoisted that effortlessly? Or pinned to the wall by such brutal strength. Too bad that long-sleeve button-down was obstructing my view. The desire to rip open those pearl snaps and get a peek at what's hidden underneath had nearly consumed me.

I lick my lips, suddenly parched. Are enemies allowed to exchange sexual benefits? Not asking for a friend…

"What's that look for?" Bianca's voice barges into my lustful musings of Brody.

The misplaced hunger in my lower belly has me squirming. "Hmm?"

"You're flushed." She circles the remaining evidence of my debauchery. "What's on your mind?"

"It's… uh, nothing. Just the summer heat. I'm burning up."

She squints. "Mhmm, better cool off. I should get going anyway. Colton is glaring at me. He probably has to poop but doesn't want to leave me unsupervised."

"Charming."

"Welcome to my paradise. I'll talk to you soon. Stay strong, Lee."

"Same to you, Bee."

Our mutual giggles ring out as the call ends. I'm still laughing when my mother sidles up beside me. The smile that curls her lips has mine pinching shut. A neon sign advertising sex is more subtle than this woman.

"Hello, daughter." Mama nudges me when I remain silent. "How's Bianca?"

"Fine." The single word is ripped from my mouth.

"Just fine? You can do better than that."

"Super-duper," I gush.

"Better." Her sharp gaze watches as I fight the urge to fidget. "That was quite the conversation. Very riveting."

"Not really. Just catching up."

"Is that what we're calling it?" She's practically frothing at the mouth while chopping at the bit. "I overheard something that sounded a lot like boy troubles."

"More like broody billionaire problems." Regret immediately tightens my posture after I incriminate myself. "I mean… uhhh, it's just been hectic at Benson Farmstead. Still settling into the job. It's a… um, process. No big deal." The reflex to thump my forehead on the table has me curling inward.

Mama June grins wider when I stomp directly into her trap. "Not getting along with your new boss? Such a shame."

Sweat prickles my scalp. "That's putting it mildly."

Brody is a storm system, arriving just in time to rain on my parade. Little does he realize that I always pack an umbrella. I'll be the one shining bright after the downpour quits.

A disturbing sigh breezes from my mom, as if she's sweeping my victory speech under the rug. "Maybe you've finally met your match." That statement has a very different meaning coming from her.

"Not even close," I scoff. "We barely tolerate each other. He's constantly on my case no matter what I do."

"That's strange. I've only ever known Brody to be mild mannered."

"He's the opposite with me."

Her focus studies me like a textbook. "I see."

"What's that supposed to mean?"

"Maybe there's a reason you bring out such a… passionate side of him."

I shudder. Mama talking about passion isn't on my bingo card. "Please stop."

"You could do worse. He's the most eligible bachelor in the Midwest."

My eye roll deserves an Academy Award. "Depends who you ask."

"Well, the entire town will soon be rooting for you to do the honors of branding him. It's about time he gets snatched off the market."

A sour taste bubbles up my throat. "Very funny. Who delegated that courageous task to me?"

"You did."

"Me?"

"Yes, dear. There's a distinct buzz in the air. You haven't been very discreet." She motions to the crowd of traffic that's created a bottleneck near the tent I'm using for shade.

My gaze scans the people who are digesting the juicy gossip I just plopped at their feet. Some are already disbursing to spread the news wider. A pit forms in my belly when I spot an unfortunate sight.

Lynn Ellen Paige is among those sticking around in case I divulge more tasty tidbits. The busybody needs three first names to get recognized in this town. To add flies on the manure pile, she wiggles her fingers at me. That gesture reveals my downfall. She's seconds away from ruining me.

How could I be so careless? As Bianca's best friend, I know better than to blab openly about private drama. The Benson name is revered. They're local celebrities. Cloverleaf Meadows was built around the livestock empire their ancestors created. Rumors about them, regardless of facts or believability, get broadcasted across the state. I only have myself to blame for providing this breaking news report.

When Brody catches wind of this, I'll need earplugs to block his tirade. I can already predict the rant that will nail me to the barn wall.

Frustration slips from me in a low groan. "Ohhhh, brother."

Ryder is suddenly in front of me. "You rang?"

"Where'd you come from?"

"The throng." He hooks a thumb at the lively bunch. "They're thirsty in this heat and I don't miss an opportunity to sell our fresh squeezed juice. Tips are stuffing my pockets."

Mama pats his cheek as if he's five. "Such a shrewd businessman."

Another pitiful sound spills from my lips. "Uh-huh, great work. Way to give them what they want." *While they plot my demise.*

"I learned from the best." Ryder wags his brows. "Thanks, sis."

"At least one of us wins. Meanwhile, I have to move. Cassidy will take pity on me. Hopefully." Or I'll offer my cousin free babysitting in exchange for her cooperation.

"Knox Creek has always been like a second home. I'll fit right in."

"And get recognized instantly," my mom drawls.

"What do you suggest?"

"Simple," she chirps. "Brush yourself off and get back in the saddle."

"Huh?"

Mama pulls me off the chair. "Go ride your horse."

"Why?"

"How else will you beat the gossips at their own game?"

"Umm…" The answer continues to evade me.

She parks her hands on her hips. "I didn't raise you to be a quitter. Save the bronco and bang a Benson."

My jaw drops. "Mother!"

"Oh, don't act scandalized. I saw you squirming." She pushes me from the tent as if I'm a baby bird fleeing the nest. "Giddy up, Paisley. Make Mama proud."

CHAPTER SEVEN

Brody

"Y OU'RE THE TALK OF THE TOWN, SON."

I slide my gaze from the computer screen to watch Dad enter the office. His choice of greeting suggests that he's aware of our latest investment statement. That isn't possible unless he decided to check his email for the first time in months. In addition, the report just arrived an hour ago. News must've traveled faster than normal through the rumor mill. Unless he's being facetious and this is his clever way of telling me something else broke at the farm.

Or I'm simply overthinking his comment, which is the most likely option.

"I'm on the edge of my seat." The dull edge in my voice betrays me. "Better spill or I'll fall on my ass and embarrass both of us."

My father ignores any sense of urgency, strolling to an empty chair across from me. His jovial expression soothes the irritable thrash in my veins. That easy grin is a sight

I wasn't sure I'd see again. I scrub over my chin while he adjusts in the seat. The change in him over these past two weeks is nothing short of a miracle.

Maybe he read the email after all…

He steeples his fingers, further prolonging whatever this is. "Guess who I just got off the phone with?"

My exhale is steeped in restored frustration. "Are we seriously playing this game?"

He chuckles and I feel like an ass. "Would you rather be a party pooper?"

"Yes."

"That isn't an option in this house." He scolds me with a wag of his index finger.

"Dad," I chide in return. "Can you get to the point? I'm swamped."

"Fine. Ruin my fun." His huff belongs to a disgruntled teenager. "Excuse me for trying to build anticipation."

"Consider me adequately eager."

My father plants his palms on my desk and leans forward. "Lynn Ellen Paige shared the latest from the farmer's market."

The nuisance's name gives me a migraine. "Did she straddle a cucumber?"

"Goodness gracious, Brody." Dad's laughter is the richest reward. "Don't be crude."

"She's done worse."

"Be that as it may, what I have to tell you is far more personal. Dare I say it's positively private."

The blink I send him is dipped in molasses. "You're beginning to sound like the blab herself."

There's a distinct twinkle in his eye when he asks, "Have you seen Paisley this afternoon?"

"No."

Dad's gaze cuts to the window behind me where a sprawling view of our property is on full display. "I find that hard to believe."

Probably because I'm full of shit. My concentration has been divided ever since the motion sensor detected her arrival. I've developed an unfortunate response to the ping from the entry gate. Once I hear the beep, my focus is obliterated. That was at least two hours ago, and the battle against my self-control rages onward. I'm fighting the pull now while Dad scrutinizes me, just waiting for a crack to appear. It won't take much at this rate.

Paisley's presence sears my back and I strangle the urge to check if she's still in the outdoor arena. Before my father walked in, she was racing barrels on one of her horses.

The sight of her wrapping those tight turns, sitting deep in the saddle, is a temptation I don't need. I'm willing to admit that she's a great rider. She's an even better adversary in an argument. Our heated banter gives me a bigger thrill than I've felt in years. That's one more reason the twinkly cowgirl needs to kick rocks.

Fuck, she's driving me crazy. Nearly the entire compound separates us yet there's a restless energy thrumming in my chest, as if she's next to me. Or maybe she left for the day. I didn't get a notification from the gate, but she could be hiding in the barn. My knee bounces in preparation to launch me upright to feed the addiction.

It's only then I realize the silence has stretched longer than a morning piss.

I force my attention to Dad. "Are we done here?"

That gleam hasn't left his gaze. "We're just getting started. As I was saying, rumor has it that Paisley sang your praises at the market."

A gruff scoff calls bullshit. "I find that very hard to believe."

"Several reliable sources claim that she's crazy about you."

"First of all, there are no reliable sources in Cloverleaf Meadows." My earlier intuition about them blabbering about me was mostly spot on, but that's beside the point. "And the second portion of that statement is only factual if they meant in the delusional sense."

Dad waves off my retort. "The town thinks you and Paisley are destined to be together, which got me thinking about your love life. Or lack thereof," he adds on a grumble.

"Since when do we listen to gossip? It's a bunch of bull."

"Not in this case."

"Agree to disagree." I recline in my seat, the leather creaking beneath me. "Is that all? I have work to do."

"Funny you mention that since it leads into my next point."

The throb at my temples gains intensity and I rub at the ache. "When will this end?"

"Very quickly if you accept what I'm proposing."

"Get on with it." I roll my wrist to hurry him along.

"Before I dive into the specific terms, I want to acknowledge how much you've done for Benson Farmstead. The investments alone have brought us to another level. I'm very proud of what you've accomplished, Brody."

"But?"

"This is a family business," Dad continues. "That's our core principle. The roots that grew a small livestock operation into a legacy. We have to honor those values."

"What do you call this?" I motion between us.

"The end of our line unless you produce the next generation."

My brain scrambles. The concept of starting my own family to keep our empire thriving isn't lost on me. I knew that's a factor I'd have to consider, but in the distant future. Not while I'm still barely getting us back on track.

"Where is this coming from all of a sudden?"

His sigh is thick while he combs through his thinning hair. "It's not a secret that I've been absent since your mother passed. You've done well picking up the slack, proving you're capable of handling the pressure. I owe the success of this company to you. But it also got me thinking about our situation. What happens once I'm gone? Life is a precious gift that can be stripped away in an instant. Our time on this earth isn't a guarantee. I need to know our name won't die with us."

"Dad—"

"I want you to get married," he interjects. "And if it's not too much to ask, I'd like to be a Pappy before I go."

Laughter spews from me in a raucous wave. The release feels good, until I notice my father isn't joining in the hysterics. That sobers me faster than an ice bath. "You can't be serious."

"I wouldn't joke about the state of our fortune."

The wind gets sucked out of me. "I'm not getting married."

"Well, not right this second. But I'm hoping we can negotiate a speedy ceremony."

"My answer is no. Period."

His exhale is resigned. "Be reasonable, son."

"What you're asking isn't reasonable," I bellow.

"It's perfectly acceptable to have contractual demands. Call me sentimental, or senile. This is what I'm requiring of you to take ownership of Benson Farmstead."

"Sounds a lot like coercion and bribery."

Dad smirks, unbothered by my temper tantrum. "Call it whatever you'd like. Won't change the fact that I have stipulations."

"You can't expect me to go along with this."

He shrugs. "Nobody is forcing you."

"I've earned this spot." My finger jabs the desk.

"Sure, but it's not officially yours."

"My own father is blackmailing me."

"It's just business," he states casually.

"This isn't the way I run our company."

"You'll be free to make changes soon enough. Or not," he taunts.

"Thanks for plunging the knife deeper, Dad."

"Hold your horses, son. I want you to be the one who carries on our legacy. You're damn good at the job. Nobody is discrediting that or trying to overthrow you, regardless of what you'd have me believe." The stern edge in his tone is almost comical.

That bogus attempt to shake Dad from the funk is biting me in the ass. "It wasn't far off. Jimmy is constantly on my ass about money. Where do you think the bonus structure came from?"

"That's true. He can't shut up about the extra cash."

"Which is strange since he has plenty already, but there's more where that came from if you leave me in charge."

"Do this for me and it's a done deal."

I narrow my eyes at his nonchalance. "What happens if I refuse?"

"If you're not interested, Jimmy is ready to fulfill my request. Your cousins will be hitched by Christmas if I give him the go-ahead."

My jaw drops, quite possibly hitting the floor. "You'd give him the company?"

Dad makes a noncommittal noise. "He's willing to make sacrifices for the family. Not sure I can say the same about you."

"That's bullshit and you know it. I've given everything to this company. There's nothing I wouldn't do, but this crosses a line."

He flicks nonexistent lint off his shirt. "Perhaps, but it's in my power to set the conditions. The choice to comply is yours. Choose wisely."

"There isn't a good option," I counter.

"Just think about it." His gaze becomes unfocused. "Your mother made me a better man. I want that for you. A real partnership. A love that burns brighter each day."

"A contractual obligation," I add.

"Don't think of this as a punishment. You'll thank me eventually."

"Doubt it." I scrub over my face, ashamed that I'm actually considering the option. "Do you already have a bride picked out for me?"

"That's part of your decision." It doesn't escape my notice when his gaze slides to the window again.

"There's no chance Paisley will go along with this." But the thought of shackling myself to any other woman shrivels my balls into raisins.

Dad raises his palms. "I didn't mention her."

"Didn't have to," I mutter.

"If you want my opinion, she suits you well. I approve." The audacity of this man makes him a true icon.

"You old rascal. Reviving your nickname?"

"Always loved that comic strip. The show wasn't bad either." He reclines in his chair, a dreamy glint in his eye.

"Dennis the Menace lives and breathes," I mutter.

He's quiet for a beat. "Gives me a reason to get up in the morning."

An ache spreads through my chest. "Fuck, that's a shot to the soul."

"The truth hurts, kid. I was in rough shape until you reminded me that there's plenty left to live for." A wry smile touches his lips. "I'd love nothing more than to see you settled with a family of your own."

"Mhmm, the message has come across loud and clear."

The wiggle of Dad's brows is unsettling. "Does that mean I can book the chapel?"

CHAPTER EIGHT

Paisley

I SLIP THE HALTER OFF RITZY AND GET HER A PIECE OF carrot. My horse loudly crunches on her treat as I drift a palm down her bald face. It's a common feature for a frame overo paint. The large marking begins at the top of her forehead and extends down to her muzzle, stretching over one eye that's bright blue. Her brown body is splashed in white patches, creating a unique pattern. She's such a beautiful sight.

"My model mare," I croon. "You belong on the cover of magazines."

The pretty girl snorts and searches my pockets for another snack. I happily oblige, more than accustomed to spoiling her rotten. She deserves extra rewards after our practice runs today.

We've been a team for six years, ever since I bought Ritzy as a yearling. She's double registered as a paint and quarter horse, which allows me to compete in exclusive breed shows. We usually win big at those events. The next one is in September and I anticipate earning a large check.

Approaching footsteps interrupt my quiet contemplation. A glance over my shoulder bursts the peaceful bubble entirely.

Brody is crossing the property grounds toward me. The cowboy king strides forward with purpose and I'm instantly struck by the raw energy he emits. Static sparks along my skin, raising goose bumps despite the heat. There's no disguising my shiver as anything but anticipation.

His green stare narrows at me from the shadows under his hat. After several days of not seeing him, I'd been silly enough to think he found someone else to torment. Now I'm realizing that he's been lying in wait until I started to relax.

Pebbles skitter from his path to avoid getting crushed under the incoming wrath. Can't say I blame the tiny rocks for retreating but I thrust myself into the fray. After a farewell pat to my horse, I slip through the gate to confront him. My heartbeat trots faster as the distance separating us narrows to a few scarce feet.

The flutters in my belly are totally uncalled for. Brody's extremely attractive appearance is a sneaky trick. That handsome shell won't distract me from what's lurking beneath the surface. This man is a condescending jerk who would gladly stomp on me if I melted into a puddle at his feet. I'll never give him that opportunity. My spine steels as I prepare for our verbal spat.

"Howdy, Twinkles." Brody's deep timbre liquifies my knees.

I grasp onto the board behind me. "Boss."

His tall frame towers over my short stature. My head is level with his chest, which always leaves me looking up at him. I'm sure he gets off on that. The urge to climb the fence and perch above him wiggles my hips. He'd probably push me down before my ass settled on the wood.

Brody hums and glances at the sky. "Nice day for a ride." His bland comment gives me pause.

"Sure is," I respond slowly.

"Mighty fine-looking animal." He gives Ritzy a thorough inspection while she preens in the paddock. "Solid confirmation. Stocky build. Bold coat. How's her disposition?"

I peer at him through a squint. This isn't what I expected. Quite the opposite. Maybe I've unlocked an upgraded level to his game.

"Calm until we enter the alley," I answer. "She's bred to run and a natural at racing the barrels."

"I saw that."

My lips part when our gazes clash and hold. "You were watching?"

"Hard not to." His admission spurs my pulse into a gallop.

"Are you feeling okay?"

"Why do you ask?"

"You're acting strange."

His lips twitch as if my observation amuses him. "How so?"

My mind whirls for a moment as I study him closer. "You don't just chit-chat like this. Especially to me."

"Is that a problem?"

"It's just unusual." And a bit concerning, if I'm being honest.

"I'm capable of being quite charming." Brody tips his hat and smooths a palm down the pearl snaps of his western shirt.

A snort escapes me. "Oh, you're joking. Okay, phew. I get it now."

His jaw ticks and I brace for impact. "We've gotten off on the wrong hoof."

"Well, look at you stealing my lines."

"Seemed fitting." Brody grips the back of his neck. "You were right then, just like now."

My mouth pops open. "Is this another prank?"

He glares. "I'm trying to mend fences."

"Why?"

"Maybe I feel guilty for how I've treated you."

My brows reach for the sky. "Since when?"

His shrug is less committed than a one-night stand. "I overreacted about your… position at the farmstead. My sister trusts you, which should've been enough proof that you're capable. I've made… unfair assumptions and didn't properly welcome you to the team."

A dry laugh trips from me. "That's putting it mildly."

His lips tighten into a firm line. "Will you accept my apology?"

"Maybe if you actually apologize."

The request is met with a harsh exhale. "I'm sorry, Paisley. You didn't deserve my negative attitude and bad assumptions based on a poor first impression. That led to me acting rude and unreasonable, which is out of character. I'll be more respectful moving forward."

His speech would come across as more genuine if he

didn't sound physically pained. My flat expression reflects the thought. "And what about all the other stuff?"

"Such as?"

"My access code to the front entrance was erased, the halters went missing, no electricity in the barn, my truck keys were hidden, the tack room was locked," I count the transgressions off on my fingers. "Just to name a few, and those don't include the random damages and mishaps around the ranch."

"I'll take credit for the first one, but the rest aren't on me."

"Who else could be responsible?"

Brody is quiet for a beat before a smirk appears. "That sneaky menace. Definitely reviving his old nickname."

"Who?"

"Not important. I'll handle it, along with everything else." That last part is muttered under his breath.

Which reminds me of his recent absence. "Is the sudden weight of your guilty conscience the reason you haven't put up a fuss this week?"

There's an unmistakable gleam in his green gaze. "Miss me?"

"You wish," I retort.

A noise that could be mistaken for a chuckle rolls off his broad chest. I gape at him and the sound abruptly cuts off.

"Been busy." He allows that explanation to hang in the stagnant air between us as tension hardens his expression. "There's a new contractual obligation that requires much of my time. We're still negotiating the terms. It's irrational and complicated."

"I'm sure it will pay off," I say for the sake of conversation.

"But it will cost me," he grunts. The frustration bleeds from his features until he's restored the impassive mask. "Speaking of selling your soul, I heard you were talking about me at the farmer's market. Rumor has it that we're a love match."

I inwardly cringe. How foolish of me to assume I'd avoided this awkward discussion. "That's trashy gossip for you."

Brody is staring at me too intently. "I bet your boyfriend is pissed."

"He would be if he existed," I mutter.

An unreadable glint flickers in his gaze. "Glad that's settled." He hooks a thumb in his belt loop and steps closer. "I have a proposition for you."

"In addition to the truce?"

His nod is slow and calculating. "I need you to pretend that we're in a relationship."

My brain misfires and I recoil. "Can you repeat that? I must have misheard you." I feel dizzy while waiting for him to strike again.

"The entire town already assumes you're infatuated with me. Might as well make it work in our favor. It's not too big of a stretch."

That explanation does little to unravel the mess in my mind. Brody watches while I grapple for a response. His unyielding attention feels like I've been dropped in a pressure cooker.

"Okay, hold on. Let me get this straight," I mumble as a throb blooms at my temples. "You want us to fake date?"

"As a start."

I'll have to circle back to that cryptic statement. "And you're proposing this sham because…?"

His jaw clenches. The slight reaction reveals more than he's probably willing to admit. "I need you to play this small part in order for me to become the owner of Benson Farmstead. Once the company is officially mine, you'll be free of me."

"Ohhh," I sputter. "The plot thickens. You *need* a girlfriend. It's not just a request. It's a requirement."

"Yes," he grates. "It's an obligation I need to fulfill."

Did I just stumble into a romance novel?

Laughter spills from me—the type that's catty and brittle. I was right to be suspicious. "No wonder you're being almost nice to me. You want to use me as a prop." My glare attempts to pierce through his armor. "The answer is no."

"Why don't you think about it for longer than five seconds?"

I count to ten just to watch his eyelid twitch. "Oh, look at that. I still don't want to fake date you."

"What can I do to change your mind?"

"Nothing." I cross my arms to ward off this ridiculous ploy. "I'm not a pawn, Brody. For you to assume otherwise is very enlightening."

"You're upset. That wasn't my intention." Sincerity is noticeably absent in his tone.

"Could've fooled me. I didn't even accept your apology, but I guess it doesn't matter since that was fake too. Your true colors are showing, and they're several shades darker than morally gray."

"I'm not the bad guy," he defends. "Blame my father."

There's a sharp hitch in my breath as I picture Dennis

making such demands. "He's forcing you to choose me specifically?"

"Not exactly."

A small slice of relief worms through me. "You and your ulterior motives can find someone else. It's probably best if she doesn't sparkle too much."

"Where's the fun in that? You're the only candidate I'll consider, Twinkles." Just the way he phrases the offer is cold and detached. A simple business transaction.

My huff is deliberate, slicing through the red tape and dotted line I'd surely have to sign. "I can't imagine why you'd pick me, not that it makes a difference."

"Convenience is a major factor. It's plausible that we'd cross the line while working together. That's why the entire population of Cloverleaf Meadows already assumes we're a couple. Why would I bother looking elsewhere when you're already cast for the role?" His gaze takes a leisurely stroll along my curves as if he actually likes what he sees. "But most importantly, you'll hate the arrangement as much as me. Maybe more. We're not at risk of developing real feelings."

"A true love match." My eyes roll twice for good measure. "Unfortunately, I'm not interested."

"Take a few days to decide." He must have cotton stuffed in his ears.

"My answer won't change," I reiterate.

The green in Brody's eyes appears to flash. "Everybody has a price, Twinkles."

"That might be true." I flutter my lashes before skirting around him to ditch this pointless debate. "But even you can't afford mine."

CHAPTER NINE

"A RE YOU SURE THAT'S HIM?" THE MOST RECENT inquirer doesn't bother to whisper.

"I'm willing to bet on it," another voice babbles.

"He's alone." As if that isn't obvious.

"Won't be for long."

My jaw clenches as I glare straight ahead into the thick crowd. It's easy enough to block out the curiosity while a loud buzz circulates around The Paddock. But then a similar conversation begins on my opposite side.

"From what I've heard, Brody hasn't left the farmstead since the funeral."

A willowy exhale steeped in pity follows. "Such a shame what happened to his mother."

"Very tragic. At least the aneurism took her fast and she didn't suffer." A double dose of sympathetic sighs fills the short pause. "It sounds like Dennis is still in rough shape," the first speaker adds.

The pit in my stomach—that I'd previously been able

to ignore—yawns with a sharp ache. What a considerate topic to discuss during happy hour. Damn gossips and their lack of boundaries. I'm not here for their entertainment, which is the reason I chose the most secluded seat in the joint. They've descended regardless.

Their incessant chatter burns at the walls I've built around myself. My mood is sour and getting fouler by the minute. If they're trying to make me uncomfortable, I'll gladly return the favor. The couple on my right freezes when I turn to face them. I flick the underside of my cowboy hat to give them a good look at what burns in my gaze. Their eyes bulge before quickly dropping.

Whatever response I might've shot at them fizzles when a commotion at the front door demands attention. The blonde bombshell strutting inside steals the spotlight. Victory tilts my lips into a rare smirk. I'll have to thank Bianca for the accurate intel. She unknowingly gave me an advantage that I plan to exploit.

My gaze follows Paisley while she weaves into the sea of people like a strand that corrals the chaos. Everyone turns to greet her as she passes. It's obvious she's a regular, but she doesn't blend in. Quite the opposite as her radiant energy glows in the dim dive bar.

Paisley's smile is blinding, aimed at the swarm like a free dose of sunshine. I'm willing to bet her expression would shutter if pointed at me. But the desire to get that joy from her solidifies into a demand inside of me. I want to earn it. Tonight. Right now.

I rise from the corner spot that's blanketed in shadows, snagging my drink to keep me company. Clusters of locals part in a rowdy wave as I stride across the packed space.

Their murmurs chase me, but I don't hear them. My riveted attention roams over Paisley with a hearty appetite.

She's not wearing her cowgirl uniform for a change. Instead of jeans and an athletic top, there's a denim dress showing off her curves. There's plenty of bling stuck to the material, confirming that she sparkles on purpose. The hem stops at mid-thigh to expose smooth, toned legs. A rhinestone belt is snug around her waist, reflecting a blinding shimmer whenever she moves. Heavily tooled boots complete the outfit that's been stamped into my fantasies.

Too damn much.

But her performance isn't done. She twirls and the briefest tease of what's hidden underneath taunts me. My fingers tighten around my bottle of Coors, imagining something much more supple filling my palm. I tilt the beer to my lips and polish off what's left. The single gulp does little to soothe the fire in my throat.

Slack jaws and dumbfounded expressions are left in my dust when I approach the rail. Paisley is leaning over the counter and speaking to a bartender. The guy is ogling her tits instead of listening to what she's saying. I toss my empty in the nearby trash, which redirects the dude's leer. One glance at me has him rushing off to do his customer's bidding. Maybe he'll bring me a fresh one while he's at it.

Once Paisley straightens and lowers her boots to the floor, I step behind her to make myself known. I bend until my mouth almost touches her ear. "Sure know how to make an entrance, Twinkles."

Paisley whirls until our gazes collide. "Brody," she gasps. "What're you doing here?"

"Appreciating the decor." I wave at the interior design

that resembles an old-fashioned saloon. Seems fitting since the place looks exactly the same in my fuzzy memories. "Maybe I'll try my luck while I'm at it." My arm arrows at a sign boasting their weekly meat raffle, which hangs above the pull tab station.

Just as predicted, the brightness in Paisley's features fades slightly as she scrutinizes my random appearance. "The Paddock doesn't seem like your vibe."

"That's presumptuous. I used to frequent this fine establishment several days a week."

One skeptical brow curves upward. "Was that in the previous decade?"

"You wound me," I deadpan. Not that I can completely discredit her assumption. "For the record, I won the Stuck on Bucky bull riding contest at least a dozen times. Most recently was two years ago. I came out of retirement for that one."

Which I only agreed to compete in as a bet. My cousin is a cocky shit and needed to be taught a lesson. The bragging rights were well worth the unwanted attention. I lost count of the phone numbers and lewd suggestions stuffed into my pockets. It's a shock I made it out in one piece.

It takes me a minute to realize Paisley is unusually quiet. She's nibbling on her bottom lip while checking me out. A deep blush stains her cheeks when I catch her in the act.

"I was there that night," she murmurs. "It was the first time I saw you."

"And you've been madly in love with me ever since."

Her laugh is loud and free. "You wish."

"Sure would make our arrangement easier," I drawl.

"We don't have an arrangement."

"Yet."

She didn't tell me her terms, which has grated on my nerves. But we'll get it settled. Eventually.

Paisley rolls her eyes as if hearing my stubborn determination. "Who are you here with?"

"You."

"Me?"

I nod. "You've been avoiding me."

A hint of her genuine smile fondles my ego. "Or you've missed me, boss."

I chuckle as she throws my words back at me. "Well, you arrived just in time. How about we—"

"Holy horse manure!" A redhead behind Paisley whistles. "Brody Benson is crashing ladies' night."

I grind my teeth at the interruption, but tip my hat at her. "Ma'am."

The woman wrinkles her nose. "Oh, you did not."

"Excuse me?"

She huffs. "I'm barely over thirty, not approaching fifty."

I glance from her to Paisley. The latter is waiting for me to acknowledge her smug grin. "Care to clarify?"

The twinkly cowgirl snorts out a giggle. "You ma'amed her."

"Is that a verb?"

"Mhmm, and it's not sexy. Makes us feel old."

"Wouldn't want that." I'm not shy about roving my blatant appreciation along Paisley's hourglass figure. "Not that there's a chance of that happening. Are you even legally allowed to be in a bar?"

"Want to peek at my license?" She leans close, giving me a whiff of vanilla and reckless abandon. "That'll prove I'm too young to fake date you."

I clench my hand into a fist to stop myself from grasping her hip. "There's nothing wrong with an age gap, Twinkles. A mature guy like me can take better care of you."

"Pretty promises for a contractual obligation." Paisley clucks her tongue and moves away to point at the redhead. "This is my cousin. Cassidy is partial to Knox Creek, but she decided to visit us in Cloverleaf Meadows for a change."

I tip my hat. "Nice to meet you, filly. I'm surprised they let you in without getting carded. You're probably breaking the law."

Cassidy nods in approval. "Now that's more like it."

"Don't let him fool you," Paisley chirps. "This charm is an act. He just wants something he can't have."

"Girl, give it to him." Cassidy lightly shoves her cousin at me. "Make sure to get yours too."

Paisley rights herself before I can catch her. "You're a horrible influence."

"I like her," I counter.

"You would."

"How about we discuss this somewhere more private? I have a table reserved in that dark corner." My thumb hitches in the general direction.

"I'm not going anywhere with you." Paisley plants her boots into the concrete floor for emphasis.

"You'd rather get more intimate where everyone can see?" I step forward until our bodies nearly brush. "Fine by me."

Her breath hitches at our proximity. She glances from left to right, most likely noticing the attention we're gathering. "What are you doing?"

"Setting the mood."

Baby blues widen at me. "You're making a scene."

"Then put an end to it," I urge.

Her unblinking gaze narrows into a glare. "You're doing this on purpose."

I shrug. "Let them talk." Maybe the rumor mill will be somewhat useful tonight after all.

"Nope, you're not using me as a pawn." Paisley shoos me toward the door. "Buh-bye."

I loop an arm around her waist, tugging until she's flush against me. "I'm not leaving without you, Twinkles."

Her palms flatten on my chest, ready to shove me away. The slight curl in her fingertips is the only sign of hesitation. Our eyes lock and hold. One breath extends into two. Her body presses closer to mine with every ragged exhale. The buzz around us goes quiet. I search her gaze while she gets lost in mine. My heartbeat quickens under her touch. Warmth spreads between us.

The urge to pull her even tighter against me flexes my arm. Paisley blinks, casting her gaze around the crowded room. Red blooms on her cheeks and she breaks free from my hold. I release her but my eyes remain glued on her fiery blush. There's no hiding her reaction to me.

"You're playing dirty," she mutters.

"Whatever makes you mine."

"Never gonna happen."

"No?" In a fluid motion, I remove my cowboy hat and put it on her head. A collective gasp ripples across the bar. I smirk as the gossips prepare to do their thing. "The town will say otherwise."

Paisley is quick to rip off my claim, clenching the straw brim in an unforgiving grip. "I can't believe you just did that."

"Ready to fake date me yet?"

Fury blazes in the blue depths she pins on me. "Not even close."

I return her stare and weigh the options. There are only so many that will confirm what I've started without pushing too far. It's about authentic presentation, which is somewhat of a specialty.

"Fuck it," I rasp and haul her against me.

Paisley inhales sharply just as I seal my lips over hers. Silence rings in my ears while our very public display is witnessed around the room. That allows me to hear her soft whimper. The quiet sound sets off a chain reaction.

Lust crashes into me, flooding straight to my dick. Paisley stiffens at the hardening evidence of my arousal but almost immediately relaxes again. That encourages me to glide my tongue along hers, obliterating the boundaries of what's meant to be a chaste kiss. She fits herself to me like a missing piece. A sense of completeness accompanies an unfamiliar craving. The comfort gives me pause until her teeth gently clamp onto my bottom lip. That slight motion spins me out of control. Lines blur in my mind to defeat the purpose.

It's suddenly unclear who I'm trying to convince. That's why I'm the one to pull away, which is more difficult than I want to admit. The cloudy haze in Paisley's eyes doesn't notice. Her heavy lids blink slowly, tempting me to steal another taste. Somehow I manage to resist. At least until she lifts onto the balls of her feet to reclaim my mouth.

I smile into the kiss. "You're mine now, Twinkles."

CHAPTER TEN

Paisley

M Y GAZE WANDERS TO THE COLORFUL BOUQUET ON the counter again. The arrangement is innocent but represents the entire inventory of Sassy Stems that was delivered to my apartment this morning. And here I thought a trip to my favorite boutique would be a worthwhile distraction.

Memories from last night float to the surface. Brody's lips against mine felt like an explosion of fireworks. That crackle sizzled in my veins and burned me from the inside out. After the initial sparks faded, a wave of relief filled me. It was intoxicating but detrimental. I'd been lulled under a false sense of satisfaction.

That moment of weakness was a major hit to my pride. As if that wasn't bad enough, I practically begged for a second kiss. The only thing salvaging my confidence is the reminder that he was turned on. There was no mistaking the solid bulge nudging into me. He couldn't fake his body's reaction.

That doesn't change the original purpose, or the harsh truth. Brody is trying to use me and I'd let myself forget. My guard slipped down as his mouth caressed mine. Damn, it felt good to be taken by surprise.

But the pleasure was fleeting. Now I'm stewing in shame. Indefinitely.

"Jeez, sis. What did the hangers do to you?" Gemma's voice startles me from the pit of regret.

It's only then I realize that I'd been whipping clothes along the rack. My reckless decision mocks me. "I'm just… frustrated."

She hums, lifting a skirt for closer inspection. "Does this frustration have anything to do with your smoochy sesh at Paddock?"

My nose wrinkles at her creative terminology. "How did you hear about that?"

"I might not be physically allowed in the bar, but that doesn't mean I miss the fun." Her brows wag.

"That's quite an accomplishment."

"The snaps and texts flooded in. I even saw a video."

"Creepy," I mutter.

Gemma scoffs. "Wouldn't have to rely on the gossips if you'd spill the beans like a lopsided can. Now's your chance, sis." Intrigue shines in her blue eyes—the bright shade we inherited from our mother. "What's going on between you and Brody?"

I feign an unwavering interest in a sweater that would be cozy for the approaching fall. It's bright pink and sparkly, which is my signature. "Nothing."

"Is that why he bought you every stem that Sassy had available?"

My teeth clack shut. If the cocky cowboy thinks an entire flower shop's supply will win me over, he's more delusional than I thought. He's tainted the romantic gesture for me.

"Those were from my secret admirer," I grumble.

"More like your partner in tonsil hockey. You're not fooling anyone." Her raised volume awards us several glances from fellow Bronco Bling customers.

I drag her behind a display of jeans to escape the curious stares. "He needs a… favor and is trying to mark his territory in order to convince me."

"Wait a minute." She palms her forehead. "Brody Benson kissed you in order to get something else from you?"

It sounds silly repeated back to me. Not that I'll admit it. "And now my tiny studio is full of Sassy Stems."

Gemma's lips curve into a coy grin. "You did the favor."

"Nope," I cluck. "Brody decided to shower me in gratitude. I guess that's my reward for not dumping a drink over his head."

My sister laughs. "Wow, you're not falling at his feet."

"He wishes."

Her humor escalates into a cackle. "Damn, I love this fierce vibe."

"What can I say? He brings out the worst in me." And I'm entirely *too much* for him to handle.

Gemma wanders to the candle section. Her face sours after she smells an orange jar. "So… what's the favor?"

My pulse skips as I consider how to answer. Brody's parting words play on a loop like a haunting omen. But I'm not his, and never will be. Fake relationship or otherwise. A gut instinct tells me he won't accept that easily. It wouldn't hurt to get people in my corner.

I push out a thick exhale. "He wants to pretend that we're a couple."

She goes abnormally still for several seconds. "And you're hesitating?"

"Obviously."

Her jaw drops. "Why?"

"For starters? To protect my dignity," I deadpan.

My sister narrows her eyes. "Is he expecting something… more explicit?"

I glance at two women hovering nearby. "No."

"Then your integrity is safe. Just do it."

"Absolutely not," I blurt.

"What's the big deal?

"I'm not interested in being treated like a pawn just so he can get richer and more powerful."

Her upper lip curls slightly. "Is that how he makes you feel?"

The heat from last night rekindles in my belly, spreading in a tingly wave that almost makes me gasp. "Not necessarily, but I didn't agree to his conditions. Who knows what might happen if I did."

"And what are you getting out of it? Besides him ravishing your mouth and flooding your house with flowers," Gemma teases.

A crease forms between my brows. "I'm not sure."

"You should find out."

"It won't change my answer."

She huffs hard enough to send hair flying off her forehead. "Fine, don't let me live vicariously through you. Who cares about bagging a billionaire. It's not like *Pretty Woman* actually happened."

"Don't make it sound so glamorous," I mutter.

My sister mumbles under her breath about a wasted opportunity. "What's your plan instead? Other than taking me on a spontaneous shopping spree to avoid your botanical garden."

I shrug and continue browsing the store. "To just ignore him. He'll realize I'm not worth the effort eventually."

Gemma snorts while trailing after me. "Brody doesn't seem like the type to give up."

"An unbeatable challenge is only fun for so long. There are plenty of other women who will gladly—and much more willingly—fill the role," I say.

"But the entire town already thinks you're dating."

"We're not."

"Could've fooled me," she chimes.

That deserves a glare. "Whose side are you on?"

"The one where you live happily ever after with Brody freaking Benson. The man is a legend. He's feeding the rumor mill and supporting our local businesses. It's no wonder Cloverleaf Meadows puts him on a pedestal."

My mind is quick to picture him standing tall and proud and capable of annihilating logic. I shiver as if his presence towers over me. Spicy musk and crisp pine infuse the air until I'm breathing him in. His influence is already too much and he's barely trying.

Gemma is staring at me. Her eyebrows raise higher with each rapid beat of my heart. There might as well be drool collecting on her chin as she anticipates the potential of a juicy reveal. I pull in a slow breath to compose myself. The last thing I need to do is give my sister a reaction she can use against me. Another flurry of assumptions will descend along Main Street soon after. Brody would be very pleased.

"Oh, shit. You're smitten." Her chirpy tone is positively giddy.

"Definitely not," I retort. "He bothers me."

My sister's audible inhale probably smells bullshit. "Then set the record straight. Find a guy you actually like and throw it back in Brody's stupid handsome face."

I'm weighing the option when my phone vibrates in my back pocket. A glance at the screen makes me wince.

Bianca: PAISLEY JANE KEATON!

Me: Uh-oh, you full-named name.

Bianca: Don't try to act cute. Is it true you kissed my brother?

Me: To be fair, he kissed me.

Bianca: Not the time to split hairs.

Bianca: Why was Lynn Ellen Paige the one to tell me and not my best friend? She provided very disturbing details too.

Nausea sloshes in my stomach while I imagine her upset about the news. Her grief is more than enough turmoil. Bianca doesn't need me dumping fabricated drama into the mix.

I slap a palm over the gurgle, folding in half to muffle the noise. A thought occurs to me when I spy several gazes assessing my position. After last night's scene at The Paddock, this crowd will probably assume I'm sick for an entirely different reason.

I straighten in a hurry and whirl to dismiss their judgment. Gemma is there to squeeze my shoulders. Her attention lowers to my screen when another text comes through.

Bianca: Don't make me spell out your full name again.

Me: Don't be mad. It's not what you think.

Bianca: I'm waiting...

Me: Brody was trying to prove a point.

Bianca: To confirm that his mouth fits over yours? Were you doing a sexy version of Cinderella?

Me: Not exactly...

Me: Have you talked to your dad lately?

Bianca: It's been a few days. Why?

Me: Did he mention any changes at the company?

Bianca: OMG! What's going on? You're freaking me out.

Unease squirms in my gut again. I don't want to stress her out. There's not much she can do about family politics while abroad. She's not overly involved in Benson Farmstead regardless.

My attention lifts to the ceiling. Sunlight streaks across the painted rafters, reflecting a glow that doesn't penetrate. I'm a jumble of uncertainty. This is something I can handle without dragging Bianca down. But hiding the truth doesn't sit well.

Me: Can I call you? This isn't something I want to text.

Bianca: I'm at a restaurant and it's really loud. Just type.

Nerves bubble up my throat and tremble my fingers.

"You're super jittery. Is your secret admirer upping the stakes?" My sister's voice is practically bouncing at the possibility.

A defeated whimper slips from me. "Worse. It's Bee."

"Is she talking some sense into you?"

I nudge Gemma with my elbow. "Aren't you supposed to be back at college this week?"

"You're stuck with me until tomorrow, but I'll let you text in peace." She blows me a noisy kiss before sauntering to the makeup section.

Me: So... it sounds like your dad is considering retirement and giving the business to Brody.

Bianca: What else is new?

Me: He added a slight stipulation.

Bianca: Which is?

Me: Brody needs to settle down, or at least give the impression he's getting serious.

Bianca: That doesn't make sense. My brother is nothing but committed.

Me: To a woman.

Bianca: What?

Me: In order to officially become the owner, your dad is requiring Brody to be in a relationship.

Bianca: Why would he do that?

Me: Not sure. Maybe you can ask him.

Bianca: Okay, but what does that have to do with my brother kissing you?

I pause to give her a moment to process. The pieces fit together within seconds. A stream of messages floods in faster than I can read them.

Bianca: OH HELL NO!

Bianca: Brody wants you to be his girlfriend?!

Bianca: Just for show??

Bianca: What is he thinking?!

Bianca: Absolutely not. I won't allow it.

Bianca: Is this a joke??

Bianca: I can't believe he'd suggest using you like that.

Bianca: Tell me you're kidding.

Bianca: Don't you dare fall into that trap.

Bianca: For real, Lee.

Me: Not planning on it.

Bianca: Gah, I'm so mad. This is probably why he's been asking about your schedule and what kind of flowers you like.

Me: Mhmm. He cleaned out Sassy Stems. Poppies are officially ruined for me.

Bianca: Grrrr. I thought he was being nice. What a jerk.

Me: It's fine. I'll figure out how to get even.

Bianca: Make him pay, babes. Don't hold back.

A slow smile lifts my mood at her prompting. Several possibilities sprout in my mind, taking shape into brilliant ideas. Brody is definitely going to feel my wrath.

Me: If you insist...

Bianca: I do, and he'll be hearing from me too.

CHAPTER ELEVEN

Brody

THE BUZZING IN MY POCKET HASN'T QUIT FOR FIVE minutes. Whoever it is better have a damn good reason for blowing up my phone during a meeting. I signal to my uncle and cousins before blindly swiping across the screen to answer. The device is barely lifted to my ear when unleashed hostility barks at me.

"Hello, brother."

"Bianca," I greet. "This is a surprise. How's the trip?"

"Cut the shit," she growls. "You kissed Paisley."

"And?"

My sister sputters. "That's crossing a line."

I scoff at her dramatics. "It didn't mean anything."

"So I've heard." Disdain drips from her tone. "She told me about Dad's demands and your brilliant idea to drag her into a scam."

A dry chuckle shakes free. "Oh?"

"This isn't funny. She's not getting involved with you and your obligations."

"Too late," I drawl.

"Is not," she fires in return. "Find someone else. Lucy will gladly volunteer."

I grimace at the name of my former no-strings arrangement. "It's been months since I've seen her."

"All the more reason to reunite."

"Lucy isn't eligible for the role. This connection needs to appear genuine and different. The one nobody saw coming. I have to make everyone believe Paisley has changed me, which includes Dad."

Bianca huffs. "She's done nothing but play nice and you're acting like a manipulative jerk."

"Sorry to burst your bubble, but Paisley is far from innocent."

"I'm willing to bet you started it."

And I damn well plan to finish it, not that my sister needs to hear about those plans. "I'm not keeping score."

Her frustration is almost audible. "What harm has she caused?"

The pressure in my chest triples. "She's a drain on my sanity and productivity. Might as well make use of her while I have some sense left."

A pathetic whimper comes from her end. "Don't do this, Brody. It isn't you."

"I'm doing what needs to be done."

"There's a better way. Find someone you can actually build a future with. Why lie about it?"

"I don't need the complications or commitment of a real relationship. Too messy," I explain.

"Well, fine. But my best friend is off-limits. Buy a cardboard cutout to pose as your girlfriend for all I care."

The idea has potential, but will ultimately fall flat. "It's almost sweet that you care so much, but Paisley can make her own decisions. She's a big girl."

"I'm protecting her. That's what friends do."

Sawdust and irritability scent the air when I inhale. "How endearing. Do you braid her hair while offering shoddy advice too?"

"We watch out for each other. Simple as that," she snips.

"Call it whatever you want, but my plans remain the same."

"You're not listening." Impatience raises her voice.

"Right back at you." I grind the toe of my boot into the dirt. "You ran off to heal and find yourself. Worry about that, Bianca. Your friend is in capable hands. We'll reach an understanding that's mutually beneficial."

Silence echoes down the line for several seconds. "I'm calling Dad."

"Be my guest," I laugh. "Who do you think suggested your precious friend in the first place?"

Her response is a jumble of colorful curses that would make a hardened criminal blush. "Don't make me fly home early."

"If that's what you think is best." I expel what's left of my patience in a long-winded sigh. "Great catching up, but I need to go."

"We're not finished."

I sigh and pinch the bridge of my nose. "Now isn't the time."

"Make time."

"Jimmy and our cousins are waiting on me. We're at the auction barn."

"Let them wait longer," she growls. "This is more important, unless you really want to earn the title of villain."

"It's a done deal, Bianca. You need to accept that. Call me every insult in the book if it makes you feel better. I can play the bad guy. That won't change the outcome."

"What's happened to you?" The wobble in her voice almost penetrates my resolve.

Instead, I square my shoulders and remember what's at stake. "You should know by now that I'll do anything for the farm. It's my one true purpose."

"Even if that means sacrificing your happiness and forcing others into dishonest situations?"

"It's not permanent."

"That doesn't excuse what you're trying to do. Leave. Paisley. Alone." Three resounding slaps punctuate the demand. The image of her smacking a fist against the table is comical.

My chuckle is rewarded with another streak of expletives. I sober and push off the wall to conclude this spiral. "As I already mentioned, it's too late. The whole town is fully invested in our little charade."

"You can undo it," she urges.

Which would defeat the entire purpose. "We'll talk later. Enjoy yourself over there, sis."

Bianca is shouting into the phone as I disconnect the call. I tuck my phone away and stroll to where Jimmy is propped against the auction pen entrance. My two cousins flank their dad as I approach. Byron is the oldest and hasn't been quiet about wanting more responsibility. It must be a new trend. But Chance isn't following along. The younger brother seems perfectly content completing whatever odd jobs are tossed in his direction, with little ambition to speak of.

I nod at the trio. "Where were we?"

Uncle Jimmy's eyes narrow on the lingering tension tightening my features. "All good?"

"Yep, just had to deal with Bianca's moods."

He offers a quiet hum in understanding. "She's still in Europe?"

"For now," I say dismissively.

The three of them resume the overview of our upcoming registered horse sale. These meetings are a formality I'm forced to endure during my father's personal leave. Once I'm officially in charge, my tolerance for nonsensical shit won't be so high. The predicted profits and current catalog entries might as well be white noise. At least until their voices come to an abrupt halt.

Dad saunters into the building as if he'd just stepped out to run a quick errand. The four of us turn to stare at his unexpected attendance. Our jaws hang slack at a similar angle.

He's waving something in his hand. "Got a package for you, Brody."

"Is it a winning lottery ticket? What's with the delivery service?"

"Not sure, but the packaging is something else." He throws the padded envelope at me.

I glance at the bold message stamped on both sides. "Secondhand sex toys?"

"Don't ask me what you ordered."

My eyes roll. "This is obviously a prank. Are you responsible?"

"Nope. I've quit the shenanigans." Dad rocks backward,

rubbing his palms together. "Open it and find out who has it out for you."

I rip at the seal with a savage yank that exposes my rising temper. A cloud of glitter explodes outward from the rough treatment. My lack of amusement is doused in the evidence, which sticks to me and the surrounding area like glue. Real fucking clever. Once the sparkly dust clears, I reach inside for the contents.

"A Bag of Dicks," I read the label aloud.

And that's exactly what it is. The rainbow candy is shaped like tiny penises. My audience doubles over in laughter as I palm the sack of peens. Dad and Jimmy are howling like a pack of hyenas. Chance has tears in his eyes. Byron is the first to gather his composure.

His low whistle pairs well with a thorough inspection of my embellished attire. "What did you do to deserve all that?"

"Depends who you ask." I tuck my chin and a river of glitter falls off the brim of my hat. "It seems someone wanted to brighten my day."

"Is there a note?"

I glare at my cousin. "No."

"Must be from someone really special."

There's only one possibility. It turns out my twinkly cowgirl likes to play dirty too. She's proving herself to be a serious contender for the upper hand. I almost smile at the acknowledgement.

Dad claps me on the back, sending another gust of glitter into the air. "Things are progressing quite quickly. I'm impressed."

My glare chastises his jolly grin. "This is your fault."

He raises his hands. "I'm innocent."

"You stuck us together with your constant repairs and mishaps at the farm."

His weathered skin twitches when he grins. "All that was just a gentle shove in the right direction. Look where it's led you."

"Smells like a love connection is brewing to me," Chance snickers.

"Maybe if you're stoned and have the munchies," I mutter in return.

This flirtation is fucking adorable, but it's getting me nowhere. We've been dancing around each other for weeks and getting nowhere fast. Paisley doesn't even know the extent of my proposal. Getting her to date me is challenging enough. But after this stunt? She's practically begging for me to ditch what remains of my morals.

Between Paisley's thoughtful gift and my sister's attempt at dissuasion, I'm ready to tie the knot on this ruse. I need her as my wife—preferably before Bianca gets home. The rushed process is going to go over about as well as if I dragged her down the aisle kicking and screaming. I'll have to make a grand gesture she can't refuse. Or earn the title my sister just bestowed upon me. At this rate, I'm choosing the latter.

Me: Need you to do something for me.

Colton: Name it.

CHAPTER TWELVE

Paisley

AFTER WRAPPING THE THIRD AND FINAL BARREL, I steer Echo straight for home. Her hooves pound into the dirt as the wind whips at my cheeks. She's so fast, the ground blurs beneath us. Emotions rise when we gain more speed.

"We're flying," I murmur into the breeze.

My blood sings from the adrenaline rush of running on a horse. It's a natural high and I'm addicted, chasing this sensation through each cloverleaf pattern. I surrender myself to the thrill thrumming through my veins.

But those fifteen seconds are over all too soon. I pull lightly on the reins after we cross the imaginary finish line. Echo slows and curves into a swift loop near the fence to complete our ride. My palm flattens on her neck, patting softly in gratitude. She ran with her whole heart and I'm grateful.

This buckskin mare is—*or was*—Marion's favorite. I feel connected to the wonderful woman whenever I'm near

Echo. It's another phenomenon entirely when I'm in the saddle, soaring astride her back. Or maybe I'm extra sensitive after recent events.

I stretch my arms out and tip my face to the sky. "Miss you, lady."

Slow applause startles me from the serene moment. Brody saunters to the arena gate in his lethal prowl that immediately sets me on edge. I force my stiff posture to relax and dismount in a fluid motion, putting us on even ground. Or that's my intention. His smirk disarms my attempt at a confident approach. A clump of dirt almost trips me while I become captivated by that uncharacteristic expression.

But then Echo bumps my elbow with her nose and the nudge gets me back on track. For the assist, I smooth a hand along her bronze face. My chin lifts as I pin Brody with a much-deserved glare.

"Hey, boss."

Brody tips the brim of his hat. "Twinkles."

I lean against the buckskin mare for moral support. "Miss me?"

His eyes flash, the green sparking into flames. "Hard not to after that delightful care package you sent me."

Laughter bubbles up my throat just picturing him opening the gift. "Same day delivery for a direct impact."

"If you wanted to surprise me, I could offer more fulfilling suggestions." The gritty rasp in his tone curls my toes.

I avert my gaze before accidentally stumbling into his provocation. "You got what you deserved."

"Message received," he rumbles. "And now I get to return the favor."

The swoop in my belly is completely uncalled for. "How might you do that?"

Brody slips through the fence and moves to stand within my personal bubble. I almost retreat, but refuse to give him the satisfaction. A hint of his crisp scent teases my nostrils and I inhale discreetly for another whiff. The wiggle on his lips reveals that I failed at subtlety.

I flash back to when he initially tried scaring me off the compound. The scales have tipped back and forth since then. It would appear that we're developing somewhat of a pattern. I find myself wondering what direction this confrontation will slide.

Brody's intense stare blazes a trail straight to my lower belly. "I'll start by thanking you." The response is staggering.

"Thank me?" My mind goes blank and I forget what we're talking about. "For what?"

"Your glitter bomb gave me a fresh outlook. The Bag of Dicks provided an insightful reflection on my behavior too."

I blink at him and his shocking admission. He tilts his head while studying my reaction. The mid-morning sun catches a few sparkles in his stubble. A giggle springs free before I realize what I'm seeing.

His scowl tries to dull my joy. "Is my revelation amusing?"

My smile stretches wider while I point at the decorated spot. "You're still bright and shiny."

"Clings worse than a needy girlfriend." He scrubs at his jaw. "Speaking of, ready to fake date me yet?"

Disbelief clogs my throat and I scoff. But it backfires into a wretched gasp. I choke, begin coughing, and fold myself in half to recover. "Not even a little bit," I croak.

Brody pats my back like a concerned humanitarian. "Do you want more money? I'll give you a raise."

I straighten in a hurry. It's like destiny is set on me starring in a reenactment of *Pretty Woman.* "I don't need your riches, boss."

"But you could be dripping in diamonds instead of rhinestones."

The sun chooses that moment to reflect my encrusted belt. "I'd choose being buckled in barbwire over getting into bed with you."

"Are you sure?" His voice is silk sliding across bare flesh. "I've never had any complaints."

A tremble threatens to quake my knees. "Positive."

"That's a shame."

"As if you expected my answer to change."

"Sure would make this process easier," he drawls.

A shadow stretches over me from his towering height. It's only then I realize just how close we're standing. At this distance, I notice the complex landscape in his eyes. The darker rim fences in a much lighter shade of green, which fades into gold near the pupil. I'm mesmerized by the hypnotic impact of the colors swirling together.

Once again, Echo saves me from becoming a mindless mess who will do whatever this man says. A gentle shove alerts me to stay strong. Supportive solidarity at its finest. Her jab also reminds my scattered wits that it's my turn to speak.

"Um," I mutter eloquently. "This is a dead end, boss. Turn around and set your sights elsewhere."

"Nah, you're the one I need. Nobody else is too much, which is just right for this situation."

"I still don't understand how that's possible. You hate me."

"Hate is such a strong word," he murmurs.

My breath hitches when he tucks hair behind my ear. "What are you doing?"

His eyes become bottomless pools that threaten to drown me. "Have you thought about our kiss?"

"No," I blurt.

"Why don't I believe you?"

Probably because I'm lying my blingy-butt jeans right off. "Not sure, but you should. There's no spark between us. The leftover glitter on your face doesn't count. Better luck with the next gal."

Low thunder booms from his chest and sends a burst of static across my skin. "Should I try again? To prove you're full of shit."

I feign nonchalance with a shrug. Meanwhile, my pulse is a stampede of wild mustangs. "It's your pride on the line."

His mouth flattens into a hard line. "Do you regret not pushing me away? Maybe I shouldn't have been spontaneous."

I consider feeding into his misplaced guilt. The pinch in my gut scolds me. My conscience won't allow foul play. "You would've known if I wanted you to stop."

That devilish smirk reappears. "Does that mean you like me, Twinkles?"

"Don't press your luck."

"Unfortunately for you, I'm going to do just that."

I brace myself for his underlying meaning to lunge at me. Brody bends slightly, the brim of his hat bumping my high ponytail. Silence crackles between us and I'm frozen within the static. All I can do is breathe, which is a mistake. He smells too good. The woodsy musk is intoxicating my common sense. I'm liable to fall for his nonsense scheme if I don't get some space.

Before I can move, he lifts his hand and I anticipate his touch. Just before making contact with my cheek, his palm shifts to land on Echo's head. A *whoosh* escapes me. Flutters erupt in my stomach as heat sizzles across my face. This man has me rattled. Again.

"It's interesting that you chose to ride this one today," he muses while petting the mare's forelock.

"Why's that?" The husky notes in my voice betray me.

But Brody doesn't seem to notice, or pretends to be consumed in stroking Echo's black mane. "I just talked to my uncle about adding her to the upcoming auction."

That sobers me immediately. The warmth traveling through my veins gets snuffed as I replay his words. But the message still doesn't compute. "What did you just say?"

"Not sure if I'm ready to sell her, but she deserves more than sitting around the compound. Mom would agree." The briefest flash of a grimace is his only sign of remorse.

I laugh. The sound is choppy and unhinged. "Wow, that's a good one. You've pulled some pranks, but joking about getting rid of your mom's favorite horse isn't funny."

"Which is why I'm taking this very seriously."

"You can't just… get rid of her. She belongs to your mom. How could you even suggest that as an option?" An emotional tidal wave crashes over me and my vision blurs against the onslaught.

Meanwhile, Brody looks bored while I fight tears. "Contrary to what you think, I'm not a total monster. I'll only consider reputable buyers who treat their herd like royalty."

My brain scrambles as I try to quickly calculate how much money I have to my name. "I'll take her."

"Doubt you can afford the asking price," he deadpans. "Unless…"

When his pause hangs in the balance, I roll my wrist to spur him on. "Good grief, spit it out and put me out of my misery."

"Marry me," he drawls.

It feels like all the air is sucked from my lungs. "Excuse me?" I wheeze.

"Forget the fake dating. Agree to be my wife and the mare stays put."

Clarity slams into me while I stare at him. I barely recognize this man looming over me like a vengeful rival. His judgment is clouded by the desperation to rule his cowboy kingdom. Or I've given him more grace than he ever deserved.

"Holy shit." I lift a shaky hand to my lips. "You're using Echo as a bargaining chip?"

Brody's face resembles a stony mask, reflecting indifference and ruthless determination. "If that's what you'd like to call it. Doesn't matter to me. I just need a bribed bride to secure the business."

A hot lash strikes against my chest and I rub at the burn. I'm not sure how I didn't catch on sooner. This man's main currency is ulterior motives. My bottom lip wobbles when I ask, "Do you feel good about yourself?"

"As I've already said, I'll do what's necessary to guarantee that Benson Farmstead is mine."

"You're actually willing to sell your soul?" I slap a palm against his chest that might as well be an icy rock. "This horse is your mother's trusted partner. She meant more to her than money or getting ahead. You should preserve every piece of her memory. They can't be replaced. Hold those treasures tight. Don't sell them off for the sake of a business transaction."

"Lovely speech. I told you at the beginning that this deal would cost me." He pinches the bridge of his nose. "What's your decision?"

My jaw hangs loose on a hollow whistle. "You can't do this."

"Trust me when I tell you that I can," he challenges.

"But it's blackmail, or coercion." I'm not sure which one is correct for this crime he's trying to commit.

His jaw clenches. "And?"

"It's wrong to put me in this position."

"Tell that to my father," he mutters. "Trust me, this isn't how I would choose to do things."

"Then why are you going along with it? You can refuse."

Brody's exhale is weary, sinking down to his bones. "Dad won't see reason."

"Must run in the family."

"Clever." He tugs at the cuffs of his Western shirt. The long sleeves are almost appropriate for the weather as autumn creeps closer. "I'm just following through on what's required of me. That's the way business goes."

"But this isn't some simple transaction. You're asking me to forfeit my beliefs in what marriage represents. I want my vows to be real."

"Which is why I've added more incentive for you to

overlook that moral high ground." A pinch tightens the space between his brows.

"No, she's not yours to sell. Please reconsider. Your mother loved this horse." My voice borders on a plea.

"Why does everyone insist on giving me too much credit?" He rephrases my earlier thoughts too precisely. "It turns out that I'm not the good guy. The sooner you realize that, the faster we can finalize our arrangement."

"I'll never agree to your terms." I tug on the reins until Echo is shielded behind me. "Once Bianca and your father hear about this, you'll be rethinking your strategy real quick."

"Don't threaten me with a good time, Twinkles."

"Have you always been this…?"

"Calculating?"

That's far too complimentary." I analyze his features, searching for a crack that reveals the truth. "This isn't you. Why are you going to such extremes?"

"My mother died. Our family is fractured. The weight of our empire now rests on my shoulders. That about sums it up, yeah?"

"Don't use your grief as an excuse to be an asshole."

"You have no idea what I'm feeling."

My gaze scans his frigid demeanor again. "I'm beginning to believe you feel nothing at all."

"Now you're finally getting it." He chuckles but the dark noise is something from a nightmare. "Rest assured, I'm fulfilling my promise to her by ensuring our legacy continues to thrive."

"She wouldn't approve of this."

His expression goes arctic and I almost shiver. "You have no idea what she wanted."

My gulp is audible, but I don't waver. "I know she wouldn't have wanted this. She wouldn't want you stooping to such levels."

"There you go again, sticking your assumptions where they don't belong." He dips until our noses almost touch. "Haven't you learned by now that you're not part of our family?"

"But aren't you trying to force me to be just that?"

"In name only."

"Not interested." I shove past him and whip out my phone. "Bianca will never believe what you're trying to do."

"And she won't until it's too late," Brody calls after me.

But I barely hear him over the outgoing call ringing in my ear.

CHAPTER THIRTEEN

Brody

"**H**OLY HAY BALES!" THE FAMILIAR VOICE BELLOWS across the parking lot and stops me in my tracks. "Are my old eyes deceiving me or is Brody Benson at a charity event?"

I turn to acknowledge Ted Malone's humor. He's been friends with my dad since they were kids and remains a permanent staple in our lives. Some of that might have to do with him being the town mayor for at least a dozen or so years.

A breeze kicks up dust while I meet him halfway to the gate. "Don't make me sound like such a Scrooge. I'm always happy to support a worthy cause."

Especially if it involves tracking down a certain cowgirl and ruffling her rhinestones.

Ted bobs his head as we walk to the park entrance. "Just busting your chops. Benson Farmstead is always the first to donate."

"And I'll be sure to keep it that way."

His meaty palm grips my shoulder. "Cloverleaf Meadows is in your debt. If you ever need anything, be sure to holler."

"You know I will." Not that I've ever called in a favor, but it's good to have in my back pocket.

"I've been meaning to ask"—he lowers his voice before adding—"is it true you're getting married?"

A chuckle puffs free and I scrub over my lips. Dad must've shared his grand scheme. "That's the plan."

Ted hums. "And Paisley Keaton is your intended bride?"

I survey the crowd gathered for the event, searching for a particular shade of twinkly blonde. "If she'll have me."

"Now that's interesting," he muses. "I talked to Bill the other day and he didn't know a thing about his daughter getting hitched."

Pressure cinches around my ribs. "Ah, Ted. You've gone and spoiled the surprise. I've got a whole spectacle planned to ask for his approval."

"Oh, shoot." The old man blanches. "I didn't mean to barge into your business."

"Nah, it's fine. I understand getting ahead of myself."

Ted wipes his sweaty brow. "Thank goodness. I'd hate to be the one who ruined your proposal."

"To be honest, you've probably made the process easier for me. Laid the groundwork I hadn't gotten around to yet."

He brightens, squaring his shoulders like a proud politician. "Glad to be of service."

My concentration wanders to the far field where a horse trailer pulls in, joining the long row of others. "Decent turnout, huh?"

"Looks that way. Some folks are usin' this as an

opportunity to ditch excess stock before winter hits. Oh, that reminds me"—he drops his tone to a conspiring level again—"are you sellin' Echo?"

Every muscle in my body solidifies into stone. It's a chore to breathe through the block of guilt now resting on my chest. "No, of course not. Who would say such a thing?"

Am I manipulating Paisley to believe otherwise? Yes. Do I feel bad about that? Only when I think about it long enough. Fuck, I really am an asshole.

Shame slams into me with the force of a wrecking ball. Maybe I'm taking things too far. I'd purposely avoided thinking about that crooked curveball I threw at Paisley. It was foolish of me to assume word wouldn't get out about my latest dick move. The evidence of my inflated confidence is mocking me. And to make the situation worse, it's been less than a week.

It's only then I realize that Ted is staring at me too carefully. "Hey, don't let the rumors get to ya. Figured it was a pile of manure."

"Right," I rasp.

He brushes off his hands as if it's that easy to drop the subject. "Your dad coming today?"

"Nope. He's out of town with Uncle Jimmy. There's a breeder in Montana who insisted we need to see their new stud in person. All too eager to spread his seed." I almost gag on my own attempt at lightening the mood.

Ted's bushy eyebrows rise to the cloudy sky. "You got him to leave the compound?"

"After much persuasion." Damn, that's one more slash against me. I'll have to beg Mom for extra forgiveness before bed tonight.

"And here you are, making a public appearance. Way to rule the roost." He pats me on the back. "Good for you, Brody."

"Mhmm, just doing what I can. What's with the barrel race on a ball field?" I lift my chin to the makeshift arena.

"Not sure," Ted laughs. "From what I've heard, they got the idea on the YouTube. Or maybe it was that clock app. What's it called? Ticky-tack?"

"TikTok," I offer.

He snaps his fingers. "Yes, that's the one. The committee brought the suggestion to several organizations. Race for the Fences was the fastest to accept."

But I'm barely listening. My future wife has revealed herself. Thunder roars in my ears as I pinpoint Paisley's position in the temporary corral. She's waving her arms in wild motions while chatting with her cousin. From the looks of things, Cassidy just got done riding. I find myself wondering why Paisley didn't enter. The best answer will come straight from the source.

"Great talking to you, Ted." I give him a crisp nod before stalking my target. "I'll be in touch about that favor."

"What favor?" he calls after me.

I lift my hand in farewell. "You'll see soon enough."

Meanwhile, Paisley is all I see. Her golden hair shines bright even in overcast conditions. She's a beacon solely meant to snare me.

My boots stomp across grass and dirt to erase the distance between us. People wisely leap from my path. The determination in my glare probably signals an alarm. It makes getting to her a short trek across the pen. Just as I'm about to make my presence known, Paisley begins backing away from her cousin.

She clips me with her elbow and immediately whirls to face me. An apology waits on her parted lips until recognition settles in. Her glare could scare unruly children into behaving. It has the opposite effect on me.

Paisley fumes when my smirk stretches wider. "What the hell are you doing here?"

As if I'm going to reveal the truth. "None of your concern."

She stabs a finger into my chest. "You better not be trying to sell Echo again."

I sweep her hand off me before I yank her closer on reflex. "It's none of your business, Twinkles."

"Don't even go there." She huffs and crashes into my shoulder on her way past me for a hasty retreat. "If I find out you're trying to get rid of her, you'll have hell to pay."

That response is almost comical. But I guess Ted was right about people using this event to test the buyer's market before winter. That hadn't been my intention upon arrival, but I sure as shit can use it to my benefit.

Just as Paisley is about to storm off, I reach for her arm and haul her against me. "Not so fast. We have an arrangement to discuss."

She yanks from my grasp. "There's nothing left to talk about."

"Be my wife, Twinkles."

Her posture becomes a rigid beam. "You can't afford me, boss. My moral compass is priceless and always points in the opposite direction of where you are."

Whispers from those nearby begin to buzz in my ears.

I turn slightly to shield her from the crowd. "You'd rather I sell Echo?"

"I'd rather you return to being a decent human and quit trying to force me."

"Not happening."

"Figures," she huffs. "You're a stubborn ass and I'm done trying to find any redeeming qualities."

"Guess I came to the right place then," I drawl.

Her eyes narrow into daggers. "You wouldn't dare."

I lean in until my cheek brushes hers. My exhale caresses her ear and she shivers. "We both know I will, just to prove a point."

She pulls away to search my gaze. Her unshed tears are a knife to the gut, but a few droplets won't stop me from pushing harder. It's only fair that she crumbles too. A single glance from this woman rips me open and exposes the ugly rot I've become.

I grind my teeth. She was wrong the other day and I fed the lie. But the truth is that I do feel. Too much, thanks to her. She's responsible for this downward spiral I'm caught in. My mother's death should've ripped me to shreds, but this burst of sunshine streaking into my life is what's turning me inside out. Whenever I get near Paisley, I have the sudden urge to kiss her into submission while simultaneously spanking her ass red. She really does bring out the worst in me.

"You're gonna regret it," she whispers.

A sharp ache stabs at my gut. It's strange and uncomfortable but I'm beginning to realize that the pain beats being numb. That's why I find myself begging for another hit.

"What did my sister have to say?" My heart pounds when Paisley dips her chin.

"Bianca is busy on her trip, which I'm sure you know." She bites her bottom lip while a rosy flush races up her throat. Fuck, yeah. That hits the spot. "But she's assured me you're just on a power trip and won't take it too far."

"When was that?"

Paisley fidgets with a jewel on her belt. "It's been a while."

"Haven't gotten ahold of her lately?" It requires villainous effort to mask a grin.

Her baby blues leap to my face, scrounging for secrets. "Have you?"

My shrug is easy. "Don't worry about it."

"Easy for you to say." Her frown flattens into a firm line. "I'm caught in a sticky trap with no escape."

"There's always a choice," I remind her.

Paisley tips her head skyward and groans. "Why are you the worst?"

"You bring it out in me, and insist on being difficult."

"Me?" Her gasp is the fakest form of shock I've witnessed since Mom's soap opera era. "You're the one playing bride or blackmail."

"I can assure you that my intentions aren't built on corrupt foundations. This is for the greater good. If my uncle is put in charge, Benson Farmstead will be ruined. My mother definitely wouldn't want that."

"But what you're asking me to do is wrong."

"Only if you bring emotions along for the ride. It's a contractual agreement. Simple and brief. You'll be compensated for your cooperation."

"Wow, that's very sweet." Her voice is devoid of inflection, which hurts me more than I care to admit. "You sound like a master manipulator."

There's a sudden lump in my throat and I gulp. "It's a recent development."

"Suits you well," she mutters.

Heat floods my veins and I widen my stance. "Careful with the compliments, Twinkles."

"Or what? You'll threaten to trap me in a tower? It would fit with the story since you're already trying to steal my free will."

I shake my head. "There's a choice. Make the right one."

Blue flames burn in her fierce stare. "I've always preferred the left."

My cock jerks behind my zipper. "Fuck, you and that sassy mouth. If the circumstances were different, I'd very much enjoy fucking that bratty attitude out of you. With consent, of course."

Her breath hitches as a fresh blush blooms across her cheeks. "Well, how about that? There are lines you won't cross."

"We all have limits. Is this truly yours?"

Before she can answer, a hush settles over the crowd as someone makes an announcement. Paisley's eyes widen and she begins hoofing it to the benches. "If you made me miss their big moment, I'm gonna put you on blast over the loudspeaker."

I match her quick stride. "You're ready to broadcast your devotion to me? Why didn't you say so sooner?"

She keeps her focus locked straight ahead. "Your skull is thicker than your ego."

"Thanks for noticing. Care for a private tour to see where else I'm hardheaded for you?"

She slams to an abrupt stop at the bottom of the bleacher stairs. "Stop following me."

"Why?" My gaze trails to the front row where several guys are looking at us. "Is someone waiting on you?"

"As if I'd pour more gasoline on this dumpster fire."

I breathe easily for what feels like the first time in months. "Saving yourself for me then?"

"Spoiler alert," she clips. "I'm not a virgin."

Desperate need has my dick trying to punch a hole through my jeans. I almost groan at the mounting pressure demanding release. "That's a relief, Twinkles."

Paisley falters but snaps her slack jaw shut quickly enough. "Why?"

A tug on her belt loop crashes her chest into mine. My lips dust her forehead as a bright future appears in front of us. "I won't have to be gentle on our wedding night."

CHAPTER FOURTEEN

Paisley

MY PHONE TREMBLES IN MY GRIP AND I PAUSE ON the porch before stepping inside. The ringing cuts to Bianca's voicemail, which leads to the inevitable beep. I hang my head as the repetitive cycle continues, but that doesn't stop me from leaving a message.

"Hey, Bee. It's me. Again. I'm starting to get really worried. Your dad is nowhere to be found either. I really need to talk to you. It's urgent. Your brother is still threatening to sell Echo. I'm not sure if he actually will, but it's freaking me out. Not hearing back from you isn't helping. Please call me. Day or night. Love you. Bye."

Just as I disconnect the call, the front door swings open. My mother stands there in her Sunday best. She blinks at me before doing a visual sweep of the surrounding area. Crickets and the setting sun streaking across the pale sky are all that keep me company.

Her sharp blue eyes return to mine. "Were you talking to someone?"

My arms wrap protectively across my middle to ward off the evening chill. "Just leaving a message for Bianca."

"Still can't reach her?"

I shake my head. "She must be really busy."

Other alternatives are too traumatic to consider just yet. It hasn't been that long since I've heard from her. But I'm nearing the point of asking Brody if he's spoken with her in the last two weeks. My stomach cramps into a painful knot. The fact that Dennis has also gone off the grid only adds to my concern.

"Well, don't worry about that now. Come in." Mom practically yanks me over the threshold. "We have a guest for dinner."

That's not unexpected but slightly disappointing. My parents are connected to everyone in town thanks to the success of their general store. They frequently have visitors stop over just to chat. She tugs on my elbow when I don't move fast enough for her liking. My sandals slip on the floor before I skid to a stop in the entryway.

The dining room isn't visible from where I stand but two recognizable voices carry down the hallway. My heart lurches as I blindly stumble forward. When Dad and the man sitting across from him come into view, I can barely breathe.

"No." My flight instincts kick in, but I only manage to retreat two steps before stumbling into Mom. "This isn't real."

"What's wrong, dear? Looks like you've seen a ghost."

It feels that way too. All of the color has undoubtedly leached from my face if the shocking numb is any indication. The scene in front of me plays like a horror film I'm forced to watch. I can't move or look away. My unblinking stare is glued to where my father recalls the glory from his last fishing trip. His audience of one appears captivated by the story. Even from here, the glint of his scheming is noticeable. This very well might be a nightmare. The only saving grace—albeit tiny—is that they haven't noticed me, too immersed in their conversation.

I duck behind the wall to hide in the shadows. "Why is Brody Benson in your house?" The question quakes off my lips, little more than a whisper.

Mom's forehead creases as she studies my expression. "To talk to your father."

"About what he caught at the lake last month?"

She appears bewildered, her mouth silently opening and closing a few times. "I figured you had at least some idea but maybe not."

"Care to clue me in?"

She clasps my hands in hers. Excitement seeps from her pores as she leans close. "He came to get your dad's permission before asking you to marry him. Such a fine gentleman. Your father gladly gave his stamp of approval. Isn't that wonderful?"

The rug yanks out from under me and the room begins to spin. Forget the horror flick. I have the lead role in an old Western where the daughter gets hitched to the first eligible cowboy who comes knocking.

"This can't be happening," I murmur.

"Are you nervous? It does seem a bit sudden," Mom admits. "But he's very eager."

"And diabolical."

She laughs. "He must've forgotten to include you in his

plans. Don't be too hard on him. Love can be wild and reckless, especially early on. You two have moved rather quickly."

"That's one way of putting it."

The man has gone from a practical stranger to my intended jailer within a month. I peek around the corner. Dad and Brody are still engrossed in their male bonding. Nausea bubbles in my gut and I choke on bile.

My single status is in grave danger, along with my sense of self. This is punishment for keeping my mouth shut. I should've told them about his attempt at blackmailing me. Now he's here, playing nice with my parents.

"I have to stop this," I croak.

Mom's grip on me tightens, drawing my focus back to her. It's only then I notice the stars in her eyes. "Aren't you happy?"

A hot sting blurs my vision and I blink at the threat of tears. "There's something I need to tell you."

She gasps. "You're pregnant."

"Mother!"

Her giggle is too innocent. "What? I'm ready to be a grandma. Sue me. Besides, it's a reasonable assumption based on how fast Brody wants to have the ceremony."

It feels like the control on my destiny is slipping from my grasp. I clap a palm to my clammy forehead. "There's no baby. He's in a hurry to get down the aisle because—"

"Twinkles?"

My shoulders take a hike to snuggle my ears. There goes the privacy protection this wall is supposed to offer. I expel a silent curse before stepping out from my hiding spot. "Yes, boss?"

His chuckle is warm, sliding over me like melted

chocolate. "You can drop the formality. We're far past that point, right?"

"Mhmm, sure."

"I've been waiting for you to arrive." His smile is soft and kind.

The unfamiliar expression boosts his devastating appeal and gives me pause. He wasn't lying about his charm being potent. My pulse gallops as I absorb the catastrophic impact. It's no wonder he has my parents fooled. But I know what's hidden underneath.

That reminder chases off the fog and I remain firmly planted at a safe distance. "I hear you've been busy plotting my demise again."

Brody rises from his seat, rushing toward me like a lovesick fool. "There's something I need to ask you."

"Don't you dare," I grate out.

But he lowers to one knee regardless of my warning. The motion is smooth and practiced as if he's been preparing for this romantic gesture. A muffled cry escapes from Mom, who's watching this train wreck from the sidelines. She's shedding tears like a winter coat in spring. A sideways glance at Dad reveals that he's in a similar state of distress. That's what I'm choosing to refer to the blubbering emotion pinching his face. Meanwhile, I'm two seconds away from fleeing the scene.

"If you don't tell them the truth, I will."

"Go ahead," he taunts.

Another peek at my parents squeezes my heart in a vise. A painful ache spreads through me as I bring my glare back to Brody. "I despise you."

His lips quirk. "I wouldn't have our blissful union begin any other way."

Clarity washes over frazzled nerves, filling me with a sense of calm. I can play the part. At least until a feasible exit strategy presents itself. Revenge is patient and often underestimated until it's too late.

A wide smile stretches my lips as I slip into the role he's so desperate for me to fill.

I fan my eyes and release a dreamy sigh. "This is very sudden, darling. It's almost surreal, like we're in a fairytale. I can't believe how much you love me, but you never skip an opportunity to lay it on extra thick. Isn't that right?"

His right eyelid twitches. "You're impossible to resist."

"Well then? Go ahead."

"Paisley Jane," he croons. "I've been infatuated with you from the moment we first met."

It takes strength I don't possess to hold back a snort. When Brody pauses to let me recover, I roll my wrist. "Please continue."

"As I was saying, your beauty is captivating. You have an undeniable sparkle—both inside and out—that illuminates any space you choose to enter. I've become addicted to that glow, wanting it solely for myself. Call me selfish and I'll admit it. You've got me hooked on you, Twinkles. But more than that, you inspire me to be a better person. One who deserves you. I had no idea what I'd been missing until you showed me. With you by my side, I'll be complete. That's what our love does to me. If you'll let me, I'll prove myself worthy of your love. I can't wait to spend my life making you happy."

I try to remain unaffected, but I'm not a slab of concrete.

The flutters in my belly expand and spread until I feel like I'm floating. This man knows how to win. That's precisely why I'm caught in this predicament. But I can't show weakness.

"What a fitting speech to describe our future together." My breathy tone is too revealing.

Brody winks and whips out a blue box from his pocket. He cracks open the lid, nearly blinding me in the process. "Will you marry me?"

"Is that meant to resemble"—I squint at the glittery band tucked in velvet—"barbwire?"

"All the better to buckle you with," he murmurs.

"You turned my contempt into an engagement ring. How appropriate," I deadpan.

"You'll also be dripping in diamonds. We both win."

"That remains to be seen." I thrust out my left hand for his taking. "Do your worst. I'm done dragging my feet."

"Is that a yes?" The sincerity in his tone almost convinces me that I have a choice. As if this is legit and I can reject him without consequences. His unwavering stare does a good job selling the ruse too.

I groan and roll my eyes. "Yes," I confirm.

Mom and Dad erupt in a chorus of congratulations. Their joy is almost infectious until the haze clears and I remember what's at stake. Brody is ruining what's meant to be one of the most memorable milestones of my life. I should cherish this moment, but it isn't real. Instead, there's a bitter taste in my mouth that I fear might be permanent.

My parents must notice that I'm struggling to choke down this wretched fate. They take the cue and disappear into the kitchen to fetch champagne. Maybe the bubbles will help me escape.

But when Brody slides the ring onto my finger, the cool metal feels like a shackle I'll never break. "Perfect fit."

With our audience preoccupied, I allow my grin to collapse under the weight of this lie. Anger consumes me as he stands to his full height. I grip the front of his shirt and yank him down to my level.

The hatred I feel sizzling in my veins demands that he burns with me. "You're such a jerk. I'll never forgive you for this."

Brody lifts my left hand to pepper kisses on my knuckles. "Lucky for me, I have the rest of our lives to make up for it."

CHAPTER FIFTEEN

Brody

THERE'S A THRUM RUSHING UNDER MY SKIN AS I straighten off the wall. The anticipation has gained momentum, clawing at me to take charge. But this is a delicate matter. An ounce of patience won't hurt me. That doesn't make it easier to stand still.

I resist the urge to check my watch again. As if rewarding my diligence, a buzz comes from my pocket. The excited chatter filling the room fades into a muted hum. A glance at the screen blocks out their voices completely.

612-543-5555: Why is there a glam squad at my apartment?

And just like that, the restless energy goes still.

Me: Good morning, fiancée. I was wondering when you'd finally use my number.

Twinkles: Answer the question.

Me: It's our wedding day.

Twinkles: That's news to me.

Me: Couldn't let you get cold feet.

Twinkles: You proposed two days ago...

Me: Did you prefer a shorter engagement?

Twinkles: Is that a serious question?

Me: I couldn't get us on the schedule sooner. Small town problems.

Twinkles: Wow. You're really something else.

Me: Apologies for the delay. Just sit back and relax. You deserve to be pampered, bride of mine.

Twinkles: We're not getting married and I'm not your anything.

Me: But you said yes.

Twinkles: To avoid disappointing my parents. Thanks again for putting me on the spot. Really nice touch.

Me: Won't they be disappointed when you don't show up to City Hall?

Twinkles: You invited them?!

Fuck, she's adorable. A grin threatens to make an appearance. I force the unwelcome expression to get gone before responding.

Me: Of course they're here. What kind of villain do you take me for?

Twinkles: One with a micro peen.

Me: Care to rephrase that?

Twinkles: I've come to the conclusion that you must have a tiny penis.

Me: Come see for yourself.

Twinkles: You know I won't. That's why you need a fake bride. You're afraid a real one would actually want to have sex with you. At least until she saw your teeny weenie. Gosh, your reputation would be ruined.

Me: Hilarious. Get your ass to the courthouse.

Twinkles: Why are you the worst?

Me: To redeem myself in the end. Best to start from rock bottom.

Twinkles: I'm going to tell my parents the truth before this goes any further.

Me: Should I tell them to call you?

Twinkles: They're already there?!

Me: We had brunch with the mayor. Dad is here too.

Twinkles: Where's Bianca?

Me: In Europe...

Twinkles: Why isn't she answering the phone?

Me: How would I know?

Twinkles: You haven't talked to her?

Me: Colton has passed along a few messages. She's fine.

Twinkles: But she isn't responding to me. What's going on with her?

Me: We'll worry about that later. Focus on getting ready.

Twinkles: I'm not getting married without my best friend present.

Me: We'll have a second wedding once Bianca is home.

Twinkles: That seems excessive. How long are you planning to hold me hostage?

Me: Ask my dad.

Twinkles: I would have but he's been noticeably absent.

Me: He's back now.

Twinkles: How convenient.

Me: Couldn't miss our big day.

Twinkles: But Bianca can? We should just wait until she's here.

Me: That's not an option.

Twinkles: What's the rush? Afraid she won't approve?

My nostrils flare as I expel a burst of frustration. Bianca will sever this arrangement faster than I can rope a calf.

There's a reason my sister has been silent, but she won't be for much longer.

> **Me:** This deal needs to get done. Let the glam squad do their thing. I'll meet you at the altar.

Twinkles: I don't even have a dress.

> **Me:** Sure about that?

Twinkles: What did you do?

Rather than answer, I wait for her to find the garment bag that should be hanging in her closet. There's no stopping my smile now. Damn, there's just something about her that gets to me.

Twinkles: I'm not wearing this.

> **Me:** Don't like it?

Paisley reads the message but the three dots to signal her typing don't appear. My blood pressure spikes as I wait for her verdict. Five seconds is the limit on my tolerance.

> **Me:** I'll send other options. Hold on.

Twinkles: No, it's fine. Be there soon.

A frown flatlines my amusement. It's difficult to decipher a tone through text, but hers definitely isn't pleased. That bothers me more than I want to admit. The disappointment is gnarled and tough to chew. Instead of analyzing the odd reaction, I focus on my accomplishment. Benson Farmstead will officially be mine by this afternoon.

I tuck my phone away and reclaim my spot against the wall. City Hall is deserted, leaving our party to socialize without interruption. Paisley's parents are still mingling with Ted while we wait for the bride to arrive. Dad separates from the group to join me in isolation. His keen awareness scrutinizes my relaxed pose. That distinct gleam appears in his gaze, which immediately puts me on alert.

"Figured you were in for a lengthy uphill battle." Dad tugs at the collar of his dress shirt, the tie probably irritating him. "How did you get her to agree so quickly?"

"Powers of persuasion," I reply.

He claps me on the back. "That's my boy. Never doubted you for a second."

I snort through a grimace. His pride is sorely misplaced. If he hears about what I did to get Paisley to agree, we'll be having a very different conversation.

My gaze turns to the large bay window where the mid-morning sky appears ready to burst with rain. Apparently, that's good luck at a wedding. "What happens next?"

"You become a family man."

"Dad," I press.

His smile is carefree, and makes this contractual obligation worth it. "I won't go back on my word, son. The company is yours."

Pressure lifts off my shoulders and I inhale slowly. "Thanks for that."

Dad scoffs. "I'm the one who should be thanking you. I

get to watch you experience one of the greatest gifts in life. If only your mom was here to witness it too."

Guilt curdles like expired milk in my gut. I haven't let on that my relationship with Paisley is fake. That would defeat the purpose. Dad wants to see me settled. The picture I'm posing for is just that, except the image will fade before the snow starts falling.

At my strained silence, he sniffles and bobs his head. "It doesn't get easier. We just learn to deal with the pain. I'll spend the rest of my days missing her."

Emotion lodges in my throat and I almost choke. "She'd be real disappointed in me right now."

"Nah, your mother is up there singin' your praises. You went after what you wanted and got it. What's not to be proud of?"

I scrub at my wet eyes. Fuck, this is getting out of hand. It's not too late to throw a stone at the deceptive mirage I've created. Guidance would be much appreciated.

That's the precise moment Paisley sweeps into the building like an avenging angel sent to rescue my soul. The sight of her so soon is staggering and weakens my knees. If the wall wasn't already at my back, I'd be crashing into it. She managed to get ready in record time, but her speedy appearance isn't what shocks me. It's just her. I'm not the type to submit, but this woman could convince me to kneel at her feet.

She's simply breathtaking. The long white dress hugs her curves like a lover's embrace. There's just enough sparkle to make her shine without overdoing it. Her golden hair is loosely braided and hangs over one shoulder. A light dusting of makeup highlights her features, somehow brightening what already glows. The pink gloss on her lips is too inviting. I force my boots to remain rooted to the carpet.

June and Neil ditch the mayor to greet their daughter in a whirlwind of excitement and expectations. Nervous energy wafts from their fumbled movements. This is a special occasion they've been waiting to celebrate and will never forget. Paisley hugs her parents, searching the small cluster of guests. Her siblings aren't in attendance. Another strike against me, but there wasn't time to include them.

"You chose well," Dad mumbles from his place beside me.

When Paisley's smile stretches wider, a strange warmth spreads through my chest. I press a palm over the inflicted area. The joyful pounding threatens to break free. It's been so long since I've experienced even a sliver of this intensity.

"She looks happy." I could almost be convinced she actually wants to get married.

My father glances between me and my bride. "Why wouldn't she be?"

Guilt threatens to weasel its way in again, but I manage to trap the pest before critical infestation. "We barely know each other," I deflect.

"That's what the honeymoon is for." He chuckles and wags his brows, making me feel sick for an entirely different reason. "C'mon, kid. Let's get you hitched."

We straighten off the wall as a cohesive unit. Neil and June escort Paisley toward us. As predicted, the stars in my cowgirl's eyes dim when she looks at me. That doesn't stop me from openly admiring her.

"You're radiant, Twinkles."

"Not too bad yourself, almost husband." Her smile is brittle and saturated in betrayal.

The tie around my neck suddenly tightens. I put that stain on her usually sunny expression. She'll be rid of me soon enough.

"We make quite a pair." My suit is entirely black to contrast her pure white. I hold out a bent elbow, which she hesitantly accepts.

Our pace is slow and leisurely as if we're headed to a blissful happily ever after rather than a corrupt ceremony. Ted stands at the front of his chambers, beckoning us forward. Paisley's steps falter.

"The mayor is officiating our sham of a wedding?"

"He owed me a favor."

Her bottomless stare attempts to burrow beneath my scowl and stubble. "You're something else."

"About to be yours," I rasp.

"In name only," she reminds on a whisper.

I nod and Ted proceeds with the farce. The vows are basic and bland, quickly leading to when we exchange rings. I grab both from my pocket, holding her delicate band aloft.

My pulse sprints, booming in the quiet space. "Do you accept this ring as a token of my unwavering love and devotion?"

Paisley's slender throat quivers from an audible gulp. "I do."

The thin loop slides onto her finger, fitting just right. I had her set custom made to appear as one when connected, like barbwire and grit. That's what she'll need to withstand our matrimony.

Paisley shifts her hand to admire her new embellishment. "Black diamonds?"

"Like my heart," I explain. "Figured you could use a reminder of me."

"As if I could forget who I belong to," she mutters.

Heat floods my veins at a dangerous speed. An image of Paisley beneath me, begging for more, slams into my mind.

"Careful with what you say or I'll want to keep you that way." Getting aroused in front of this crowd is shameful, even for me.

Ted coughs into his fist. "It's your turn to repeat after me, Paisley."

She studies the band I chose for myself. The black gold is inlaid with parallel platinum lines. It's a relatively plain design except for the yellow diamond set in the center. Her polished nail rubs over the small stone.

"It's a symbol of you," I explain. "Now you'll be with me wherever I go."

She sucks in a sharp breath, eager gaze leaping to mine. "That's very romantic."

"Maybe I'm not so bad, hmm?"

Her eyes narrow. "Why are you being sweet?"

"I might've taken a few crooked turns to get here, but it's not my intention to remain enemies. We can be civil. There's nothing for us to fight babout."

"Stealing my lines again?"

One shoulder lifts in acknowledgment. "I'm finally taking your advice. When applicable," I tack on.

The mayor clears this throat again. I shoot him a warning glare. Paisley is much more considerate of his time. She repeats the required phrase while bumping my fingertip with the metal like a taunt.

My gaze sears into hers as I recite the words that unite us. "I do."

Paisley slips the thick band over my calloused knuckle. The weight of it on my finger is foreign, but not uncomfortable. Almost like a rite of passage I never planned to seek.

Ted concludes his spiel, reaching the pivotal point. "It gives me great honor to pronounce you as husband and wife. You may kiss your bride, Brody."

"With pleasure." I lift her left hand and peck the spot above the ring I just gave her.

"You can do better than that," Neil jests.

I quirk a brow at my bride. "Should we give the crowd what they want?"

A fiery blush stains her cheeks. "If you insist."

"Need to hear you say it. Won't steal another liberty, even if it's part of the tradition."

Her chin lifts in offering. "Kiss me, husband."

I cradle her face between my palms. Her lashes flutter at the gentle touch, followed by a soft whimper. Anticipation crackles along my skin again. No more delay.

In a swift motion, I swoop down and seal the deal. She's stiff and unyielding until I smile against her lips. Paisley surrenders, melting into our first—and possibly last—kiss as a married couple. Hoots and hollers strain my ears as I enjoy her taste for a bit longer. When we pull apart, the restlessness inside of me is subdued. At least temporarily.

"Congratulations, Mrs. Benson." I drift the pad of my thumb along her rekindled blush. "You're even more beautiful as my wife."

CHAPTER SIXTEEN

Paisley

"**I**'M NOT GOING." MY ARMS CROSS TO ADOPT A defensive stance against this bridal abduction.

This entire day has already spiraled out of my control. The ink is still drying on our marriage license but now I'm expected to hop into an Escalade limousine without hesitation. We're about to be whisked away to an undisclosed location. I've read too many dark romances to willingly fall for this script. The urge to stomp my heels into the concrete is strong.

Dennis frowns. "You don't want to go on a honeymoon?"

"That's not what this is," I state.

"Call it whatever you want," my darling groom interjects. He bends until his lips brush my ear. "Afraid to be alone with me?"

"Very much so." My jaw juts forward at a stubborn angle. "Especially when I'm kept in the dark about where you're taking me."

I take a moment to glare at my husband. He isn't

wearing a hat for a change. That accessory seems permanently attached to him, except for this special occasion. His hair is longer than I thought—on the right side of unruly. The dark chocolate shade looks warm and inviting, but that's not true. Dressed like this, he's a ruthless businessman in a custom suit. A downward glance reveals he doesn't belong in a stuffy boardroom. His cowboy boots tie him to his country roots.

Brody's flat stare finds mine. "I had nothing to do with this."

"But you know our destination."

His expression remains impassive. "Your guess is as good as mine."

I blink at him. "And you're okay with that?"

"Contractual obligations," he grumbles.

"What type of clothes should I bring?" I'm hunting for clues like any sane person about to be snatched.

"Already taken care of." Brody gestures to the trunk.

"You packed my things?"

His nod is a single dip. "And the rest will be delivered to the farmstead while we're gone."

"That's invasive."

"Or proactive," he retorts.

"You just assume I'll move into your mansion." The desire to stomp my feet resurfaces.

He snorts. "Would you prefer we wedge ourselves into your studio apartment? Your horses are already at my place. Might as well join them."

"That's just temporary."

He swoops down until his breath tickles my ear. "Much like our arrangement, hmm?"

"You can discuss living arrangements in the limo." Mom approaches and wraps an arm around my shoulders. "Dennis planned this trip to be a surprise, dear. I'm sure it's somewhere very romantic."

"Spared no expense." The man I previously thought was on my side suddenly resembles an instigator. "You'll have the time of your life."

Or I'll never be heard from again. Not that I can voice my concern out loud without unraveling this entire debacle. It's a bit late for that.

I'm outnumbered, which rouses my flight response. A quick stop at the bathroom might be in order. Then I can scurry down the fire escape before they notice I'm gone. That's when I notice all eyes are on me. My swift exit strategy must show on my face.

Mom tugs me closer. "Are you worried about the expectations of your wedding night? Don't worry, dear. I'm sure your husband will be a perfect gentleman."

"Good grief," I mumble as my face bursts into flames. "No, that's not the issue."

She exhales loudly, fluttering a palm to her chest. "That's a relief. For a second there, I thought we'd have to review sex education."

"Please stop."

Her giggle has me bracing for more humiliation. "Don't be shy. You're a married woman now. Make me a grandma and I'll be tickled pink."

I'm about ready to demand entry into the stretch SUV just to escape this conversation. "This has been fun and all, but I have to use the ladies' room."

Brody grips onto my waist before I can attempt to flee. "We'll stop on the way."

"To this mysterious place that could be anywhere?"

"It's close enough to drive." He tips his head to our chauffeur.

The wind whips at my braid, pulling more tendrils loose. "That's something at least." I can hitchhike back to town as a last resort.

"Better get going to beat the rain." My groom points to the sky that looks angrier than me.

"We'll miss you!" Mom almost suffocates me in a tight hug.

"Be sure to call once you arrive," Dad says while tucking me into a farewell embrace.

My smile feels forced. "Fingers crossed there's reception."

Dennis grins, giving me a fatherly shoulder squeeze. "No need. Your husband will keep you occupied."

"Make me a grandbaby," my mother croons.

"Not gonna happen. Love ya!" I blow Mom a noisy kiss and haul ass to the Escalade.

Leather and luxury swaddle me as I climb inside. The scent of wealth drips off the mirrored ceiling onto the plush carpet. Windows provide a panoramic view. If I'm forced to travel, this fancy ride isn't too shabby.

Brody follows me in, but sits at the far end of the opposite couch seat. The distance eases the tension radiating between my shoulders. A low groan has me sliding a peek at him. He's tugging at the knot of his tie and tosses the black silk onto the bench beside him. The top two buttons on his dress shirt are next. I try not to watch the fluid motions but something about him loosening up is very attractive. It also makes him appear more… real. He needs to unwind just like everyone else. That doesn't mean he's approachable.

The limo pulls away from the curb, leaving Cloverleaf Meadows and my freedom behind. Familiar landscape fades into an unknown blur out the window. Brody doom scrolls on his phone while I stew in silence for a solid hour.

The steady motion and thump from the tires lull me into forced relaxation. My eyelids grow heavy and I rest my head against the cool glass. Maybe I'll doze for a bit.

"Champagne?"

I jerk upright when Brody's voice shatters the quiet. He's holding up a bottle of Dom Pérignon for my inspection. My mouth practically waters at the sight. Never in my wildest dreams did I imagine getting the chance to try the expensive label.

It's difficult to contain my enthusiasm when a giddy squeal is crawling up my throat. "Sure, why not."

Brody grunts and shakes his head while ripping off the foil. His motions are smooth and efficient as he pops the cork. Not a drop is spilled. I almost want to applaud his talent, but he doesn't need the stroke to his ego.

After filling a crystal flute to the top, he lifts the glass for me to take. The only problem is that I'm far out of reach. I quirk a brow, not making any indication to change that. Brody doesn't move either. We stare at each other from opposite sides of the vehicle. Static crackles in the tense pause. This is a power struggle, one of many I picture in our near future.

His stubbled jaw clenches, a muscle leaping under the pressure. He slides along the supple leather to deliver my beverage. I accept it with a victorious smile.

"Don't say I never did nothin' for you," he mutters. It doesn't escape my notice that he stays in the spot beside me.

"My darling husband is such a sweet man," I croon in response.

But then my sole focus turns to the Dom now in my clutches. Bubbles tickle my nose and I giggle. I force myself to only take a small sip. This type of delicacy is meant to be savored, and I immediately understand why. Crisp sweetness bathes my tongue in a cool caress that leaves me wanting more. A moan slips free and I don't even care. It's just too delicious.

"Good?" Brody's voice is a deep rasp.

"Heavenly," I sigh before treating myself to another taste. "Best thing I've put in my mouth."

Brody chokes on his champagne. Green flames heat me to my core when he looks at me. "Challenge accepted, wife."

I snort into my drink. "Good luck with that."

"You should know that once my mind is set on something, I don't give up until it's mine."

"Is that what you think I am?" I give him a slow once-over. "Yours?"

"Yes," he clips. "I have the certificate to prove it."

"In name only," I taunt. "That's all you wanted from me."

"We'll see." He downs his entire glass and pours himself another. "Things change."

Warmth pools in my belly, but I blame it on the liquor. My gaze wanders from the fizzy bubbles to the bling adorning my ring finger before scanning the Escalade's posh interior. "Sometimes I forget how rich you are."

"*We* are," he corrects.

A shrill laugh escapes me. "Um, no. What's yours is definitely not mine."

Brody's stare smolders into mine. "Did I make you sign a prenup?"

My eyes bulge. "Holy shit, you're crazy."

"Figured it was the least I could do."

The reminder of our situation sits like a rock in my stomach. "I'm going to donate every penny to charity."

His broad shoulders lift carelessly. "Go ahead. It's your money."

"I don't want it." My hand waves absently at the pristine interior that symbolizes his lifestyle. "I don't want any of this."

"A little late for that, wife."

I'm about to sulk back into silence when a thought occurs to me. My pulse takes off into a gallop. "The horses!"

"What about them?"

My posture goes straighter than a fence post. "Who's taking care of them while we're gone?"

"Bianca."

I freeze. "Bianca?"

"Your best friend," he drawls.

"Don't be an ass."

"Might as well ask me to quit breathing." His full lips slant into a smirk.

My next exhale is a sputter. "Was that a joke?"

"Must be the champagne." He glares at the gold liquid as if it's tainted.

I swat at our digression. "When is Bianca coming home?"

A spark dances in his gaze. "Her flight lands tonight."

"And you're just telling me this now?"

"You didn't ask."

The urge to throw my drink in his face twitches my fingers. But I couldn't do that to the Dom. "I very specifically said I didn't want to get married without my best friend present. We could've waited a day."

"Didn't know she was headed home until an hour ago." His nonchalant tone grates at my fraying nerves.

"How is that possible?"

"Colton sucks at using the phone."

"Why hasn't Bianca called?" It's the same question I've been asking for almost two weeks.

"You can ask her when we get back."

"We should turn around." I make a spinning gesture with my index finger.

"Not happening." His legs splay wider, almost covering the entire length of the couch. The extreme man-spread makes it clear we aren't going anywhere.

"What aren't you telling me?"

"I have to see this through." He adjusts on the seat again. If I didn't know better, I'd assume he's uncomfortable.

I narrow my eyes at this expert in deception. "Where are you taking me?"

"Not sure, Twinkles." Brody glances out the window. "But we're about to find out."

CHAPTER SEVENTEEN

Brody

A GRUFF CHUCKLE PARTS MY LIPS AS I STEP OUT OF the limo to admire our home for the next week. My dad sent us to an isolated cabin in the woods. But calling this place a cabin is an insult to the builder. The log structure is massive and modern. It's the type of spot that someone with money owns to escape the daily grind. Comfort and luxury are combined.

I do a visual sweep of the area. There's nothing else to see except the lake and trees. No sign of people or civilization. Only nature in its purest form. We're alone, which is far from peaceful.

At least there's a truck in the driveway. That must be Dad's doing as well. It's awful considerate to provide us with a means of escape.

I turn back to the Escalade, peering through the open door. "Planning to join me, wife?"

"No," Paisley mutters from her seat. "And quit calling me that."

"That's what you are, I'm afraid."

Her baby blues narrow into feisty slits. "For how long?"

"Why don't you get out and we'll talk."

She sniffs, still not moving. "I'd rather go home."

"And I'd rather we never met but here we are."

Paisley sucks in a sharp breath. "Rude."

"Accurate." I stretch my arm, fingers curling to beckon her. "C'mon."

"No."

"You've already come this far," I grit. "Might as well enjoy the scenery."

After several disgruntled huffs, my bride slides across the leather and accepts my hand. I hoist her from the vehicle like she's a sack of feathers. She squeaks at my gentle treatment but the sound cuts off when her gaze locks on our lakeshore home.

"Wow," she breathes.

"Not too shabby, eh?" Even I can admit that Dad chose well for us.

"It's stunning." Paisley's steps are clumsy as she blindly walks toward the A-frame cabin. "We get to stay here?"

"Oh, now you want to stay?"

Her wide stare moves along the log base, lifting skyward to the tall peak of the roof. "I might've been a bit hasty at first."

My chuckle confronts her feigned indifference. "Wonder what you'll say after seeing the rest."

"Ready when you are."

"It's okay to admit you're excited."

"Just cold." She shivers and I'm reminded that it's much

cooler in northern Minnesota compared to the southern region.

Her wedding dress does little to conserve any warmth she's cooking. My suit jacket can be a quick fix to that problem. I have a hunch that the gesture will get shrugged off instantly. A blanket of burrs would be better received.

"Dammit, woman." I gesture to the cobbled path. "Get your ass inside."

Our driver unloads the bags and we trail after him to the front door. He unlocks the deadbolt, stepping aside to grant us entry. I pass him a hefty tip in exchange for the keys, and then he's backing away to allow our honeymoon to begin. Just fucking great.

Paisley is held captive again once we cross the threshold. To be fair, the view straight ahead is worthy of her awestruck expression. The entire back wall is made of glass. Beyond the window is a deck that's large enough to host a Benson family reunion. There's a hot tub sunk into the right side that might get some use.

"What a view." Paisley's voice is sweeter than spun sugar as she appreciates our private patio surrounded by nothing but trees and the bay.

"Damn fine indeed." But my gaze is on her.

That realization has me turning my focus to the kitchen, which occupies half the square footage. A lounge area fit with a fireplace sits opposite. There's not much else. My skin is suddenly stretched too tight. I'm cramped in this crowded floor plan. It's cozy and intimate and clearly meant to keep us in close quarters.

At least the interior design reflects the same upscale quality as the outside. Not that I expected less with Dad responsible. Meanwhile, my wife appears impressed with the expensive shit arranged around the room. I'm reminded that we come from vastly different backgrounds. Is this the way into her good graces? My gaze finds its way back to her as she gets a feel for the layout.

Her fingers drift along glossy countertops and stainless-steel appliances. A plush rug stops her short, toes curling into the thick fibers. She pets the fuzzy blanket hanging over a chair as if the cashmere knit is the softest thing she's ever felt. Even the light fixtures get an adoring glance. The burning in my gut certainly isn't jealousy. Hell, I'm glad she's distracted. That leaves me to do as I please.

Paisley wanders off to explore the lofted den or whatever's up the staircase while I settle onto the couch and flip on the news. While the anchors drone on, I take a moment to breathe. It's quiet and still and awkward.

Nothing needs my attention. I haven't sat idle since influenza bit me in the ass four years ago. But even in a fever haze, I was keeping tabs on the business. That's not an option now. Dad insisted that I treat this trip as a true vacation. Anyone who bothers me—excluding my bride—will face his wrath.

A dull throb kicks against my temples at the reminder of who's sharing this space with me. My thumb spins the ring on my finger, and I consider removing the strange weight. That impulse vanishes faster than it formed. If I ditch the symbol of our marriage, Paisley will be quick to follow. She's just looking for an excuse to flee. The drive up here was tense, just like every other battle I've fought against her. I slip off my jacket and try to get more comfortable. The cuffs of my shirt are too tight, just itching to be rolled up. That would require me to expose more than I'm willing.

But I'll have to let my guard down eventually. We're stuck in this cabin together. Being alone with her for days on end will dry hump my last nerve. I've been trying to trick myself into believing it's a bad dream.

The approaching slap of bare feet on hardwood dissolves that illusion. "There's only one bed."

My eyes shift from the screen to where Paisley broods. "Is that a problem?"

"Yes!" She tosses her arms in the air like that should've been obvious. "Where will you sleep?"

"In the bed."

Her outraged squeak is more appropriate for a mouse in a trap. "Absolutely not."

I recline into the cushions, disguising the fire in my blood as I picture her curled against me. "You're my wife, Twinkles. We'll share like a happily married couple on their honeymoon. No touching unless you initiate, though."

Blonde hair whips back and forth with her refusal. "That doesn't work for me."

"Consent is important," I chide.

"The sleeping arrangements, *husband*." Her tone on that endearment twitches my lips. Damn, she's feisty.

"I guess you'll find somewhere else to rest your pretty little head."

Paisley's jaw drops. "You'd make me sleep on the sofa?"

"No," I state calmly. "You'd make that choice on your own."

"I can't believe this," she huffs. "How long are we supposed to stay here?"

"A couple days at least. Just for show," I add for the sake of calming her tits.

But then she goes and asks, "What are we going to do with ourselves?"

My gaze heats on her curves in the dress I picked out. "I could think of a few things."

"Hey! You said no touching."

I lift my palms. "Just looking. No harm in that."

"Leads to trouble."

"Only if we let it." My voice is a coarse rasp that raises goose bumps along her exposed flesh.

She mumbles something under her breath while pinning a glare on the vaulted ceiling. "Is there a town nearby?"

For whatever reason, I like that she asks me rather than find out for herself. "Hacken isn't too far away. Ten miles or so."

"Is that truck ours to use?" She swats in the general direction of the driveway.

I nod at the hook by the front door. "Want me to take you somewhere?"

"Nope, I'll manage on my own." She begins backing away. "You've done enough already."

"Too much," I mumble absently.

"Yeah, yeah. I'm about to give that phrase fresh meaning." My twinkly wife snorts and turns for the stairs. "Right after I take off this wedding gown, I'll be out of your hair. Don't wait up."

I tense. "It's three o'clock in the afternoon."

Paisley winks at me over her shoulder. "Gonna be a long night."

CHAPTER EIGHTEEN

Paisley

IT'S JUST GETTING DARK WHEN I ADMIT DEFEAT AND take the next turn that leads back to our cabin. The clock on the dash mocks me. Try as I might to waste the entire night, there's not much to do in a town that makes Cloverleaf Meadows look like a big city. Four hours was a struggle. Surrendering this soon after my dramatic exit will be equally difficult.

A streetlamp ahead on the right catches my eye. I ease off the accelerator and squint into the dusk to get a better view. The spotlight exposes a narrow driveway that opens to a wide lot. That's where a quaint bookstore is nestled in a clearing just off the road. I'm sensing a theme in this neck of the woods, and take it as a nudge to stop in.

My blinker is loud in the silence as I creep forward along the gravel path. I pull up next to the only other vehicle and shift the truck into park. Illuminated in bold lettering on the roof are the words Chase the Storm. It includes a cute logo of the sun poking through rain clouds. A sense of familiarity settles in my gut.

The open sign is on, which I accept as an invitation. A chime announces my presence as I enter the shop. My lashes immediately flutter shut as another strike of awareness hits me. I inhale deeply, allowing the worries to melt away for a moment. The crisp scent of paper and imaginations running wild hang in the air. When I open my eyes, there's a security guard sitting on a chair beside me.

"Holy shit." I rest a palm over my pounding heart. "You scared me."

The guy doesn't respond, or even blink. I'm about to retreat in a hurry when a woman pokes her head out from between two shelves.

"Oh, hi!" Her smile is wide, severely contrasting the mean mug still aimed at me. "Welcome to Chase the Storm."

"Uh, thanks. Is it okay that I'm here?" My gaze bounces off the guard for emphasis.

"Don't mind Nash. He takes his role too seriously." She approaches at a wobbly snail's pace, which is most likely caused by her pregnant belly. "Quit scaring my customers, Thorn."

His stare moves to her and instantly softens. "Sorry, Darlin'. It's late and you need to rest."

"We're just fine." She pats her baby bump and then ushers me toward a table stacked with paperbacks. "I'm Penny, by the way."

"Paisley," I say on a laugh. "With names like ours, we should probably be book besties."

"Couldn't agree more. It's nice to meet you. Is there anything in particular that you're looking for?"

Other than delaying the inevitable? Not really. I don't say that, of course. "Do you specialize in romance novels?"

"Oh, yes." She clutches her hands over her heart. There's a dreamy glint in her eyes as well. "Love stories are my absolute favorite. I've become even more obsessed with them now that I'm living my very own fairytale."

A rumbling noise comes from Nash as he looks at Penny like she's a ripe piece of fruit he wants to devour. The temperature in the small shop spikes while they exchange a heated glance. This is what I'm missing, and might never experience.

It's a daunting realization I was hoping to escape. Envy pricks at me instead. Their obvious adoration is strong enough to get me intoxicated from one sip. It's an elixir that any hopeless romantic would guzzle by the gallon.

"Phew, excuse me." Penny fans her face. "I'd blame it on the hormones, but it's honestly nonstop whenever he's in the room."

Jealousy nips at me again, which is totally ridiculous. But a change in subject couldn't hurt. "How's business? If you don't mind me asking," I tack on for the sake of decorum.

"Probably what you'd expect. Summer is our busy season. The rest of the year is a bit slow, but I'm not in this for the money. It's about spreading the joy of reading."

I nod in understanding. "Kinda off the beaten path, huh?"

She flips through a book absently. "My husband doesn't care much for people. This is the closest to town he would build the shop."

A choked exhale sputters from me. "He built this place?"

"Sure did." She beams with pride. "We've owned this little slice of heaven for a few years."

I glance around the store with a fresh perspective. "Wow, that's—"

"Daddy, Daddy!" A little girl no older than three appears out of nowhere, rushing toward Nash at lightning speed. She's waving a piece of paper that's covered in colorful squiggles. "Gots a pitcher. Here go!"

The ice king at the door melts into a squishy teddy bear before my eyes. The doting father leaps off his stool and crouches onto the floor. His daughter flings herself into his waiting arms. Their tight embrace brings tears to my eyes.

"Mhmm, that's how this happened." She points at her protruding tummy. "Can't resist him when he gets gooey."

The conundrum winks at her before pinning me with a scowl as if I'm ruining a special family moment. He's probably right. At this rate, I might beg Brody to have babies with me if they can cure intolerable grumpiness.

"Maybe I should go." My sandals slip on the carpet as I prepare to flee.

"Wait." Penny hovers her hands above my arms to form an invisible barrier. "Did you find what you were looking for?"

That's putting it mildly, but I shouldn't leave empty-handed. I blindly reach for the nearest book. "This will do the trick."

Her brows lift. "Interesting choice. I approve."

A quick glance at the cover explains her reaction. There's a mostly naked, very male alien hovering over a swooning woman. The title doesn't hide the fact that she's about to be blasted with his astronomical laser beam. My cheeks go up in flames when I give the image another peek.

"I like to expand my horizons," I croak.

"You're in for a treat. This one gets credit for putting my second bun in the oven." Penny strokes the girthy spine longingly. "There's something extra stimulating about reading dirty scenes while ovulating."

Just what I need. I dig out more than enough cash and push the money into her grip. "You've been really… um, informative. Extremely helpful. Keep the change."

Penny's mouth opens and closes as she inspects the wad. "Thank you!"

I offer a backwards wave before dashing out of Chase the Storm. The evening chill allows clarity to return but I'm still overheated. My motions are jerky and rushed as I get settled behind the wheel. The truck roars to life, swerving slightly when the tires kick up gravel.

Darkness envelops me on the road. I spend the drive lost in thought. It's unfortunate to admit that Brody fills entirely too much bandwidth in my brain. Maybe I'm still feeling the effects of Penny and Nash. The love potion they infuse into their shop could be dangerous to my resolve. I'll have to be careful about what stores I stumble into.

The cabin is quiet when I arrive and slip inside. Nothing appears out of place, just the same as when I left. There's not even a single dish in the sink. Guilt slithers around my ribs and squeezes. We didn't go shopping for food. The least I could've done was get him takeout. Not like I would've known what to get. My eye roll is reserved solely for me and my misguided concern. If he was hungry, he could have told me.

I wander around in search of Brody but can't find him. If not for his suitcase on the bed, I'd assume he took off. His woodsy scent lingers as I absently descend the stairs. My phone gains ten pounds in my pocket, demanding I relieve the weight and send him a text.

A splash yanks my attention to the deck. It's pitch black out there except for the soft glow from the hot tub. That's where I spot my husband, submerged in the water up to his broad shoulders. His head is tipped back onto the stone ledge. This might be the first time I've witnessed him unplugged and relaxing.

I don't want to disturb his peace but the insistence to check on him is too powerful. The cool sweep of autumn drifts along my bare legs when I sneak onto the patio. Brody hasn't noticed me yet, which allows me to shamelessly admire him. His dark hair is wet and slicked back away from his face. I shuffle closer while appreciating the unobstructed view. The reclined position puts his angular jaw on display. Sooty lashes seal his eyes shut while he soaks. Sweat or stray droplets sprinkle his forehead. Steam rises off the churning surface, making him look even hotter. Too bad the jets are on or I'd get a glimpse at much more of him.

"My beloved wife returns," Brody rasps.

A jolt rushes through me and I suck in a sharp breath. "How did you know I was here?"

"I'm always aware of you." But his eyes are still closed.

"That's a creepy sentiment coming from my fake husband."

When his lips curl into a full smile, my knees threaten to buckle. "What did you expect? You sparkle like a disco ball wherever you go, Twinkles."

I glance at the lace shirt I've paired with a pink denim skirt. It's a fairly plain outfit by my standards. "But you can't see me."

Hooded lids barely lift when he decides to grace me with his stare. "Heard those bracelets jingle on your wrist like a Christmas carol."

I shake the glittery bangles, which make a racket. "Okay, that's fair."

His grin spreads. "How was town?"

Suspicion prickles the back of my neck. "Fine."

"Did you get me a present?" He sinks lower until his chin touches the water and proceeds to blow bubbles at me.

"No?" I'm beginning to question this strange version of Brody.

Which makes him double down, an exaggerated pout sticking out his bottom lip. "But it's customary for the bride to get her groom a gift."

"Oh, really?" I cross my arms. "And what did my groom get for me?"

"It's down there." He dips his head to indicate the general vicinity of his lap. "You have to unwrap it."

My mind goes blank as alarm bells clang. I rove my gaze over him, taking note of his sluggish blinks and dopey smirk. Maybe he's dizzy from too much chlorine and not enough caloric intake.

"Are you feeling okay, boss?"

"I'll be a lot better if you join me." Brody pats the roiling space beside him with a sloppy palm.

My tongue twists over several responses. I settle for, "Did you eat dinner?"

"Worried about my well-being?"

"Don't let it go to your head. I'm concerned about you passing out and leaving me stranded in the elements."

Booming laughter explodes from him, shocking me into a solid block. "Wouldn't do that to my wife. You're my responsibility now."

This semi-sweet, chauvinist behavior is spinning me faster than a baler. "I can take care of myself."

"Afraid you're stuck with me, Twinkles."

"Temporarily."

Brody's shrug is lopsided. "Sure, but we're in this together for now. There's plenty of food to keep us afloat for weeks. That includes drinks."

He lifts his arms from the water and stretches along the smooth rocks framing the jacuzzi. The sight renders me immobile for a few reasons, but I choose to prioritize the tattoos decorating his skin. I can't tell what the designs are from this distance in the dark. Before I can sneak a closer peek, a bottle of Dom appears in his grip to distract me. The puzzle is solved as he swirls the remaining contents before bringing it to his lips.

Brody guzzles the expensive champagne as if it's cheap beer. Watching him do so is another travesty entirely. Even in the piss-poor lighting, I catch every subtle movement. His fingers clutch onto the wide base in a possessive hold. The flow of alcohol floods his mouth like an open tap. I'm transfixed when a droplet escapes his lips, trickling down his chin as he swallows. The urge to lick that path beckons me to the edge of the shallow pool.

My concentration zeroes in as his Adam's apple bobs under the pressure to chug the liquid gold. Drool collects on my tongue and I gulp. I'm suddenly very thirsty.

Brody finishes the bottle and sets it aside. That snaps me out of the wrongful hypnosis.

"You're drunk," I accuse.

He tips his head to one side and squints. "I'm buzzed."

"Wow, never thought I'd see you smashed."

He snorts. "I'm not a total square."

The outdated term makes me giggle. "Gosh, you're old."

"Why do you think I married you? Wanted to keep myself young."

"Just using me," I murmur.

The reminder should be sobering, but he's too captivating in this state. Especially when he turns up the heat.

"Feel free to use me in return, wifey." For whatever reason, that endearment sounds cute.

When he tacks on a wink, I almost swoon again. Boozy Brody is an incorrigible flirt. I might just like it. At my extended silence, his eyebrows wag.

"C'mon, Twinkles. I'm not so bad. Unless you want me to be." He drifts his palms along his torso, disappearing under the water to touch areas I can't see.

But it's not a worthless tease. The seductive motion puts his arms in better view, allowing me to examine his tattoos. I never knew he had any until tonight.

Once the details register, my breath whooshes as I drop to my knees. "Are those…?"

"Strands of barbwire," he confirms. His right arm shifts to show how the design coils up and around his entire limb. "Got all these during my rebellious phase. Probably when I was about your age." He laughs while I roll my eyes.

"As if ten years is that big of a gap." I wrinkle my nose. Ugh, that sounds like I'm defending our relationship.

"You're twenty-three?"

"Isn't that something you should know about your wife?"

"Got me there. I failed to do proper research." He snaps his fingers as if scolding himself.

"Yet here we are." Rather than step deeper into that manure pile, I refocus on the thick lines etched into his skin. "Are these why you're always wearing long sleeves?"

"Cover up my mistakes."

A crease forms between my brows. "Is that how you see them?"

Brody's eyes grow a bit distant, as if memories are calling to him. "They remind me of when I thought the future was mine. It was meant to be symbolic, like I couldn't be fenced in. Crock of shit that turned out to be."

"Why's that?"

"Look at us, married against our will."

"We had a choice." There I go again, defending us. I bite my tongue before more nonsense slips through my filter.

His chuckle is a breeze slipping through leaves. "Mom and Dad gave me more responsibilities when I turned twenty-five. I liked the work, quickly demanding more. That's a damn slippery slope. Years went by before I realized the job became my identity. Nobody's fault but my own. Hours behind the desk and on the road replaced nights out with friends. Before I knew it, I was addicted to the trade. By then it was too late and I just poured more of myself into the business. How do you think I tipped Benson Farmstead into billionaire status so quickly?"

The story sheds new light on him and he looks almost normal. Like a weary man who needs a break. Maybe I've been too hard on him. I rip my gaze off his solemn expression. Nope, not falling for that. Talk about a slippery slope.

I pick at a rhinestone on my skirt to avoid petting him. "Do you regret it?"

"Nah, I've got nothing to complain about."

"It's okay to be honest and vulnerable." I wince at the supportive force in my tone.

Brody's exhale is heavy. "Want to hear something crazy?"

"Always."

"I'm starting to think barbwire might be tying us together. Like fate." He nods at my glitzy ring finger.

I move my hand and the diamonds sparkle on cue. "You believe in fate?"

"Maybe. There might be something greater at work here." His gaze lifts to the sky, scanning the blanket of stars.

I can tell his thoughts rest on Marion. The relentless desire to offer comfort perches on my tongue but I don't want to pry. Whenever I've tried, it's backfired.

"That's a nice thought," I murmur instead.

A lazy smirk spanks his lips. "You might save my soul yet, Twinkles."

Emotion catches in my throat. Brody is an open book right now. I find myself wanting more before he closes himself off again.

"So, why are you drinking by yourself in the hot tub?"

Brody sends me a blank stare. "It's my wedding night. I'm celebrating."

"*Our*," I correct on a whisper.

He leans forward slightly. "What was that?"

"It's our wedding night."

"Does that mean you'll celebrate with me?"

I roll my lips between my teeth and consider the options. "Maybe I should… go to bed."

But running away doesn't sit right in my gut.

Brody must agree, choosing that second to splash me. "Get in here. I'm lonely."

That stops me short. I've never heard Brody claim a weakness other than needing a wife to own his company. This is… vastly different.

He's being somewhat vulnerable, especially for him. It makes me want to toss caution to the wind.

"I don't have a suit."

He scoffs. "Bra and panties will do."

"You're not seeing me in my underwear."

His palm glides along the stone pavers, inches from my leg. "Find something else to wear."

"How about a compromise?" I kick off my sandals and sit on the ledge, slowly easing my feet beneath the surface. Warmth instantly shoots through me and I sag into the comforting embrace. "Ohhh, the temperature is just right."

"See? Not so bad."

I nudge him with my elbow. "Boozy Brody is nice."

"That's the effect of the whirlpool talking. It's very persuasive."

"Really? I was thinking we were headed to a truce." Which is a huge leniency on my part.

Brody scratches at his jaw. "Oh, we're back to that?"

"We don't have to fight," I reiterate.

"Couldn't agree more, wife for life. This calls for a toast." He pulls out a fresh bottle of champagne from behind him.

"Where are you getting this stuff?"

"In the cooler." He hitches a thumb at the hidden compartment carved into the deck.

"Fancy ass lodging," I mumble.

"Hmm?"

"Not important. We'll discuss it tomorrow."

"And tonight we drink," Brody booms.

Nimble fingers get busy unwrapping the foil. His impressive talent has the cork popped before I can blink. Bubbles spill along the sides, revealing that he's not perfect. He hammers it home by slurping the excess as it trickles down. It's entirely too provocative but I can't look away.

Once the fizzy stream stops, he holds the bottle out to me. "Want some?"

"I'll get a cup." My voice is scratchy.

Green settles on blue as we lock eyes. "Afraid to get my germs?"

"Very. You might rub off on me."

Brody's lips curve into a devastating smile that roots me in place. "What if I promise to be gentle?"

CHAPTER NINETEEN

Brody

PAISLEY IS ABOUT TO KNEEL AND UNDO MY JEANS when a loud buzz yanks me from the dream. I groan as the illusion fades, leaving me hanging. My hips shift in search of friction and bump into lush curves. A muffled grunt complains about my movement but tapers off into a breathy snore almost immediately.

Clarity sweeps at the fog in my brain. As I come to, I recognize the weight sprawled on top of me. Paisley is still out like a light and using me as a pillow. My mouth curves into a satisfied smirk.

That expression flips into a frown when the buzzing begins again. I'm reluctant to move but the commotion won't quit. My hand blindly searches for the source on the nightstand. I silence the incessant rattling and enjoy a moment of peace. Just as I'm about to chuck the device over the railing, another attempt to reach me vibrates my palm.

"Fucking cock blocker," I grumble while slipping out from under Paisley.

The instant I stand up, I'm smacked with the consequences of my choices. A sharp throb pounds behind my eyes, scolding me for that third bottle of Dom. Worth it seeing as my wife kept me warm all night.

She doesn't so much as twitch while I stomp from the room like a poked bear. I'd been really damn clear about no disruptions. Someone forgot the memo.

Once I'm out of earshot, I swipe to accept the call and put him on speaker. "This better be urgent, Colt."

"Guess again."

I pause on the stairs. "Bianca."

My sister huffs. "What took you so long?"

"Give me a break. It's"—I squint at the screen—"ten in the morning?"

"Does that surprise you?"

Like a pheasant jumping out of the bushes, not that I'll admit it. Fuck, I slept deeper than a well. My groggy mind struggles to focus while I amble into the kitchen. Except this doesn't feel like the lingering effects of a drunken stupor. I lift my gaze to where the woman responsible lies. It's too damn much, which is just what I need.

"Hello?" Bianca's shrill voice stabs at my aching head.

"Coffee," I mutter and shuffle to the counter.

"Did I wake you up?"

My body is on autopilot as I go through the motions to get caffeine injected into my system. There are too many buttons on the machine. "Rough morning."

"It's about to get worse," my sister warns.

"Mhmm, great." I'm barely listening while trying to get this machine to brew. This model is too complicated.

"Care to explain why you're out of town with Paisley?"

The cinch wrapped around my skull squeezes when the complicated contraption remains silent. "Work trip."

"Just the two of you?"

"Consider it a reward retreat for the best employee." It's impressive that I can come up with this shit in my current state.

Her laugh lacks humor. "You're a worse liar than Dad."

"Uh, thanks?" The beans finally start to grind and I give myself a round of applause.

Frustration spews from Bianca and I'm betting she wants to throttle me. "What did you do while I was gone? I want the truth."

"Made money. Fixed random shit on the farm. Herded cattle. Kept the horses alive."

"And?"

"Tolerated your new hire," I add just to be a pain in her ass.

"Rumor has it, you've done a lot more than that," she mutters. "Why isn't Paisley answering her phone?"

A chuckle almost slips free to betray me. "Have to ask her."

"Put her on then." Bianca's tone is a cheese grater against my last nerve.

"She's still asleep." I'm ready to beg this machine to go faster.

"At this hour?"

"Guess she's tired."

"And why might that be?"

My knuckles bleed white as I grip onto granite, trying to borrow its strength. "Dunno."

It sounds like Bianca pounds on a hard surface. Maybe

Colton's loyalty to me. I'd pay to see that fight. My sister's labored breathing suggests she's losing the battle against his iron will.

"What's up with you lately, Brody?"

"Didn't we already go over this?" By some miracle, the second mug is almost full. So. Close.

She huffs before inhaling deeply. "You've been really cagey whenever I mention Paisley. Why won't you let me talk to her? Are you hiding something? If you are, I'm going to find out."

And that's my cue. "What was that? The service is spotty."

"Oh, don't you dare hang—"

I stab at the screen before she can finish her threat. Before her persistence can call me back, I shut off my phone and toss it in a drawer. It's been the better half of a decade since I've had a real vacation. I'd say it's long overdue. This also allows me to delay the inevitable for another day or two.

Paisley is beginning to stir when I return to the lofted den. I stand back and watch as she escapes the clutches of sleep. She stretches in an exaggerated arch across the sheets. An ear-splitting yawn raises the roof to notify the other wild animals in the area. When she's done howling, her tongue smacks the roof of her mouth. I bet it's drier than a July pasture in there.

"Water," she croaks.

"That'll require a second trip." I lift my full hands.

Her baby blues are bleary while she tries to focus on me. Blonde tangles frame her face, which has me thinking about a roll in the hay. I'd have her far more disheveled if that were the case.

Paisley struggles to prop herself on an elbow and manages to sit semi-upright. A sloppy palm scrubs at the drool crusted to her cheek. My wife is mussed and messy and never looked sexier. Damn, I'm a simp for this bundle of sunshine.

"Look good in my shirt, Twinkles." The fact she's wearing something of mine is icing on the cake.

She squints down at the white tee covering her upper half. "Aw, shit."

"Hungover?"

Her nod is jerky while she massages her forehead. "I think we overdid it on the celebrating."

"Maybe this will help." My bare feet pad across the carpet and I sit on the edge of the bed.

Paisley sniffs. "Coffee?"

I pass her a steaming mug. "Don't know how you take it, but figured you like it creamy and sweet."

She lunges forward as if I'm holding the cure to her illness. "I could kiss you!"

"All it takes is a cup of Joe? Wish I'd known sooner."

"Hush," she mumbles and inhales the rich aroma. Her lashes flutter shut while she sips. "Ohhh, this hits the spot."

Warmth spreads through me as if I'm the one savoring every drop. I'm captivated by my wife drinking the coffee I made for her. My gaze is latched onto her upturned mouth, waiting for another sound of approval. It's startling to realize that I want to see her happy.

As Paisley drinks and a moan parts her lips, satisfaction like I've never felt thrums through me. It's worth suffering through the process of making another cup. What's wrong with me? She's not doing anything out of the ordinary. But the pleasure she gets from such a mundane act is irresistible. I want more.

Which is when she whispers, "Thank you. I needed that."

Our eyes meet in a swift collision. The impact is an electric shock to my heart, but I manage to stay still. It's a familiar game we've played before. Static sparks between us, crackling with tension. There's a question in her gaze and I wonder if she'll find the answer in mine. The anticipation mounts into a demand the longer we're caught in this trance.

Paisley is the first to break, her stare dipping to my bare chest. Her interest explores lower and screeches to a halt on the distinct outline of my dick. That's what she gets for turning the simple act of drinking coffee into an erotic spectacle. The reminder strokes me to half-mast and a blush paints her cheeks a rosy hue.

I can't help but taunt her after the damage she's done to my composure. "Like what you see, wife?"

"Umm…"

"Still think I have a teeny weenie?" I thrust to make it extra clear I'm packing more than a cocktail wiener.

"Uhh…" Paisley's gulp is audible.

"Need a closer look?"

"You're wearing gray sweatpants," she blurts.

"And?"

"Nothing else." If she stares any longer, my cock will pitch a tent for her to stay indefinitely.

"Is that a problem?"

Her gaze skitters away like a frightened virgin. "Only for our boundaries."

"Obliterated quite a few last night." Along with my guard against her.

She freezes, her mind probably working overtime. "We didn't do anything."

My chuckle is gritty and I finally take a sip of my own coffee. "Depends on your definition."

Her wide eyes take stock of our proximity. "I blame the sleeping arrangements for this."

"Could've taken the couch."

"Didn't seem like an option at the time," she admits on a breathy exhale.

I preen like a proud peacock when she brazenly ogles me again. "You remember?"

"This"—she motions between us—"was just a cuddle party after too much champagne."

"And a bedtime story."

Her entire face ignites into flames. "That part slipped my mind."

"That's some sexy shit you brought home."

"The shop owner warned me about that," she mumbles.

"But you picked it anyway."

"To be fair, she told me after I'd already committed to the title." Paisley swats at the rising temperature in the room. "It was the first thing I grabbed."

My eyes narrow on her evasive maneuvers. "I think my wife likes her romance spicy and extraterrestrial."

"Or maybe I just like it when someone reads to me." She swaps her mug for the paperback on the nightstand. "Can't believe you broke the spine."

"You wanted it rough."

"I said *gruff*," she corrects. "As in your voice. You didn't need to manhandle my book."

"Hard to hear over your demands."

"At least you fulfilled most of them." She pets the cover. "We'll call this a honeymoon hazard. It's easy to get carried away in the moment."

After setting my coffee aside, I sprawl out beside her on the mattress. "Should I read the next chapter?"

Paisley stiffens. "That's not a good idea."

My lips twitch. I'm becoming fond of just talking to her. "Why not?"

"Look where last night got me." She gestures at her outfit like I haven't been constantly staring at her. "I can only imagine what will happen to my resolve during the light of day."

"We should find out."

"No way, mister. You're too handsy." Her nail taps a deep crease on the book's spine.

"I'll be more careful."

"Sounds a lot like your promise to be gentle." She taps my nose, giggling when I attempt to bite her finger. "See? You can't be trusted."

And she doesn't know the worst of it. My gut clenches into stone, reminding me of what stalks beneath the surface. The shit with Bianca will hit the fan soon enough. I can't keep them apart much longer. That will require major damage control, and I'm not sure our shaky truce will survive. But why should I care? This is what I wanted.

Paisley gasps as if hearing my betrayal. "My phone!"

Relief I shouldn't feel sags my shoulders. "Ah, yes. It took an unfortunate swim in the hot tub."

Which I had nothing to do with. Paisley saved me the trouble of expanding my deceit by dunking her device underwater. It was very convenient, almost like I planned that too.

"I can't believe it's ruined," she whines.

"No sweat, wife. Your new one is already on the way. It'll arrive at our house on Friday."

Confusion pinches her drowsy features. "What?"

"Ordered it before I fell asleep."

"Oh." She smiles, but it's weak. "Thanks. I'll pay you back."

"You better be joking."

Her chin tips to a defiant angle. "I'm not."

"Listen, Twinkles. My money is yours. Spend it freely."

"That's not possible."

I tuck some unruly hair behind her ear. "You'll get used to it."

Her breathing goes shallow. "I could say that for a lot of things, but what's yours isn't mine."

I lean in, trailing my nose along her neck with a deep inhale. "You smell like mine." My fingers tug the hem of her borrowed shirt. "Look like mine too."

"In name only." But she doesn't pull away.

Contentment pulses under my skin. I could get used to this. "Until I convince you otherwise."

She hums while inspecting my half-lidded stare. "Is Boozy Brody still here?"

My palm drifts along her side. "I don't mind having you around whether I'm buzzed or not."

"Careful or I'll think you like me."

I trail my fingers to her hip, fisting white cotton instead of her bare flesh. "And if I do?"

Her laugh is a lie. "Don't get attached, husband. This isn't real."

"Maybe it should be," slips from me without warning.

Paisley peers deep into my eyes, peeling away layers to reach what I keep hidden. Our breaths mingle while seconds stretch the silence. I let her search until she grows tired of trying to find any semblance of good. After what feels like hours, she squints and a grin stretches her lips.

"I see you," she whispers.

"Kinda hard not to when I'm right here."

She shakes her head. "The real you."

This time, I'm the one to avert my gaze. "Doubt it."

She shoves my shoulder and hops out of bed. "I'm just messing with you. Don't be so serious."

My pulse drums to the beat of her skipping down the stairs. "Where are you going?"

"Wouldn't you like to know," she croons.

I sit upright, about to give chase. "Yes."

Her laughter taunts my concern that she's leaving me again. "I'm going to make us breakfast. Feel free to join me when you're ready, old man."

My heart jolts at her playful tone. "Old man?"

"Do you prefer ancient?"

Oh, she's going to get it for that ridiculous endearment. I spring to my feet like a young stud just to prove a point. My heavy stride pounds on the steps as I prowl after my wife. I skid to a stop when she comes into view.

Paisley is swaying to her own tempo in front of the stove. I never thought that watching a woman cook would turn me on. But she isn't any woman. It's becoming arousingly obvious that I have a crush on my wife, especially while she's wearing my shirt and frying bacon.

I genuinely like her, which is a problem if she insists on ending our marriage as soon as possible. Last night shifted our dynamic. She can deny it but I'm not alone in this. That means I'm going to enjoy her company while she allows it.

Paisley must sense my attention and glances at me over her shoulder. "Like what you see, husband?"

"Very much so." Now I just have to convince her to stay.

CHAPTER TWENTY

Paisley

WE GLIDE ACROSS THE LAKE LIKE IT'S A SHEET OF ice. Wind whips through my hair as Brody pushes for more speed. It's chilly but refreshing. I tip my head to the gray sky and stretch my arms out. If not for the slight bumps and splashes, I could convince myself I'm racing on horseback.

Nobody else is on the water, which doesn't surprise me considering the isolated area. That allows me to be swept away by the natural beauty at every turn. Green and brown still hog the landscape, but my favorite season has entered the scene. Trees along the shoreline offer pops of fall colors as their leaves begin to change. It's comforting and peaceful, except for the other person onboard.

Warmth churns inside of me, burning hotter as I glance at my husband. Brody sits in the captain's chair like a king on his throne. Thick fingers drum on the wheel before re-gaining a loose grip. The stubble on his jaw is thicker than normal. I shiver while recalling the rasp of that coarse scruff against my neck when he smelled me earlier. Desire had pumped through me, much like now.

When another gust hits me, I tighten my scarf to avoid squirming. Gosh, I cannot fall for this man. Absolutely not.

"What else is on our agenda today?" I shout over the breeze.

In a fluid motion, Brody yanks on the throttle and cuts the engine. My body rocks on the waves from our abrupt stop. The absence of sound captures us in a bubble that my husband doesn't burst. I'm about to repeat my question when he swivels his seat.

His steely expression softens when he focuses on me. "You're not going to ditch me when we dock?"

I narrow my eyes playfully. "Wasn't planning on it unless you give me a reason to scoot."

"It's barely noon. A lot can happen in one boat ride."

"Speaking from experience?"

He shrugs, more carefree than I've seen him. "And our… volatile history."

"That's one way of putting it," I chide. "Besides, we have a truce."

"Indefinitely?"

The urgency in his tone raises suspicion like a red flag. It's unlike him to be vulnerable unless several bottles of champagne are involved. I study him through a squint. A lazy smirk greets my perusal. Brody's posture is slouched to match the wide spread of his legs. The long sleeves of his shirt are rolled up, putting his tattoos on display. He's unbuttoned and unbothered and… almost unrecognizable.

I dissect his mixed signals again. "What are you worried about, Mr. Benson?"

He casts a sideways glance at his phone that's abnormally quiet. "The usual."

"Is it work?"

A subtle shake of his head disputes that theory. "Dad has it covered while we're here."

My brain misfires. "You took time off?"

Brody stretches, appearing completely at ease. "It's our honeymoon."

"But it's not real."

"Crushing my hopes and dreams, wife." He clutches his chest.

"You're a goof."

"Bet you didn't think I had it in me."

I roll my eyes. "Not sure why you're still laying on the charm when the deal is done."

"Maybe I want you to stick around. Willingly," he emphasizes.

Welp, that settles it. There's an undeniable change in him, which adds to the contradiction. My gut instinct tells me that he's hiding something. He'll probably do whatever it takes to keep the secret buried. But that's not where my concentration rests right now.

"This trip is good for you, boss."

Brody scowls at the nickname, reminding me of his grumpy self. "I think it's more about who's with me. You're an unexpected relief."

"There you go again," I laugh.

"Can't I compliment my wife?"

"If you actually mean it."

"I do." His smolder could make me sweat in a blizzard.

My mind reels under his bold claim. I can't take my eyes

off him once he's captured me. We're coasting along dangerous territory and not for the first time. It would be too easy to let him sweep me off my feet, if only for the duration he needs a wife. The risk to my heart overrules the fantasy.

But I wonder how love would look on him. The deep, unconditional kind that makes us reckless. Has he ever fallen that hard for someone? Doubtful, but not impossible. Would his heart shine through those bottomless green depths I'm currently drowning in? Damn, I need to quit staring. There's just something very irresistible about my husband.

I shift my gaze over his shoulder in search of a distraction. "Do you know what our private bay is called?"

Brody scans the slice of paradise. "Do you?"

"Lover's Cove," I croon. "A local told me yesterday, along with more information than I needed."

"Sounds about right," he chuckles.

"Mhmm, the cabin has a reputation. I got quite a few looks after revealing where we're staying. Rumor has it that couples come here when they're seeking an intimate vacation." I wiggle my brows to a sultry beat.

"Might as well be a sign posted in the front yard."

"Or a public service announcement." I cup a palm around my mouth and shout, "Can anyone hear me? We're about to bang beyond boundaries." Amusement stretches my lips into a megawatt grin. "We're in the clear."

My husband shifts in his chair. "Leave it to my dad to find a place fit for the occasion."

A blush burns my cheeks, which has little to do with the autumn chill. "Only one bed. Dennis is definitely a menace."

Brody scrubs over his mouth to stifle a smile. "That he is."

"He wants us to catch feelings."

"Something like that." His gaze slides to his phone again.

It's strange that he turned it off completely. I'm getting jittery without mine, but choosing to use this opportunity to be off the grid. That urge to check notifications proves how addicted I've become. I can't remember the last time I unplugged from technology. Even now, I want to snatch his cell and call Bianca. She's home and we haven't talked. But it can wait another hour or two.

If there's an emergency, Brody has his available.

"Well, this swanky pontoon is a nice touch." I exhale the demand to doom scroll, stroking the cream leather to occupy my hands. "Pristine condition. Wherever your dad rented it from must have strict rules."

"Didn't I tell you? This stud is fresh off the lot." He pats the steering wheel. "Dad got it for us as a wedding gift."

"Another present for a sham marriage. Why did he bother?"

"Keep up appearances," he mumbles absently. "This way, we'll be seen cruising around Lucky Lake back home."

"A town spectacle."

"It's about authentic presentation." His flippant tone suggests he's familiar with the phrase.

Which sprouts a random thought. "Does your dad want grandchildren?"

Brody grunts and motions to our secluded surroundings. "Isn't it obvious?"

I scrunch my face. "Please don't tell me that's the next contractual obligation."

His shoulders bounce with soundless humor. "Nah, he didn't push the limits."

"Phew, I was about to jump ship." I wipe fake sweat off my forehead. "I'm surprised he doesn't care that our marriage is fake."

Brody's jaw works to the sound of grinding gears. "He would…"

A daunting realization bulges my eyes. "Hold your horses. He doesn't know?"

His carefree expression shutters. "Don't blame me for his assumptions."

"Oh, please. You didn't bother to be honest and reveal the truth."

"Why would I? He wants to believe we're crazy about each other. There's no harm in letting him."

A pit forms in my stomach. "He's going to find out. We're not paid actors."

The sparkle dims from his gaze. "Do your parents know the truth?"

"Of course not." I throw my hands in the air. "You didn't give me the chance to tell them before shoving this rock on my finger."

He glares at the diamonds I shove in his face. "What's the difference?"

"Are you serious?" The impulse to throttle him fists my hands. "This isn't about me or my parents."

"How do you figure? You're deceiving them just the same."

"Nope, not happening. Quit trying to turn this around

on me, master manipulator. I wouldn't be in this mess if it wasn't for you and your blackmail."

His shrug couldn't care less. "But you could've set the record straight."

"We'll share that honor when we get an annulment," I huff.

He bolts upright, posturing going rigid. "We're not getting an annulment."

"Excuse me? You're not keeping me in this phony matrimony."

"Not forever, but we need to stay married until I take ownership of Benson Farmstead." A vein throbs in his neck.

"Which is what? A month? Maybe two? How long will it take to convince your dad that we're not meant to be?" I tap my chin. "A week should do it. Let's hope he gives you credit for trying."

Brody pinches the bridge of his nose. "Twinkles—"

"Holy shit," I blurt. Realization dawns on me while the sun remains tucked behind the clouds. "Bianca thinks this is real too. Is she pissed at me?"

My darling husband takes a sudden interest in checking the gas gauge. "Beats me."

"Oh, you're an ass. That's why she hasn't talked to me in weeks."

"Or maybe she was just busy in Europe," he evades.

"I need to call her." My upturned palm beckons for his phone.

Brody makes no move to fulfill my request. "Wait until you see her."

"You better be joking."

"It's for the best. Trust me," he presses.

The desperate edge in his voice gives me pause. Bianca must be really mad. Maybe my husband is trying to protect me from his sister's wrath. That seems far-fetched, even for this unlikely scenario I'm trapped in.

I rake trembling fingers through the snarls in my hair. "How can I trust you? This is all your fault."

His stare implores mine, convincing me to search his soul. "Am I that bad?"

"Yes!" Which immediately stabs me with guilt. Not that he deserves my empathy. "You tricked me into this marriage and now my best friend won't speak to me."

Brody's swallow is thick. "My intentions weren't great at the beginning, but I think there's something real between us, Twinkles. Give me tonight to prove it to you. We can leave in the morning."

My cringe shuts him down. "I'd like to go home now."

After a solemn nod, he hangs his head. The weight of his bad decisions appears to crush his spirit in this moment. He twists his wedding ring and the fidgeting motion seems purposeful. When he peers up at me, his eyes are glassy. It's more unexpected than a punch to the gut. I choke on a gasp, trying to muffle the reaction.

"Please," he murmurs. "I can't force you to stay but I would really appreciate it."

My exhale is mostly steamed frustration. "One night isn't going to change anything."

"It might." Brody scoots to the edge of his seat. "We won't know until we try."

I cross my arms, warding off his approach. "What are you suggesting?"

"We get to know each other."

"It's a little late for that."

"Only if you're not interested." He inches forward until our legs are almost touching. "We might be married, but we're practically strangers. That's how I wanted it at first. From what little I know, I can tell you're different from the rest. Unique."

"Too much," I add in a mutter.

His lips twitch. "I feel something when we're together. That's never happened to me before."

It's difficult to keep a straight face during his seemingly heartfelt speech. "How do I know you're being honest? Maybe this is just another ploy to get me to play by your rules."

Brody reaches for me but I shrink back. "Fuck, I'm sorry. Okay? I really am, Paisley. It's my fault that you don't trust me."

I roll my eyes. "Duh."

"Give me a chance to fix this between us," he pleads.

"There's no us, husband." My tone is resolute.

"But there could be." His gaze begs me to reconsider.

I blow out another heavy breath and glance upward. Just then, the sun shines through the clouds. It's just a small section fighting against the gloom. But streaks of light quickly break apart the gray in a dominant display. The sight has me thinking of Marion. She would want patience and understanding for her son. I've been raised to offer both freely, along with kindness.

As I continue contemplating the message in the sky, my chest tingles and a strange sensation spreads through me. Almost like an uplifting force. If I were more religious, I might consider it a spiritual awakening. My faith suggests it's a sign to be compassionate.

I glance at Brody to see if he feels it too. His gaze is locked on me, waiting for my decision. I'm aware of the change in him. It's sudden but can't be ignored. If I reject him now, he's going to rebuild his walls and reinforce them stronger than before. That's not something I can have on my conscience.

"One night?"

Brody expels a breath that sounds like a bag of bricks. "That's all I'm asking."

My smile is slight but visible. "Make it count, husband."

CHAPTER TWENTY-ONE

Brody

MY GAZE IS HOOKED ON PAISLEY AS SHE SPEARS A forkful of elbow noodles and slips the bite into her mouth. I lean closer, holding my breath while she chews. Her lashes flutter shut on a moan. That sound pumps me full of heat, traveling south to twitch my dick.

Blue clashes with green when she opens her eyes and looks at me. I wait for her critique like it's a backstage pass into her good graces. Paisley leaves me hanging. A quirked brow is the extent of her feedback as she stabs more pasta from the bowl. That's probably a good sign. Or she's indecisive.

Since when do I give a shit about gaining approval?

The answer is sitting right in front of me. I care about what this sparkly cowgirl has to say. This newfound affliction is far worse than that based on my recent behavior. Fuck, I'm weak for this woman. Or just that taken. She's proven to be too much, which I'm realizing is exactly what I've been missing.

"So?" I jerk my chin at her dinner that's already half-way gone.

Paisley hums, tipping her head left to right. "Want me to be honest?"

"Please," I grind out.

Her laugh strokes my fraying nerves into submission. "It's delicious, husband. Much better than I would've given you credit for."

My smile is a slow grower, sprouting under her praise. "That's what I needed to hear."

Paisley freezes, her fork hovering in mid-air. Her wide stare is feasting on me rather than the food. It takes a full minute for her to recover, which stretches my grin higher.

"Good grief," she mumbles and drops her gaze. "Watch where you're pointing that thing."

I blindly skewer a bite for myself, unable to take my eyes off her while she stuffs her mouth. "Is my wife flustered?"

"Too hot for your own good." Paisley blushes, still avoiding my blatant attention.

"I'm all yours, Twinkles. Might as well get your fill."

"It's just temporary." The hushed tone is mostly meant for her ears, along with her resistance.

"We'll see," I counter and shove the pasta past my lips.

Her focus flickers to me as I taste my first attempt at homemade macaroni and cheese. She appears to be on the edge of her seat for a change. I'm about to celebrate that accomplishment, but a burst of flavor momentarily distracts me. It's savory and creamy. Packs an appetizing punch. Definitely passable for the beloved comfort food.

I'm quick to scoop more into my mouth. "Not bad."

Paisley huffs another laugh. "Are you surprised?"

My nod is absolute. "Figured I'd burn the place down before serving something edible."

Considering I barely cook for myself, this is unfamiliar territory for me. It seemed fitting that I prepare our last meal together. Luckily, Paisley's favorite dish isn't too complicated. She gobbles more pasta, a pleased noise offering compliments to the chef. My gesture seems to be hitting the spot. Come tomorrow, she'll want nothing to do with me.

I've been thinking about coming clean, ripping off the bandage. It felt like a wasted effort. My shot in the dark is focused on showing her what she's done for me in such a short amount of time. A month ago, I never would've seen myself playing house with a woman. The idea was inconceivable. Not until Paisley blinded me with her blingy sunshine. My future is brighter now, but only if she stays in it. Damn, look at me getting caught up in foreign feelings.

"Well, I'm about to burst." She pats her flat stomach. "Thanks for making dinner. It was very tasty."

I finish mine before gathering the bowls and utensils. "You're welcome."

She gawks when I rise to clean my mess in the kitchen. "And you're doing the dishes?"

My gaze finds hers while I begin scrubbing at the cheese stuck to the pot. "I'm not worthless, Twinkles."

Paisley snorts into her cocktail. "Nobody would suggest otherwise."

"Only care what you think."

Her exaggerated throat clearing pairs nicely with her

lofted glass. "You're a very rich man, husband. Wealth drips from your pores. I can smell success on you. Money follows in your footsteps, just waiting to be spent. You're flush with cash and charm. It's an honor to be a cent in your dollar. Cheers!"

I grunt but raise my beer for her toast. "Clever."

"What can I say? You inspire me." She polishes off her beverage in a swig.

My palm rubs at the sudden pang in my chest. "Guess I'll drink to that."

Paisley's attention drifts out the window, dismissing me and my sullen tone. She might believe I'm putting on an act to get what I want. I don't blame her for assuming my purpose is self-serving. That's been my motto since setting my sights on her for this scheme. But my position at Benson Farmstead is no longer the only prize at stake.

"Would you like me to make you another espresso martini?" That phrase can get added to the list of things I never thought I'd ask.

Her smile finds me with the shaker already in my hand. "Sure."

"Coming right up." I grab the Tito's and coffee liqueur. "Go make yourself comfortable on the couch. I'll be right over."

"Such service," she croons.

My concentration splits between mixing the contents and tracking Paisley as she crosses the room. Her soft sigh derails me completely. Golden hair fans around her while she gets situated in the corner seat. She tips her head back, eyes sliding shut for a brief reprieve. It's only then I realize that I'm fixated on her rather than completing the task at hand. Rookie mistake.

Her explicit instructions play on repeat while I shake the concoction like my marriage depends on it. After adding a chocolate swirl to the bottom of a clean glass, I fill it to the rim with her choice of cocktail. Two coffee beans get dunked in foam on top for the garnishing touch. There might be a career behind the bar for me yet. If my dad were here, he'd be laughing his ass off. Mom would shove me out of the kitchen and directly into Paisley's arms. She always knew what was best for me.

I fetch myself a fresh beer before joining my wife on the sectional. Her gaze isn't shy about stalking my approach. She's particularly interested in what's swinging beneath my sweats, and it's more substantial than the drawstrings. I'll have to buy more if this is the response I get. At this point, I'll use any means necessary to win her over. Other than further coercion. She has to come willingly.

I barely manage to stifle a groan while covering the distance between us. But damn, the visual of Paisley begging me for relief is too tempting. Especially with her sprawled on the cushions like she actually wants to be here.

"Oh, my," she purrs while accepting the drink. "You're spoiling me."

My scoff calls bullshit while I take a load off beside her. "This is nothing."

Her eyes narrow. "Why do I have the feeling this is more than you've done for all your previous relationships combined?"

"That's a low hurdle," I chuckle.

"But it's true?" Paisley's eyes sparkle while she tastes the martini.

"Twinkles," I drawl. "Don't mistake me for a romantic."

"Yet you cooked my favorite meal from scratch and whipped up not one"—she counts on her fingers—"but two very yummy cocktails."

"Is it that easy to please you?"

"What? No." She scoffs, but her blush betrays her.

I drop my voice to a rasp and murmur, "You haven't been properly pampered? Such a shame. I'll be fixin' that right quick. Pull out all the stops."

Her giggle is shrill. "You sound like a country gentleman."

"And you sound impressed again."

Paisley squirms and refuses to meet my gaze. "I can't help it. This is strange."

"What is?"

Her sigh is drawn out. "Just sitting here as if we're a normal couple. You're being semi-sweet to me. Gosh, and we're married. That's really insane."

My chuckle startles her. "How strong did I make your drinks?"

"Oh, hush. I'm having a moment. Fantasy and reality are clashing." Her hand clenches into a fist before popping open to mimic an explosion.

The dots she's connecting are invisible to me. "You've lost me, wife."

"I have a confession," Paisley murmurs.

"Now that I can understand." A creak sounds from the couch as I turn to give her my full attention.

Her bottom lip gets tortured between her teeth. "Promise not to let it go to your head?"

My snort is instant. "Absolutely not."

"Fine, I won't tell you." Paisley redirects her focus to straight ahead.

"It's not nice to tease, wife." I shift closer until our thighs bump. "Tell me."

She shakes her head, and a blonde curtain hides her from me. "No, I changed my mind."

I tuck the fallen hair behind her ear, my fingers brushing her red cheek in the process. "C'mon, Twinkles. Spill the beans."

"I had a crush on you," she blurts. Her exhale is loud as if she's pushing a weight off her chest. "If I can even call it a crush. It was more like an infatuation. You were just so hot riding that mechanical bull. Really left an impression."

"Ah, yes. The first time you saw me."

"And one of the only times until recently," she clarifies. "I always knew Bianca had an older brother and there were plenty of rumors, but you were an enigma until that night at The Paddock. That drew quite a crowd. No wonder why. Once I caught sight of you, I was hooked. Never told a soul. It was silly and shallow."

The past tense isn't appreciated. An irrational spike of jealousy boils in my gut as I listen to her babble on about a former version of myself. I put my beer on the coffee table, giving this issue my undivided attention.

"Why didn't you ever try talking to me?" Not that I would've been receptive, especially to my little sister's best friend who I frequently compared to an infected pimple on my ass. Damn, I deserve to be stomped under her sparkly boots.

Paisley's flat expression reflects a similar thought. "I approached you at your mother's funeral. We know how well that went."

"Not my finest moment," I admit on a wince. And prior to that, I avoided her overly optimistic attitude like she would plague me.

Her brows lift in acknowledgment. "My so-called crush was squashed after that."

"Have I redeemed myself?"

"Hardly." She swirls the liquor in her glass. "It's going to take more than a few nights of you being civil toward me. I'm not that easy."

Did someone give me a shovel? I'm digging myself into one hell of a hole. My palms rub together, and I stretch out in a vulnerable position.

"Clean slate, Twinkles. Ask me anything. I'm an open book for you to pry apart."

"That doesn't benefit me."

"I'm trying," I murmur. "Doesn't that count for something?"

"Maybe a little bit." Paisley holds up a pinch.

My exhale ends on a grin. "I like that you make me work for it."

"Can't imagine the last time you had to."

A faded memory surfaces. "Ninth grade."

"Oh, wow," she laughs.

I nod. "Misty Johnson needed to be dined and dated before I could touch her tits."

"How romantic."

"Goes to show there's room for improvement."

Her snort becomes a dry laugh. "Like an entire estate worth."

"We've gotta start somewhere." I motion for her to let me have it. "What do you wanna know?"

She flounders for a moment. "I can't think of something on the spot."

"Not so spontaneous, hmm? Fine, how about I ask you?" I peer deep into her eyes. "Tell me about yourself, Paisley Benson."

"First of all, I didn't agree to change my last name." My sassy wife wags her finger. "And second, that's not any better. I need a helpful prompt."

My brain takes a deep dive into the past when I actually cared about getting to know the person across from me. "Would you rather…?"

Her gasp brightens her features. "Oooooh, a game? I didn't peg you as the type."

"There's a lot you wouldn't guess about me," I taunt. My hand signals for her to go ahead. "Ladies first. Take your time. No pressure."

"What about rules?"

"Do we need them?"

"I can play fair if you can."

"Spoiler alert, babe. I prefer a dirty twist."

"Fine," she concedes. "But I get the option not to answer."

"And then you drink."

Paisley sputters. "This is heavy on the vodka."

"You can switch to something weaker," I offer as a compromise.

"Or we can just behave ourselves." Paisley glares, just waiting for me to argue. Her lips twitch at my feigned obedience. "Would you rather ride a bull or a bronc?"

"Bull," I answer automatically. "More of a thrill."

"Figured." She rolls her eyes, mostly at herself. "That was too easy."

"Am I supposed to make it hard?" Her coy tone gets me halfway there.

"You won't hear me complain." I spread my thighs to hide the evidence stacking against me.

Paisley nudges my shin with her painted toes. "It's your turn."

My palm catches her ankle before she can pull away. Once she's secured in my grasp, I start massaging. Her skin is softer than velvet, even on the bottom of her foot. My thumbs dig into her arch and add more pressure.

She sags into the cushions, her mouth hanging open. "Ohhhhh, yes. Right there."

Desire slams into me and I almost grind against her heel. "You like that?"

"Yes!" Her lashes flutter while she surrenders to my touch. "Harder. Please."

The need to hear her utter that phrase in a very different context has me upping my game. I repeat the motions, and she practically melts in my hands. Her whimper begs for more. A haze of lust descends as I gladly satisfy her plea. While she's lenient and agreeable, I settle on a question.

"Would you rather kiss me or reveal a secret?"

"Secret." The response is barely a wheeze.

"Go on then," I urge.

"That's not how the game works."

My focus shifts from the bliss slacking her features to the color of her pedicure. Glittery pink polish, of course. "There aren't any rules, Twinkles."

She whines when I slow my kneading. "You make a really great pillow."

"Did you sleep well?"

Her head bobbles loosely. "Best sleep I've had in ages."

Pride swells in my chest until it's difficult to breathe. "Same for me."

"Just sayin' that," she mumbles.

My fingers pause their assault on a tough spot. "Wouldn't lie about that."

Her eyes fling open to pin me with a threat of bodily harm. "Don't stop!"

"Never, wife." I grab her other foot to provide the same treatment. "I've got you right where I want you."

"Until tomorrow." Suspicion gleams in her gaze, and it's my fault.

I built that barrier between us. Hell, it's been there from the start. We never had a chance. Not when I forced her into this situation. She hates me for it, or should. I deserve her spite.

A weary exhale does little to ease the strain on my guilty conscience. Maybe she can learn to trust me again. We can build a solid foundation after I reveal the truth about Bianca. Or I can keep dreaming.

"It's your turn." The stony edge in my voice alerts her to the mounting tension.

Paisley fights a courageous battle between staring at me and surrendering to relaxation. "Would you rather own Benson Farmstead without any strings attached or be forced to marry me as a contractual obligation?"

I almost laugh at her strategy. "That would've been another easy one if you asked me two days ago."

Her baby blue depths beckon me to take a deep dive and never resurface. "But now?"

"You're my wife and the best decision I never would've made for myself. No regrets about buckling you in barbwire, Twinkles." I glance at her ring while my palms run along the top of her feet, drifting across her legs. "Now that you're mine, I never want to let you go."

CHAPTER TWENTY-TWO

Paisley

"Would you rather turn around or get whatever this is"—I wave my hand straight ahead—"over with?"

Brody's hand tightens on the wheel. "Don't give me the option."

My sigh matches the clench in my husband's jaw. Frustration has been brewing since we packed the truck this morning. I've been trying to lighten the mood and failing miserably.

His agitation appears directly related to where we're headed. That's spiked a hefty dose of suspicion in me, rattling my nerves until I can barely sit still. Two hours is a long time to sit on the edge of my seat.

Each mile that brings us closer to town adds another brick to his recognizable defense. He's quiet, stoically guarding the vulnerable pieces of himself. Long sleeves hide his rebellious phase while a steely glare paves our way home. His shaggy hair isn't tucked under a hat but I'm sure that's coming soon. I thought we were past this phase. It hurts my heart, as if we're shifting into reverse.

A glance in the side mirror twists my stomach into knots. Just yesterday we were on that boat, speaking freely. Now the tension is so thick I can barely breathe. Whatever he's afraid to tell me must be significant.

By the time we pull into Benson Farmstead, my legs are a pair of coiled springs. I'm ready to jump out of my skin while Brody types in his access code. We don't exchange a word as the quiet hum swings the gate open.

Nothing appears to be out of sorts, which should offer a sliver of relief. Brody's stormy expression grows darker as if the sprawling green acres are a black hole. Tires thump on concrete when he eases off the brake to face the inevitable. The truck crawls forward at a pace that elevates my pulse. If I stay inside this pressure cooker for another second, I'll burst beyond measure. I'm unbuckled and reaching for the escape latch before he comes to a complete stop.

"Twinkles?"

I startle at his low tone, popping the stress bearing down on me. "Yeah, boss?"

The harsh lines in his features soften. "Thanks for last night. I needed it."

My body instinctively shifts toward his. "I'm glad I stayed."

"Remember that, okay?"

A furrow dents my forehead. "What are you afraid of?"

"Losing you."

My heart pangs and I quirk a brow to mask the turmoil. "You don't really have me. Last name only, husband."

"Planning to change that."

Before I can question him, he cups the back of my neck and hauls me in. Our foreheads bump as green collides with blue. There's so much swirling in Brody's stare. He's open to me again, if just for a moment. I watch the conflict spread until he looks pained.

"Let me kiss you." It's not a request, but he wants permission.

My exhale hitches and he breathes me in, waiting. "That isn't the explanation I expected."

"It's a need." His hold tightens on my nape. "Something to soften the blow. Real feelings are forming. I want to prove it."

"Okay," I whisper.

"Okay?"

My nose nudges his when I nod. "Kiss me like you mean it, husband."

Brody's mouth slams onto mine. The brutal intensity shocks me. He takes advantage of my gasp, our tongues meeting in a sensual glide. Heat blasts through me and I mewl at the feverish rush.

The kiss is passionate and raw—an explosion of need. The tension that's been brewing for weeks detonates. Teeth clamp onto lips while desire bursts between us. A thrum streaks under my skin in a static ripple. I whimper and he swallows the sound on a groan. The grip on the back of my neck clenches, making me feel controlled. That sensation is a hot streak of arousal pumping into me.

Brody lifts his other palm to cradle my face. The tender touch has me surrendering completely. Within the lust, I realize that we're too far apart. He must sense the distance too. Leather creaks as we shift for a deeper connection.

There's so much left unsaid but we understand each other in this moment.

His taste is addictive, much like the man in general. I sip on peppermint while inhaling woodsy spice. He's everywhere but it's not enough. My fingers fist at the front of his shirt, yanking to demand more. His fingers tunnel into my hair, pulling gently. That slight sting expands into a burning ache. I squirm to get closer, chasing the warmth.

Brody seems just as demanding. Hands drift and rove to map as much of me as possible. It's electrifying. I'm dizzy. Consumed. Lost. He's pouring so much into this embrace. I can feel his hunger stroking mine. It's enough to make me forget where we are. The need builds and grows until I'm ready to climb onto his lap.

That urge must slap him and he jolts. Brody pauses his assault before breaking the kiss entirely. The separation is slow, like pulling apart molasses. It feels like he's forcing himself to stop. A bitter chill fills the space he shoves between us.

His thumb traces over the swell on my bottom lip. "That was more than I deserve."

I shiver as the lingering warmth fades. Confusion muddles with desire while I struggle to compose myself. "What's happening?"

Brody nods at the windshield. "My sister is about to raise hell."

And then he lets me go.

My heart hurts when his gaze ices over. The need to know what's wrong traps me in suspense. It's tempting to stay and pry, the words perched for flight. But there's someone else I need to see right now.

When I turn to look, Bianca is leaving the barn and walking in our direction. A different type of nervous energy floods me. The long-distance silence leaves me guessing how she'll react. Only one way to find out.

I open my door and a blast of cool air hits my flushed cheeks. The chill is barely noticeable as I focus on my best friend since elementary school. Her stride is a fast clip that syncs with the pounding in my chest. Uncertainty weighs me down, which sucks. It's never been like this between us.

But then Bianca begins jogging, a smile lighting up her face. Relief whooshes out of me and I hurry to cover the distance to meet her. We crash against each other in a hug that's painfully overdue.

"Holy shit," she breathes. "You're alive."

I pull away and laugh at her bewildered expression. "Did you assume otherwise?"

"Um, yeah. Brody hauled you off into the woods for a reward retreat while the entire town—" Her gaze swings to my hand clutching her upper arm. "No way. Tell me it isn't true."

"Which part?"

Bianca grips my fingers, gawking at my new jewelry. "You married my brother?"

It's my turn to stare blankly. "You didn't know?"

Her gaze bounces from my ring to my face. "Last I heard, he was bugging you to fake date him."

"Oh, no." My stomach sinks.

"The locals were quick to update me when I went to the bar last night. Figured it was a horrific rumor." She shudders. "How did this happen?"

"As it turns out, your brother didn't need a girlfriend

to take ownership of the company. He actually needed a wife. After much"—I deliberate on my word choice for a breath—"persuasion, he convinced me to fill the role."

Her eyes bug out. "You agreed willingly?"

"Well…" My brain scrambles for an excuse that won't make this worse. "He made it difficult to refuse."

Her frantic stare slides to my rings again. "Is that barbwire?"

I fiddle with the bands. "It's somewhat of an… inside joke."

"Real funny. I can't believe this." Bianca yanks at her dark hair. "Why didn't you call me?"

Frustration rises in a wave, crashing against my already frazzled nerves. "I tried several times a day. You never answered."

She exhales roughly. "Ugh, right. Sorry. My phone was stolen. Colton was a real shit about letting me use his."

"Why?"

"Good question. He's been better about it since we got back, but you weren't answering yours."

"It got into a fight with the hot tub at the cabin. Do not recommend," I sigh.

"That's… strange."

"Too much champagne."

Her brows spring to the clouds. "Wait. Was this secret getaway your honeymoon?"

"Um, yeah. I guess?" Even though I'd been hell-bent against admitting it originally.

"Did you have sex with him?" Bianca gags almost immediately. "Nope, don't answer that. I'm already assuming the worst after you ran off with him. Gross."

"We're married in name only," I say to reassure both of us.

"Doesn't matter. A fake relationship would've been bad enough."

"This is just temporary."

"Uh-huh, keep telling yourself that. Something isn't adding up. Why didn't we talk for almost two weeks?"

"I couldn't get ahold of you," I reiterate.

"Maybe that was on purpose. He knew how I felt about his plan to use you. I didn't want you involved in his messy business." Her glare shifts over my shoulder. "Care to correct me, brother?"

As my pulse kicks into a lope, I follow her focus to where it landed behind me. Brody is there, leaning on the truck, just waiting for recognition. A cowboy hat shadows his eyes and reclaims the broody indifference he oozes like testosterone. The shield is locked in place but I see beneath it. I know him better now. Sort of.

My breath hitches when Brody's stare smolders into mine. I don't bother fighting the urge to fan my face. Damn, this man gets me hot and bothered. Nobody can deny that after the onslaught of heated arguments that kicked off our… situationship. Not even his sister.

"Ewwww, no. Not the sex face. Stop looking at her like that. Fake my ass," Bianca huffs. "He's not giving up without a fight. But lucky for you, I'm home now. No more limits on our communication."

Brody's flinty stare hardens into steel when he glances at her. "I didn't take your phone."

"But you didn't help the situation. All of my accounts were frozen and Colton basically held me captive over there until you got us a flight home. Where the heck was Dad during all this? That's super suspicious too."

One part of her speech stands out. I whirl to face my husband completely. "You booked their return flight?"

"Not technically." He doesn't sound concerned in the least.

"Don't split hairs. It's a yes or no question."

His jaw clenches. "Yes."

"You lied to me." The pain in my voice echoes in the space separating us.

Brody tips his chin, the image of unapologetic. "I did what had to be done."

"Wow." My laugh is hollow. "Does that mean you made Bianca's phone disappear? To make sure she wouldn't get in the way of your plans?"

He straightens, taking a meaning step forward. "Twinkles—"

"Stop." I hold out my palm and he halts in his tracks. "This is what you were hiding."

"I was going to tell you."

"Uh-huh, sure. Right after we figured it out on our own." Another realization hits. "Why did you let me think Bianca was mad? Just to jerk me around a bit more?"

He flinches, exposing a crack in his armor. "You came to that conclusion on your own."

"But you could've corrected me. That's lying by omission, husband. You're really earning that master manipulator title."

"And you wanted to leave, but then you were glad we stayed. Just told me," he reminds on a lazy drawl.

"That was before I had all the facts," I counter. "Not sure what I expected, but this is pretty low. Even for you."

"Let me explain."

My head shakes to deny his request. "I've already heard plenty. You're exactly who you claim to be. It's my fault for assuming this could be more than a contractual obligation."

His boot takes a purposeful step in my direction as I begin to turn around. "Where are you going?"

"Away from you."

"We need to talk about this."

I roll my eyes at his authoritative tone, not that he sees it. "Maybe later. I need space."

"And we need to catch waaaaay the hell up." Bianca hooks her arm through mine.

"What's that supposed to mean?" Brody isn't shy about following us to Bianca's car.

"None of your business," she tells him.

"Paisley is my wife," he bellows in return.

Irritation prickles along my spine. "Only as a convenience for you to get ahead by any means necessary."

Bianca bristles beside me. "Such bullshit."

Brody flanks my other side. "Don't do anything reckless. Your behavior is a direct reflection on me now."

"Aww, you care about your pawn staining your reputation?" The smile I give him is deranged, which is how he makes me feel. "Don't worry, husband. I won't tarnish your image."

He glares when I get in the passenger seat and slam the door in his face. A bent knuckle taps on the window. "Call me if you need a ride home."

"She won't. Stay here and plan your next big moves

for Benson Farmstead. I'm sure you're chomping at the bit to get back at it. That's all you care about." Bianca shoots her brother with a punishing glare that I can hear cracking through the air like a whip. "Maybe find Dad while you're at it. He ran off again or is avoiding me. Probably your doing along with everything else."

"Haven't talked to him since we left." Fury sparks in his green eyes until he glances at me. "Can we—?"

"Don't follow us," Bianca interrupts while sliding behind the wheel. The engine roars to muffle any response he might've made. "Gosh, he's such a dildo."

"That's an insult to my most reliable boyfriends," I laugh.

"You're right. He's more like a constant wedgie you can't yank free." She flips him off as we flee the scene.

"Where are you taking me?"

"Didn't get that far, but we need cocktails or coffee for this discussion. You pick."

My gaze trails to the familiar landscape blurring beyond the window. "I could use a stiff drink."

"Booze it is. We're going to take a serious load off. Screw those douche canoes for trying to rule our lives." Bianca cranks up the radio.

We spend the ten-minute trip to Main Street belting out the best of Taylor Swift. Nobody does girl power anthems quite like her. That's probably why the knot in my stomach is looser when Bianca parks in front of The Paddock. I slip the barbwire rings off my finger and lose ten pounds of pressure.

"Ooooh, such a rebel. The honeymoon is over!" Bianca dances in her seat while I tuck the bling in my purse.

"It never really started," I grumble.

Her shimmying stops. "You didn't bang like bunnies?"

"No." Is that disappointment in my voice? Impossible.

But the upward lift of her brows confirms it. "Yikes. We're going to need several rounds for this conversation."

"Can I order a tub of ice cream too?"

"Whatever you want, babe." She kills the ignition and pops open her door. "To the bar!"

Which is mostly empty when we walk inside. Late afternoon on a Thursday is apparently the time to swing by The Paddock. I'm all for drowning my sorrows in semi-private. We have our choice of spots and immediately stride for the rail where our stools await. A guy steps in our path before we make it halfway.

He lifts a plastic spoon to offer a recognizable treat, perched for effortless consumption. "Gummy bear soaked in vodka?"

"Absolutely!" Bianca cheers. "This is the proper way to kick off happy hour."

"Don't eat that!" I knock the lofted utensil away from her mouth.

She pouts, her lower lip sticking out far dramatically. "Why not? It's a boost in the right direction."

"You never accept candy from a stranger," I scold. "No wonder Brody sent a chaperone to follow you around Germany."

"Oh, stop. This dude is harmless." But when she glances at the boozy bear distributor and sees his gaze on her tits, my bestie changes her tune. "Hey, buddy." She snaps her fingers. "Eyes up here."

His expression turns sheepish, a blush staining his cheeks. "You're really pretty."

"Aren't you sweet," she croons.

"But passing out from whatever he put in those is not." I narrow my eyes at him and his jar of bloated gummies.

Bianca bumps me with her hip. "Get yourself married and turn into a fun sponge."

"I'll soak some sugar in liquor for you myself. C'mon." I tug her to our seats.

"Now we're getting somewhere," she chirps.

The moment my ass meets the leather cushion, a familiar face is on the opposite side of the counter to greet me. "Hey, Paisley."

My smile comes automatically. "How's it going?"

"Just fine." Tyler's stare takes a noticeable dip to my bare ring finger. A furrow creases his forehead before a wide grin replaces the confusion. "Much better now."

Bianca thrusts her hand between us. "Um, hello? We're thirsty."

He blinks from whatever fantasy is playing in his mind, swinging his focus to my friend. "Hi, Bee. Back from your trip?"

"I was in here yesterday and you didn't notice." She flutters her lashes.

"Ah, sorry about that." He scrubs at the back of his neck.

"It's okay to have favorites, but we're on a mission to spill secrets and alcohol would be handy."

Tyler's attention returns to me while he begins mixing our usual drinks. "I'd heard you got hitched. Glad to see that's just a rumor."

A lump in my throat makes it difficult to form words. "Umm—"

"And why is that?" Bianca cuts in, her concentration fixed on something behind me.

The bartender pours our cocktails into chocolate-drizzled glasses and slides them in front of us. "Maybe I'll finally gather the courage to ask you out."

"Oh," I breathe. In a fluid motion, I pick up my martini and get gulping. The smooth flavor does little to take the edge off. "That's not a great idea, Ty."

He leans on the bar, bringing us closer. "Why not?"

"It's… complicated."

Heavy footsteps approach, almost loud enough to quiet the pounding in my ears. "I'd reconsider hitting on my wife if you're a fan of breathing."

CHAPTER TWENTY-THREE

Brody

"T HE PARTY POOPER COMMITTEE HAS ARRIVED." Bianca scowls at me, but looks downright homicidal when she glances at Colton. "And he brought reinforcements to stand guard. How typical."

Paisley swivels on her stool, almost toppling off in her haste to face me. "What are you doing here?"

The truth is that I can't stay away from her. When my sister drove off with my wife in the car, I was compelled to follow. There was no stopping me. That blistering ache transformed into blind fury when I saw the bartender try to steal what's mine. He's lucky to still be standing and wisely scurries off like the vermin he is.

The urge to punch him subsides slightly until I take another glance at Paisley's naked finger. "Where are your rings?"

"I took them off."

"Why?"

"They don't mean anything."

Fire bursts in my veins. "Bullshit. You're my wife, Mrs. Benson."

"Say it louder. The folks in the back booth might've missed it." Her eyes roll in that general direction. "I don't need diamonds on my finger to prove I'm a contractual obligation. This sham has spread far and wide, just as you intended."

"The bartender thought it was a rumor." I stab my finger at the guy who's brave enough to test the limits. If my glare could spit nails, he'd be pinned to the wall.

"And he's been swiftly corrected. See how that works?"

"It's not always that simple."

"It really is," she insists. "You just choose to do what's best for your scheme. Is it lonely at the top?"

"Twinkles," I sigh.

She crosses her arms, staring me down. "What else are you hiding?"

"Nothing." But then I think better of it and turn to my sister. "I told Paisley that I'd put Echo on the market if she didn't marry me." My focus boomerangs to my wife. "I'd never sell that horse. It was just a ploy to get you to agree."

Bianca's jaw drops. "The fuck?"

"That's really shitty," Paisley mumbles.

"It is," I agree. "I've made a lot of shitty decisions lately, most of them involving you. I'm not proud of myself, and I'm hoping you can forgive me."

My sister clucks her tongue. "Mom would be so disappointed."

"I'm aware," I grit. "She would've understood my reasoning."

"You can't just… assume that." Bianca flounders like a fish out of water.

My chest heaves under the pressure of defending myself. "I've made my peace with her."

"How convenient for your guilty conscience," my sister grumbles. "What did Dad have to say about that stunt?"

"He doesn't know." Forgot that tiny detail during my confession earlier.

Paisley's brow knits. "Is that why he was nowhere to be found before our rush down the aisle?"

"Yes."

"The secrets keep spilling out." She huffs hard enough to send stray hairs flying off her forehead.

"Can't believe I missed your wedding," Bianca complains.

"Don't fret. It'll give you premature wrinkles. Our nuptials were more staged than a ceremony on Real Housewives." Paisley's humor belongs in a comedy skit.

My chuckle is dark. "Sorry to disappoint, but you're legally bound to me, wife."

Baby blues narrow into slits, hacking at my amusement. "I'm still not sure how you got the mayor to give you a marriage license before I signed it."

"He owed me a favor," I remind.

"Which trapped me in a loveless union." She slams the rest of her espresso martini and signals for another. "What are you doing here, darling husband of mine?"

"Does that taste better than the ones I made you?"

"Not telling."

"C'mon," I urge.

"You didn't answer my question and it's the second time I've asked." She holds up two fingers.

"I can't let you walk away from us." The urge to rephrase that statement, changing *can't* to *won't*, burns my tongue. But using force isn't going to win her heart.

"We've already been over this. There's no *us*," she reiterates.

"That's gonna change."

"Do I get a choice?"

I grind my molars until an ache blooms in my jaw. "Yes."

A coy smile curves her lips into a picture of satisfaction. I'm about to be served humble pie. She might toss it in my face before leaving me to choke on every bad move that led me here. It's what I deserve for dominating our relationship up to this point.

Irritation spikes when whispers tickle my ears. It's only then I realize we're putting on a show that the entire town will binge by tomorrow. This isn't the type of dirty laundry I want aired.

Stares avert when I look at our fellow patrons. Bianca got popcorn from the machine at some point. She's munching loudly while waiting for what comes next. A glance behind me catches Colton watching her. The bartender picks that moment to drop off Paisley's refill, lingering beyond common sense. Pressure builds into a bomb that's ticking down to detonate. I'm about to make the scene worse.

Before that happens, I whip out my wallet and slap ten hundreds onto the glossy wood between us. "Shut the place down."

The bartender falters, eyes bulging at the money on the counter. "I can't close early."

"You can, and will. Now," I demand.

"What are you doing?" Paisley whispers.

My gaze heats on hers. "Getting you alone."

"We can go somewhere else, like the park. That'll cost less."

I shake my head. "You chose to come here. This is where we'll stay."

My wife quirks a brow. "*We?* I asked for space, husband."

"Want me to leave?" If she does, I'm not sure I can follow through.

"It's for the best," she murmurs.

"I dunno, Lee." Bianca's gaze shifts from her friend to me. "My brother is ruffled and riled. He might've caught real feelings. Damn, this is getting juicy."

Paisley exhales a laugh as my sister resumes chomping on popcorn. Her eyes flick over me before she turns to the guy behind the counter. "Can you help us out, Ty?"

He gulps. "Uh, well… three servers and another bartender will be on the clock soon. Cooks are in the kitchen. The dinner shift starts in an hour."

"Let me worry about them." I push the cash toward him.

He nods and cups a palm around his mouth. "Everybody out! The Paddock is reserved for a private event starting now."

A collective grumble rises from the crowd when they lose their free ticket to the shambles of my wedded bliss. Most are quick to exit, tossing a last look over their shoulder. Others drag their feet as if caught in mud on their way out. While waiting for the room to empty, I text the owner about my plans. He assures me that his staff won't be an issue. The sound of pots and pans clanging from the back suggests a quick cleanup.

"Getting rid of the riffraff just to have a conversation

with your fake wife. Well played, brother." Bianca makes no move to get off her stool.

"That includes you, Bee."

Her mouth pops open. "You're giving me the boot?"

"Take Colton with you." I hitch a thumb at the man hovering on the sidelines, more than ready to whisk her away.

My sister wrinkles her nose. "I'd rather be saddled in secrets and spend eternity alone."

Colt strides forward and sets her confiscated phone on the bar. "This belongs to you."

Steam practically spews from her ears. "You're such a twat waffle."

"Just did what I was told." His stoic expression doesn't falter and demands respect.

Bianca has a very different reaction, shoving him away from her personal space. "Now I'm telling you to get lost. Permanently."

He backs up but doesn't leave her side. "Let's go, princess."

She gnashes her teeth. "You're off duty, Colt. Go hound someone else."

"Only care about hounding you," he mumbles.

Bianca gives him a cold shoulder, turning her attention to Paisley. "I'm going to rip him a new one. Can you handle Brody on your own?"

My sparkly cowgirl rolls her lips between her teeth, gaze roaming over the determination in my wide stance. "Mhmm, he's all mine."

The rumble brewing in my chest makes my sister retch. "Ick, that sounds sexual."

Paisley reaches for her fresh martini. "It's just a business arrangement."

"Which includes dipping his company pen into your untainted ink." Bianca dry heaves again. "I can see what's happening here. You're a big girl and can make good choices."

"I'm not going to sleep with my fake husband." But there's no mistaking her blush as she notices the bulge below my belt.

Bianca finishes her popcorn and hops off the stool. "Get some. What's the harm?"

My wife squints at her before glancing at Colton. A smile splits her lips. "Ah, okay."

The instigator blanches. "What? No. This is about you making nice with my brother. He's a grumpy asshole, but I think he means well. Maybe don't divorce him quite yet. It's kinda cool that we're sisters."

Paisley grins. "We can share your wing in the mansion."

A glance at my scowl and Bianca snorts. "I doubt that's gonna fly, babes. Good luck."

They exchange a hug before my sister trots away with Colton hot on her heels. My wife squirms on her seat, taking another sip of her drink while avoiding my stare. Desire thrums in my veins as I shamelessly admire her. She's not immune to the static charge gaining intensity between us. Another shift from her hips suggests she might beg for relief from this standoff.

A throat clears, ruining the moment. The bartender hasn't left his station. "You good, Paisley?"

Anger rushes under my skin, replacing the gratification of her proximity. "*You* won't be if your eyes don't quit fucking my wife."

The cowgirl in mention has an answering glare aimed at me that promises to maim if I don't behave. That earns her a smirk. She rips her upset off me, swiveling to face the other man's concern. I'm crowding her in the next breath. An elbow jabs at my ribs and I chuckle. My wife is feisty.

"You can go, Ty. Thanks for the drinks." She taps the stack of cash, nudging it toward him.

"Have a great night," he murmurs.

"We will." The growl in my voice has him shrinking away.

"Don't mind him." Paisley pats my cheek while coddling his overstayed welcome. "My husband doesn't like to share his toys."

I glower at the sugary tone she gives him. My animosity trails his hasty retreat out the door. "You're not a toy, Twinkles."

She turns until our gazes clash again. "Could've fooled me with the way you insist on playing with me and my emotions."

Those words hit me harder than a sucker punch. My mouth clamps shut for a beat. "I'm sorry for making you feel that way, and for everything else too."

"Are you really?"

"Wouldn't be here if I wasn't," I whisper.

"I can't just forgive you." Her exhale is weary. "And what's there to fight for? Our entire marriage, or whatever this is, serves a sole purpose."

"It did, but not anymore."

She shakes her head. "You don't need me. The deal is done. Benson Farmstead is already yours."

"I've realized that owning the company isn't all that matters."

Her scoff calls me a liar. "Since when?"

My palms flatten on the wood counter, caging her between my arms. "Since I started falling for you, wife."

Paisley sucks in a sharp breath. "You expect me to believe that?"

"Maybe not yet, but eventually. We can start over. I'm just a guy in a bar, hitting on the woman of his dreams." I swoop down until our noses almost bump. "Do you come here often?"

Her chest rises and falls rapidly. "Only when I need a release. A stiff cocktail usually takes the edge off."

The martini made by another man mocks me. "Are his better than mine?"

She grins, a snarky brow arching. "I wouldn't have guessed that your ego is this fragile."

My hand grabs hers to press against my chest, sliding down along pearl snaps and the ridges in my abdomen. "There's nothing soft about me, wife."

Paisley studies the descent of our linked fingers like it's a map to the promised land. "Mhmm, my mistake. You're very… solid."

"Makes it easy to sweep you off your feet." I release her palm, drifting my fingers along her upturned jaw. "Allow me to regain your trust."

"Who says you had it to begin with?"

"Then give me a chance to earn it."

Paisley's hand clamps onto my shirt but doesn't push back or release me. "Another chance? You must think I'm very gullible."

"More like understanding. This is new for me. I'm bound to fuck up. It's an uncharted course, but you'll be my compass. Be patient with me and I'll make it worth your while." I sweep some hair off her shoulder, fascinated by the goose bumps that pebble over her skin. "No more fighting."

Her lashes flutter shut while she savors my touch. "That seems like all we do."

A low hum agrees with her. We did at first, but now my sights are set on redemption. "That means there's something worth salvaging."

"Maybe…" Her breath hitches when I dip down until my face is almost nestled in the crook of her neck. "This feels familiar."

I inhale vanilla and sunshine. My favorite indulgences. "You still smell like mine."

Just then, a recognizable glint ropes my focus. Her purse hangs from a hook under the counter, beckoning to me. The unmistakable sparkle of diamonds is trapped in an open pocket. I pluck the rings free from her hiding place before straightening. Paisley blinks from her stupor and narrows her eyes on me.

"Will you buckle yourself in barbwire with me, wife?" My determination positions the custom set at her fingertip.

She tortures her bottom lip over the tough decision. "Are you actually asking?"

"Yes. I'm going to nurture what I didn't bother to nourish before. It will be different now. I want all of you, Twinkles."

"Then I'll consider it." She smiles, but then jabs a finger into my chest. "But I'm not gonna forgive you overnight. A few gentle touches and semi-sweet words won't cut it."

"It's a start." I return the bands to where they belong, kissing her knuckle in the process.

Paisley sighs, expelling what I assume is leftover frustration. "What now?"

My attention swings over her shoulder to what sits in the far corner. "How about a solo competition to rekindle your crush?"

CHAPTER TWENTY-FOUR

Paisley

MY BOOTS ARE ABOUT TO WEAR A HOLE IN THE MAT surrounding Bucky. I whirl to pace in the opposite direction as Brody gets himself situated on the mechanical bull. He's a calm and collected cowboy up there—exactly how I remember. I can't look at him for too long or I'll get flustered. Again. The only one getting hot and bothered in this situation is me.

I wring my hands while fighting a fever. "Don't you need to sign a waiver or something?"

Whenever I've hopped on that thing, there was a stack of papers for me to complete first. It's a bit of a pain but I'm sure a lawsuit is worse.

Brody grunts. "Nah, the owner is a family friend. We have unlimited access."

"Of course you do," I deadpan. "This entire town is in your pocket."

His shrug doesn't deny it. "I don't abuse that power unless necessary."

"Like snagging a marriage license in a day?"

"Exactly." He winks before tucking his hat lower on his head. "Okay, I'm ready."

It's only then I realize that he expects me to manage the controls. A peek at the console provides relief I didn't plan to need. Labels and instructions are listed to make this a job for anyone who can read.

"Seems self-explanatory," I mumble while flipping the power switch.

"Use the remote."

That gives me pause. "There's a remote?"

"I paid for an upgrade after my last win. Figured they needed the top of the line to keep my legacy going. It might be one of a kind like me," he brags.

"Oh, please." I roll my eyes to the rafters, but grab the device as directed. The handheld version is even simpler to operate. "Hold on tight, husband."

He rolls up his sleeves and I almost purr. His forearms roped with veins and ink feel like a sight he only allows me to see. "Gonna give me a wild ride?"

My nod is a bobble while he slips his fingers under the strap. "If you can walk straight afterward, I didn't do an adequate job."

Brody's chuckle quakes my knees. "Let me have it."

And that's my cue. A tap to the green button rouses Bucky and the machine whirs. I immediately push left to set the bull in motion, simultaneously jabbing at the bucking force. Hoots and hollers spill from my husband as he flings his free arm into the air. He captivates me while I blindly switch directions on him. His butt doesn't even bump off the back. This kicks off a personal challenge to dismount him, and fast.

I shove the knobs in every which way. My methods aren't smooth or systematic or successful. The broody billionaire swivels forward and back, flowing into each motion as if he's in charge of the controls. A panty-melting smile stretches his mouth to giddy levels. He takes off his hat, whipping it in the air like a lasso. Based on his reactions, this might be the most fun he's had in ages.

The scent of fantasy slamming into reality smacks me in the face. Gosh, he's too sexy for his own good. I'd be filming if I had my phone. Drool puddles in my mouth until I almost drown myself. And that's not the only place that's wet. Phew. I fan my heated face.

But he's just getting warmed up. Brody's hips snap forward as he rides like a pro. He rocks into the disjointed gait, letting a groan slip free. The seductive rhythm gets me frantic. There's an itch under my skin that needs to be scratched.

Good grief, I'm turned on. I grapple with my composure that's fraying at the seams. It's useless against the scene spread in front of me. If this isn't a preview of how the man fucks, I'm not sure what is. My inner muscles clench in a desperate craving. I squirm and try to focus on the remote, waiting for him to fall off. It only takes seconds for my rapt focus to return to Brody.

His eyes burn into mine as his actions become more obscene, mimicking sex. He's totally doing this on purpose. I'm suddenly glad he cleared the place out. If other women were watching, I might have to claw their eyeballs out. Look at me getting possessive. Nobody would blame me while his fluid motions rocket my arousal into orgasmic levels.

I crank up the speed and intensity to the maximum. It does nothing. His body continues to follow the spastic maneuvers. There's a decent chance he's attached to the rawhide.

"Is that the best you've got?" He grinds into the next buck.

"Cocky cowboy," I mutter.

"If I didn't know better, I'd think you're trying to get me off." He thrusts forward with passion. "You're gonna have to do better than that, Twinkles."

My fingers smash at the buttons. I'm exerting myself more than he is. This isn't even a challenge for him. Bucky spins this way and that, bouncing erratically. The man barely slips from the center. No matter what maneuvers I try, there's no bucking him off.

I can't watch much longer or I'll combust. Brody's breathing is labored as I slow Bucky to a stop. At least he's somewhat winded after that performance. I refuse to be the only one panting like a dog in heat.

His grin doubles in size as he puts his hat on, flicking the brim. "Did I win?"

"Does that make me the loser?"

"I'd prefer if we both come out on top," he rasps. "What's my prize?"

Would it be too forward if I offered to climb on his lap? Might as well get some use out of this arrangement. The idea holds appeal and I squeeze my legs together. Brody notices as I squirm, his gaze turning molten.

"C'mere, wife." His finger crooks to beckon me. "And bring the remote."

I stumble forward to follow his command before I even realize I'm moving. Inflatable padding surrounds the bull and knocks me more off kilter than I already am. My stride is unsteady, wobbly like my intentions, but I arrive at his side unscathed. His stare is famished and I'm about to be plated as his next meal. I shuffle closer, willingly leading myself to slaughter.

Brody pats his thighs. "Get on."

That's easy for him to say. Our height difference is bigger than our age gap. He vaulted up there without trying, and didn't have an extra hurdle to jump. I'd be scrambling over him in a very unladylike fashion. While wearing a dress, I might add. This might've been my plan but I don't want to make it that easy.

Mama June didn't raise a quitter, though.

I grip the safety strap and bend into a squat. Before I can launch myself upright, Brody cinches an arm around me and hauls my body over his. The abrupt boost stuns me, especially since he plucked me off my booted feet as if I weigh ten pounds. My legs swing in an arch before spreading to prepare for landing. A pleased noise rumbles from him as he gets me situated in the desired position. I'm straddled astride him when I regain my bearings. Just like riding a horse. Backward.

"Took too long," he grumbles as I adjust my seat on him.

"Uh, well… thanks for the lift." The skirt of my dress keeps me modest, but the hardness prodding between my legs is indecent. "This is… interesting?"

That unsatisfied hunger ignites his gaze into green flames. "This what you had in mind?"

I wiggle to test our stability. That earns me a choked groan and his hands clench into fists. The restraint is admirable, but I want him to crumble. My temptation bumps into his dick again and I'm rewarded with a grunt.

"Fuck." Strain flexes his neck as he denies himself more friction. "What do you want from me, wife?"

That's an excellent question. I hit pause while deciding how far this should go. It's doubtful that he'll take anything from me unless I initiate. He already set the scene to get me yearning for him. My husband wants me eager and willing.

The honor of the first move across the line belongs to me. It's difficult to suggest being intimate, especially after the rocky day we've had. I probably shouldn't. Once I do, there's no taking the words back. Instead, I should harness the desire and race out of here. Then I can unleash the tension in private.

Brody lied and deceived me. But this can be about just sex. Why can't we make each other feel good for a change? Just for a little while. Not sure who I'm trying to convince. He's admitted there's more between us, that he's falling for me. Those vulnerable confessions could be another betrayal. It's wasted energy considering I'm already sprawled across his lap, but I can protect my heart.

We can go slow and see what happens. I lift my palm to trace the edge of his jaw, but halt with my courage suspended in midair. He took the reins earlier and put my hand on him. That doesn't mean I'm granted free roam.

"Touch me," he urges.

Heat sizzles through my veins when I do just that. His

coarse stubble prickles my skin when he nuzzles me. A soft exhale breezes from him and his eyelids get heavy. It's such a tender display. I want more, lifting my other palm to drift along his chest. He leans against me while I stroke up his nape and into his hair. The quiet hum that escapes him sounds like relief. It sparks my curiosity.

"When was the last time you let a woman—?"

He silences me with a kiss. "It's just you for me, Twinkles."

A thrill shoots up my spine at his sincere tone. Our eyes lock like many times before. There's nothing blocking me from searching for more secrets. All I find is his vow to try. That's enough for now.

Brody's voice is fresh gravel when he asks, "Do you still see the real me?"

My nod is absolute. "I think you like me, husband."

He smiles into my hand that's cupping his face. "Told you as much."

"Maybe I like you too," I admit on a rushed breath.

"Does that mean I'm not rotten to the core?"

My lips curve into an easy grin. "Desperate for compliments?"

"From you? Always." His thumb brushes along the smattering of freckles on my nose. "You're so beautiful."

"And you're laying it on thick." I shift against him to remind myself where we stand… or sit. This isn't about unconditional devotion unless we're discussing a simultaneous climax.

He grips a handful of my skirt, still not asserting much pressure in any particular direction. "What do you need?"

I swallow his minty taste when he exhales. "I'm not sure."

His lips ghost along the corner of mine. "You are. Tell me."

"Can enemies exchange benefits?" I finally decide to voice that question aloud.

"Is that what we are?"

My shoulders lift and drop, pushing me flush against him. "It's a bit blurry. We're definitely not lovers."

"Yet," he amends.

"Only if there are no expectations or strings attached. I don't need more obligations from you."

His chuckle bounces me against him and I trap a moan. "You can use me for sex, wife. I don't mind."

"Just once?"

He laughs louder. "Whatever you've gotta tell yourself."

Any lingering reservations swerve off course and lust gets behind the wheel. "Okay."

Another pleased sound comes from him as his hand begins wandering under my dress. "Want me to soothe the ache?"

Fire singes my cheeks as I gather the boldness that's required to blurt, "I want you to be the boss."

He stills for a moment before a slow smirk stretches his lips. "That can be arranged."

Talented fingers slip beneath my panties, gliding along my slick heat. The confident touch slips forward and back in a smooth motion. I shudder from the slightest jolt of friction.

Brody rumbles his praise. "Ready and waiting for me."

"Yes," I whimper. "Yes, yes."

My toes curl when he lightly swipes over my clit. I'm already on edge. His performance on this bull was the ultimate foreplay.

"Please," I press.

His stare devours mine while I begin to quake. "My needy wife likes to beg?"

A confusion of denial and acceptance thrashes my head in a wild circle. "This is new for me."

"You know just what to say." His teeth nip at my upturned jaw. "Gonna make you come for being such a good little wife."

Those words spur desire into a gallop. Brody Benson rules over his cowboy kingdom with a dirty mouth and steel-toed boots. Now he reigns over me too.

Pressure builds in my core when he slides a finger into me. After a few shallow pumps, he retreats and sweeps through my sex again. It's a maddening pattern meant to tease pleasure from me. The movements are steady but slow… not nearly enough.

"More," I plead.

"Demanding," he rasps against my throat. "Tell me what you need."

"Keep going. Faster," I wheeze.

At least two fingers thrust into me, and I release a soundless scream.

He croons in approval. "That's more like it. Is this what you wanted, wife?"

A sloppy nod is the only response I can manage. His expert touch is sending me to the peak. This man plays with me like I'm actually his favorite toy. In this instance, I don't mind the comparison. I'm all too willing to let him use me. Pleasure is the name of this game.

Brody sucks and licks along my neck while his hand continues to fuck me. But this feels like worship. Each action is meant to fuel my passion. His fingers scissor, demanding the release to pour out of me. A spasm clenches my empty core and I mewl. I sag into his onslaught, giving him complete control. His thumb swirls over my clit and I shatter.

My palms scramble to grip onto his shoulders while the waves threaten to pull me under. Ripples of warmth flood through me. I grind against him, seeking every ounce of relief. The orgasm seems bottomless and I almost cry from the intensity.

Eventually, the tingles subside and I'm sated for a beat. My bleary gaze finds Brody watching me consume the pleasure. I open my mouth to sing his praises but I'm too breathless.

"My wife is very responsive." He brings his wet fingers to his mouth, sucking my release from the skilled digits. "And delicious."

"Gosh, you're filthy." But I don't look away.

"Just getting started, Twinkles. Take out my cock."

I quirk a brow. "If you're about to demand a blowjob, be warned that I choke on small objects."

He swats my ass. "That sassy mouth. Can't wait to stuff it so full that you gag on me."

"Promises, promises," I taunt.

"Lucky for you, I'd rather fuck your pussy if this is a one and done." His playful tone doesn't match his crude intentions.

But I'm here for it. "Save the bronco and bang a Benson."

"Giddy up." Brody drops his hat on my head.

"I want you inside of me. It's about time we consummate this marriage. Fake or not." The urgency spreading from my lower belly is definitely real.

Desire smolders in his unwavering stare but then dims slightly. "I don't have a condom."

It takes all of two seconds for me to consider the options. "We don't need one."

"Are you sure?"

My fingers get to work on undoing his belt and jeans. "I have an implant, and I'm clean."

He palms my ass, snapping the silk layer keeping us apart. "This will be a first for me."

"Same," I mumble distractedly.

It's a challenge to reach his cock in this position, but I'm a woman on a mission. The end result is well worth the struggle. My jaw drops as his dick stands proud for me to fully appreciate. I don't need a ruler to confirm that this man is extremely well hung.

"Oh, my." There's no disguising the awe in my voice.

"Will my teeny weenie satisfy you, wife?"

I lick my lips while admiring his thick girth. "We should probably find out."

His chuckle is smug, and rightfully so. An unmistakable yank, followed by a rip, discards my underwear. Brody bunches the fabric of my dress in one hand while the other grabs my hip. I'm positioned over his jutting shaft when the last of my restraint demands attention.

"Just for the record, this goes against my better judgment."

"Happy to be the best bad decision you'll ever make." And then he shoves me down on his length.

Shock lodges in my throat and I gasp. My hand whacks his arm to halt his entry. "Slow down. You're too much."

"Takes one to know one, hmm?" Brody gives me a shallow thrust that forces me to accept more of him.

My body struggles to stretch around his intrusion. "That's far enough."

"I don't think so. Just gotta loosen you up more." He snags the remote that's looped around my wrist. "Allow me."

A single tap alerts Bucky to join in the fun. Another click sets his speed to a gentle sway. It's just fast enough to assist our desperation to fit.

"Holy shit," I breathe.

Brody massages my lower back. His length slides in a bit more with each lazy motion from the bull. "Like that?"

I nod and bite my lip. "You're going so deep."

"Take all of me," he rumbles.

For whatever reason, I don't think he's only referring to his impressive endowment.

"Too much," I remind.

"You can do it, wife. Just a bit more." He's determined to make me split in half.

My exhale is thick while I ease myself lower. Almost there. A dull ache spreads, but the slight pinch just encourages me. I widen my legs, sinking more. Brody's hand at the base of my spine guides the careful pace. A final dip snaps us together. We share a relieved breath and slump into each other.

"There we go," he croons softly. "You're incredible."

Emotion stings my eyes, which is completely uncalled

for. It's just so much at once. I tilt my face to avoid knocking him with the brim of his hat. Our lips meet in a kiss that's too tender for what this is supposed to be. But I surrender to the heat of the moment.

We rock to the easy tempo. It's an adjustment to have him inside of me. There's a frenzy brewing but the pleasure is a comforting lull. I'm becoming intoxicated by the steady in and out.

Brody's calloused palms drift across my exposed flesh, awakening a shiver. My nipples harden into stiff peaks. There's suddenly a weight on my chest that's distracting. Through hooded lids, I catch where my husband's focus rests.

"I've been admiring your tits in this dress all day." His gaze is hot on my cleavage.

"Can't say I'm surprised. I have a great pair."

My shoulders roll with purpose, sending the loose sleeves down my arms. Too bad my bra isn't so easy to remove.

Brody doesn't hesitate to unclasp the restrictive band, allowing my breasts to spill free. "Fuck, that's more than a mouthful. Feed them to me."

I thrust forward to shove a nipple past his lips. He tongues the pebbled point before sucking. *Hard.* Electric shocks shoot outward and I tremble in his grasp. His chuckle vibrates through me as an added bonus.

"Don't stop." Panic rattles me when the pressure fizzles. My hands shoot up to cradle his head against me.

Brody detaches from my nipple to give the other equal attention. "Tell me you feel this."

Agreement clenches my inner muscles. "I do."

His groan is gratifying to my unraveling composure. "Whose cock are you riding?"

"Yours, husband."

He presses several kisses against my chest. "Is this real between us?"

I falter, afraid to admit too much. "Give me more."

He pistons his hips. "Every inch is yours, whether you admit it or not."

"How many"—I gasp at his harsh invasion—"inches is that exactly?"

"We can measure when I'm done with you." He increases his speed, timing each stroke to the bull's bucks.

"Harder," I whimper.

"Not gonna last with your bare pussy strangling my dick." Brody clamps my tortured nipple between his teeth. "Not to mention these tits in my face. Damn, you're perfection."

Those semi-sweet words inject a thrill into my bloodstream. I want him to lose control. That's why I begin riding his cock like it's a race to finish. Give me a whip and I'll make us go even faster.

My competitive spirit knocks Brody's hat off my head, allowing me the freedom to really move. His jaw clenches as he tries to hold on. I almost laugh, but he swipes at my clit. The unexpected stimulation throbs in an unrelenting pulse.

Between the mechanical rocking and Brody's fuckery, I'm coaxed to let go. My hips swivel to gain more friction. His motions become jerky as relief nears. We battle for control but it's useless. The push and pull sends us soaring. I squeeze around him just before toppling over the edge. That clench triggers his release and he's tumbling along with me.

A burst of heat rushes in, whisking me away into oblivion. Brody jerks underneath me while he succumbs to his own pleasure. Minutes pass in silence. Only our rapid breathing proves that we survived such an extreme climax.

His soothing touch coasts along my back as awareness returns. I shiver and cuddle closer. In the afterglow, I feel like a blob of jelly.

"You won, Twinkles." His voice is groggy while he shuts off Bucky.

I pry myself off him to admire his relaxed features. "Really?"

Brody presses a kiss to my forehead. "There's not a chance I'm walking straight after that ride."

CHAPTER TWENTY-FIVE

Brody

MY WIFE IS QUIET BESIDE ME WHILE I DRIVE US TO the house. The silence isn't awkward, but it's not reassuring either. What's left unsaid is beginning to sound like regrets.

Paisley appeared properly fucked and satisfied as I carried her out of the bar. Her loopy smile was blissed out. Each breathy sigh told me she's content. But the last seven minutes have provided too much time for me to assume otherwise.

I'm stuck behind the wheel with my own doubt as company. It's not a partner I appreciate or entertain willingly. Lately, and often, these uncertainties hammer into me whenever a certain bundle of sunshine is involved. This woman has a way of twisting me up inside until I barely recognize myself. The reflection in the mirror smirks at my demise, but the warmth spreading through my chest doesn't feel like doom.

A soundless chuckle mimics disbelief. Look at me being

contemplative and shit. She might've gone and actually saved my soul.

Which means there's not a chance in hell I'll ever let her go.

A sideways glance finds her staring out the window. It's not dark yet but the landscape is nothing out of the ordinary. I want her eyes on me. Always.

The palm I have glued to her thigh gives a gentle squeeze, feeding off our connection. "Twinkles?"

Paisley blinks from the stupor. Her gaze shifts to me, soothing the insatiable craving. "Boss?"

My dick twitches reflexively. That nickname has taken on a new meaning. I fight the heat surging under my skin, concentrating on the road ahead.

"Are we still enemies?"

Her plump bottom lip gets caught between her teeth. "What do you think?"

"I'd prefer to be lovers." My hand drifts higher to slip under the hem of her dress.

She clamps her legs shut, trapping my fingers and halting their advance. "We agreed to just once."

"Can we expand the restriction to cover one night instead?"

"Not satisfied?"

My palm roams along her satin skin. "I'll never get enough of you."

Paisley hums, poking her tongue into her cheek to provoke me. "How much sex are we talking about? It's barely seven o'clock. Does this deal end at midnight?"

A noncommittal shrug answers her. "Let's not limit

ourselves more than necessary. At this rate, I have hours to worship you."

"Good grief," she exhales. "I suppose I can be flexible with our nonexistent rules."

"That's my good little wife." A thought occurs to me, swiping at the lust before it clogs my brain. "Are you sore?"

Her thighs clench again and I groan. "Not really. Just sensitive."

My fingers tighten on the steering wheel. "I'll be gentle."

"Or not," she murmurs.

I swerve when my foot slips off the pedal. "Fuck, you can't say shit like that to me when I can't do anything about it."

"Better hurry before I change my mind."

The truck roars when I slam on the gas. Paisley laughs and reaches over to boop my nose. I bite at her, making her squeal louder. Arousal pumps hotter in my blood with each passing mile. It takes entirely too long to reach the gate.

My fingers tremble as I jab at the keypad. The code isn't working, which spurs my irritation to enter it wrong again. "Dammit."

"Did you forget? Or did someone change it?" Her lashes flutter to the beat of her taunting.

I narrow my eyes on her sassy mouth and blindly punch at the buttons. The soft whir of the mechanics clicking into gear signals my success. Paisley huffs at the gloating smirk aimed at her. I blow her a kiss before gunning it toward the garage.

"Offer the man unlimited sex and watch him haul ass," she mutters under her breath.

"Damn straight." I've barely cut the engine before

I'm out and rounding the tailgate. My motivations nearly wrench her door off the hinges.

"What the—?" She's unbuckled and flung over my shoulder before finishing the statement.

"Hang on, wifey." I lightly spank her upturned ass.

"I… can… walk," she sputters.

"This is faster." My jog jostles her in my grip but I'd never let her fall. "Every moment is precious."

"Aww-wwahh." Paisley's croon resembles a hiccup. "How semi-sweet of you, and not a bad view."

I almost trip when she pinches my rear. "Careful, woman. I'm carrying priceless cargo."

Her giggle gets extra bouncy when I climb the porch stairs. My free hand begins tapping at the lock pad. It only takes once and I pump my fist. Just as I'm stepping inside, Dad pushes past me as if waiting for the opportunity to escape.

I turn to watch him flee, swinging Paisley around with the motion. "Where are you going?"

"Bingo at the community center," he calls in return.

"Bingo?"

"Don't say it unless you mean it. They'll fine you for that." Dad wags his finger in jest.

My stunned expression slackens further. "What…? Who…?"

"Your in-laws invited me. Mighty fine folks." He rocks on the soles of his boots. "I'm retired now, and taking time to smell the clover."

"But… how?" I've lost the ability to form a complete sentence.

"Looks like you've got your hands full, son. I'll leave you

to it." Dad tips his hat and begins whistling on his walk to the truck, giving me a wave over his shoulder. "Don't wait up."

My wide eyes watch him leave but there's nothing else to say.

"Um, excuse me?" My wife bucks against me, ready to get on with the fun. "Can you put me down?"

"Not a chance. I'll give you a tour later."

She mutters under her breath about my grumpy ass. "You act like I've never been here before."

"Whatever happened before me doesn't matter. I've got big plans to prove that."

And then I'm back in motion. My boots pound on the steps as I race to the second floor. Paisley grips onto my shirt when I take a corner too tight. Hallways stretch on for what feels like miles. This house is determined to make me work for it.

Relief punches at me when we finally arrive at our suite. The French doors have never been a more welcome sight. I turn the knob, rush forward, and stop dead in my tracks.

"The fuck?"

Paisley struggles against me in an effort to see what's earned my expletive. With a hand braced on the wall, she manages to turn herself enough to get a peek. A gasp tumbles from her parted lips. Laughter soon follows.

"Oh, I'm all moved in. That's convenient."

My shock spans the area in an arc but I still can't believe it. "Everything is…"

"Pink? Yes," she chirps. "That's somewhat of a signature for me."

"I can see that."

This is what a tragic makeover looks like. My domain has been taken hostage by a pastel princess. Bright splashes of her favorite shade litter every surface.

There's a neon rug laid out in front of my black leather chair in the corner. Model horses form lines all over my formerly organized shelves. Rhinestones gleam under the overhead light. My gray drapes are tainted with gauzy fabric. It even smells like sunshine and sugar.

Paisley's sigh is far too pleased. "I love what they've done with the place. Not that I saw it before."

A grunt is the extent of my reply. It's reminiscent of that glitter bomb she sent me. Sparkles stick to everything, never to be bland again. A crooked grin touches my lips. This room is much like myself.

Her giggle is sweet enough to make me momentarily forget about the horrible injustice. "Guess they mixed my things with yours. What do you think about the color scheme?"

"Pretty damn symbolic," I mutter.

I'm a minimalist, which used to be evident by my lack of clutter and belongings. Dark in style. Not to mention clean and simple and straightforward.

Meanwhile, she's splatters of bright sunny hues and radiance spread over every surface. I'd complain about my retinas burning if I didn't halfway love this woman. Fuck, maybe this arrangement isn't too bad.

She doesn't realize how much control she holds over me. Or maybe she does but chooses not to use it. My wife isn't the type to hold a person's weakness over them… unlike me.

But her soft snicker isn't necessary. "Your space is all mine, husband."

If that's how she wants to play it…

My arm bands tighter across her legs. "And you're really stuck with me now, Twinkles."

She stiffens and flops slightly as if trying to retreat. I almost dare her to defy me and run across the estate. The chase would end with her splayed in a very different position.

As if hearing the threat of my hunt, she clears her throat. "Your bedroom is bigger than my entire apartment."

"Which is why you fit right in." I glare at a fuchsia lampshade as if it offends me.

Paisley wiggles in my clutches again. "Isn't this what you wanted?"

Egyptian cotton sheets covered in a frilly blanket? "Beat my expectations once again, wife."

My stride is a purposeful stomp toward the atrocity. She huffs but doesn't complain about her upside-down predicament. At least until I toss her onto the California king.

"Hey!" She immediately flings upright, batting blonde hair from her face. "That's no way to treat priceless cargo."

"Don't get your tits in a twist, Twinkles. I'm about to show you how it feels to be mine. All. Night. Long." I prowl toward her, my rapid pulse throbbing in my cock. "And just to be clear, you'll never want it any other way ever again."

Her gulp is audible. "I want to take a shower."

My forward motion slams to a halt. "Alone?"

"You can join me," she whispers.

That's all I need to hear. My fingers circle her ankle and pull her to the edge of the mattress. Paisley squeals when the abrupt movement lifts her dress. In an upward swoop, I remove the unwanted garment completely. That leaves her in nothing but her bra. The scraps of her ruined underwear are tucked safely in my pocket. A fiery blush almost has her blending into our newly improved background. Her legs cross as if that will contain her modesty, but my wife can't hide from me. This growing obsession could find her in soundless pitch black.

My mouth waters at the sight of her exposed flesh. The urgency to taste her has me rushing to strip bare. I grip the bottom of my shirt and yank. Pearl snaps fly open in a dutiful surrender. A shrug slips the parted fabric off my shoulders, adding it to the discarded pile. Then I'm reaching behind me for the collar of my white tee to wrench the material over my head.

Paisley's eyes pop wide at the slick motions and my naked torso. "Very efficient."

"The faster to fuck you, wife."

Practiced routine undoes my belt, whipping the leather free from the loops. Paisley shivers at the crack splitting through the air like anticipation. Her stare is laser-focused on the bulge in my jeans. I'm harder than a fence post and eager to ditch the confinement.

"Wanna do the honors?"

She's already nodding while scooting toward me. Delicate fingers open the button, sliding the zipper down with careful precision. The gentle touch slides under the elastic waistband of my boxers, shucking off my pants and briefs in one fell swoop.

"Is this for me?" Her breathy tone strokes my dick.

"All yours," I confirm as precum seeps from the tip. "Every inch."

She stretches her hand along my shaft, which doesn't cover the length. "Has to be more than seven."

"Nine last I checked."

"Wow." She sighs while ogling my cock like a foot-long with all the fixings.

My thumb roams the shape of her jaw. "Hungry?"

"I could eat." She smacks her lips, preparing for a meal.

Desperate need tightens my balls and I wrestle the demand to fuck her before fulfilling her request. "Gotta hose you down first."

Baby blues fling to my face. The naughty gleam sparks all sorts of filthy ideas. There's time for that under the spray.

"Up you go." After I've kicked away the shed layers, I heft Paisley in my arms and turn for the bathroom.

She giggles, kicking her feet. "My legs are good for more than spreading."

"This is where you belong." I drop my mouth onto hers, nibbling before licking at the inflicted bite.

"The least I can do is turn on the light." She flips the switch, revealing that her interior design influence spread here as well.

More girly shit is stacked all over the countertop. Pink towels and mats to match. The list goes on. I ignore what looks like a crochet penis proudly displayed in the basket of washcloths.

"Totally worth it," I mumble while setting her down in front of the half wall.

Paisley is busy gawking at the custom shower that occupies a third of the large space. The doorless walk-in is worthy of admiration but the digital controls are the best feature. I only have to tap once for my saved settings to kick on.

"Three rain spouts?" Her eyes bulge at the overhead faucets.

"You just need the one." I stroke a fist over my cock.

She nods obediently while watching me. "Yes, that's all I need."

"Get in," I command with a lift of my chin.

Her fingers fumble to unclasp her bra. I'm mesmerized as her breasts bounce from the cups. Her nipples tighten, begging for my mouth. A quick downward swoop latches me onto one. Paisley squeaks, fingers spearing into my hair. A slight tug at the roots trails down to my dick and I nudge the insistence for more against her. She bows into me on command. I clamp down on her skin before wrenching myself away. If I don't stop, we'll never get clean.

Steam quickly gathers and billows toward us. The center head pours a heavy stream, beckoning to my wife. It's large enough to fit both of us underneath.

Paisley stumbles backward with me hot on her toes. Whatever she sees in my gaze has her reversing faster. I stalk her until the water hits her ass and she jolts. The fact that she's skittish pumps me full of the desire to be in control.

"Am I still the boss?"

"Yes," my wife states automatically.

I duck under the spray and yank her flush against me. Our wet bodies slide together like gentle waves. One of my hands cuffs her wrists behind her back. The other trails along her stomach before palming her breast. She bends back and thrusts into my touch. A pinch to her nipple has her gasping, clutching onto me like she might fall.

"You'll tell me if I do something you don't like." It's not a request.

"Should we use a safe word?" Paisley sounds entirely too excited about that possibility to refuse her.

"Just call me *old man*. I really hate that and I'll stop on principle alone." Then a more desirable outcome sprouts. "Or want to punish you." I release her from the restraint to swat at her ass.

Her freed palms rub along my abs, gliding higher to rest against my neck. "My husband is very dominant."

I turn my head to kiss her outstretched arm. "Does that turn you on?"

"Yes," she purrs. "I haven't explored many kinks, but it's sexy when you're in charge."

"I've never put it to use in the bedroom. Not sure what specific categories I'd fall into."

Paisley laughs, lifting to bite at my chin. "Probably all of them, but we don't need more labels, husband. We can just do what feels right."

That spurs me into action. My mouth fastens onto hers, swallowing a surprised breath. Tongues glide in a lazy caress. Water soaks us from above while heat spreads through me. Insatiable hunger has me pulling her impossibly closer.

She grabs onto my shoulders while I knead her ass. Her mewls spill against my lips as my cock grinds into her. We're slippery and hot hand needy. I consider hoisting her up against the wall to thrust deep, but that can wait.

"Need to wash you." The reminder is just as much for me as it is for her.

My palm blindly grabs a bottle of soap and a fluffy pink loofah. I squirt too much on in my haste. The lather spills over my hands while I begin scrubbing her skin. Paisley stands dutifully, allowing me to bathe every crevice.

"Can I clean you in exchange?" She holds a soapy sponge aloft.

"Only if you get me dirty afterward."

"Of course," she whispers while scrubbing at my chest.

Fire infuses my veins when she pays special attention to my dick. Her palm is slick, grip sliding in quick bursts to tease me. It's enough to draw my balls up tight.

Once we're both covered in suds, I grab the handheld sprayer. The added spout heats the room into a sauna. Bubbles slip down Paisley's curves and pool in the nearest drain. Her skin is flushed, nipples pebbled. I bring the water between her legs and adjust the pressure. She gasps, grabbing onto my wrist. My stare is riveted on hers as I swivel the stream to hit just right. Her mouth drops open on a soft moan.

"Good?"

She bites her bottom lip and steps back to get support from the tiles behind us. I'm quick to follow. We're out of the direct spray, but moisture still clings to us.

Her hips rock against the nozzle. "I might come already."

"Can't have that." I drop the sprayer while lowering to my knees.

Her protest fizzles when I drape her leg over my shoulder. She parts for me like a flower in bloom. I'm all too eager for her nectar to quench my thirst.

"Do you like praise?" I kiss her inner thigh. "Compliments?" A peck to the opposite side. "Romantic sentiments?"

"All of the above," she breathes.

"This pussy is perfect." I spread her folds with my thumbs. "Tight. Pink. Mine."

My exhale drifts across her heat and she trembles. On my next breath, I bury my nose to inhale her sugary aroma. Flattening my tongue, I taste her from pucker to clit. Tangy arousal floods my mouth.

"Fucking delectable," I groan. From this day forward, I only want to drink from her bottomless well.

"Ohhhh, my." Her upper body slumps against the tiles.

"That's right. Just relax, beautiful." One arm cinches around her waist to keep her steady. "I'm gonna take really good care of you."

Paisley's lashes flutter shut and she surrenders to my control. "O-okay."

My lips attach to her clit with expert precision. She jolts from the onslaught. I swipe over the swollen bud, spilling sweetness onto my tongue. Hard suction is met with a spasm and sharp cry.

"Do you feel like my toy now?" I murmur into her slick heat. "Or do I need to play with you more?"

"More," she whimpers. "More."

"I'll never share you, wife."

Paisley quivers. "No, never."

"Just the thought of another man touching you makes me enraged. You're mine." Feral need tightens my grip on her.

"Yours," she parrots.

The acknowledgment thrums through me and doubles my efforts. Jittery hands grasp my hair as an anchor. Her trembles are already starting. That urges me to sink a finger into her pussy. Shallow thrusts rip mewls from her, getting louder when I increase the pace. I add a second digit on the next entry. She hisses, jerking her hips.

That pauses all movement. "Too much?"

Blonde hair flings side to side with her refusal. "Just sensitive. Keep going."

"What the lady wants…"

"She gets…." Her voice trails off into a whimper. "Ohhhh, there. Yes, yes!"

That shout is hoarse, pushing me to lash at her even harder. Her unique flavor is candy melting in my mouth. I work my fingers against the clench of her inner muscles. She's drenching me but I'm still thirsty.

My groan vibrates through both of us. "I'm going to wring you dry and swallow every drop."

"Please," she begs. "I'm almost there."

Paisley's need for relief is directly connected to mine. That thrum beneath my skin pushes me faster. I slide my fingers in and out to the frantic beat of my pulse. Hard suction attacks her clit, feasting without apology. It's a sloppy mess, and I fucking love it.

My methods notch higher to get her to the peak. She squeals and bucks against me. I drag my pinky back to her ass, teasing the puckered rim. That's all it takes for her to gush in my mouth.

Paisley's head lolls against the shower wall as the orgasm washes through her. Limbs twitch while pleasure sweeps in. A thick exhale tapers off into a contented sigh. She's sated and pliant. If I wasn't holding her upright, she'd fall right to her knees.

"Well done, husband." She pats my head with a sloppy

palm. "If you expect me to move anytime soon, you'll need to carry me. I won't fight you."

I gaze up at her, caught in the blinding sunlight she reflects. "Thank you."

She blinks her bleary eyes. "For what?"

"You give me something I haven't had in a long time, if ever."

"A vagina in your face?"

My chuckle bursts free and I nip her skin. "That sassy mouth is trouble."

"Gonna stuff it full?" She pops her lips.

That visual distracts from the strange flutter in my heart. "Wouldn't mind."

Paisley unhitches her knee from my shoulder and tugs me to my feet. Her fingers are quick to cinch around my cock while she sinks to sit on her heels. The insistent demand for relief has me thrusting gently. It's slippery, better than lube. She tightens her grip and uses that slickness to pump faster. Tingles gather across my lower back, spreading warmth and the need to come.

"Shouldn't take long," I grunt.

"What do you like?" She glances up at me from under lowered lashes.

"The sight of you kneeling in front of me while holding my dick."

"Hmmm," she muses. "Is that all?"

My brain short-circuits when she kisses my tip. "Uh-huh."

"Gag me," she exhales against my rigid shaft. "I want to feel you in my throat."

My knees almost buckle and I slap a palm against the tiles. "Fuuuuuuck, Twinkles. Are you sure?"

"Mhmmm." Her tongue swirls around the flared crown before pulling me past her lips.

I'm captivated while she slowly sucks me in. Her cheeks hollow from the effort. Halfway and pressure begins to collect, warning me the end is closer than I'd like.

"Look at my good little wife," I croon. "Mouth stuffed full of me. Gonna choke on that big cock?"

She bobs her head, taking another inch in the process. Her hum of approval benefits both of us. Stars explode across my vision when she takes me deeper. It's getting difficult to hold back. Between her taste lingering on my tongue and her lips stretched wide around me, I won't last much longer.

I clench my hands into fists while leaning forward to brace against the wall. My dick bumps the back of her throat and I feel her gag reflex try to spit me out. But Paisley swallows the urge, along with more of my length. Her eyes were already wet but a stray droplet escapes to trickle down her cheek. It's enough to make me pull back.

Hands slap on my ass to halt the retreat. A feisty glare swings up to punish me. Determination shines bright in those blue depths. Who am I to deny her?

But she struggles to shove me beyond that point. An uncomfortable gurgle sounds when she tries. I wait for her to adjust or quit. Her breathing is harsh and loud, even over the pounding stream beside us. It's a major conflict of interest as I watch her sputter again.

"Relax," I murmur. My palm wraps around her throat, fingers massaging gently. "Go slow."

Her nostrils flare with a heavy exhale. She pushes forward, gulping when my dick nudges the sensitive passage. That's when I slide through her resistance. A shudder ripples through me. So. Tight. Under my hand, her neck bulges from the intrusion. It's too tempting not to press against that strain. Just the slightest bit.

Paisley's stretched lips lift at the corners when she jams the rest of me down her throat. Her rapid breaths puff against my pelvis and I jerk from the sensation. The tension seeps out of her after reaching the accomplishment. My length thickens at the slight change in angle. A steady throb squeezes and suspends me just at the edge. I'm seconds from losing it.

"Gonna come," I warn on a rasp.

Rather than withdraw, my wife drags her tongue along my cock and sucks. As if that's not enough, she cradles my clenched balls in her hand. Her fingers latch on just like my grip on her neck.

"Holy shiiiiiii—" My garbled speech cuts off as my release rushes forward.

I can't think or move as warmth floods me. My eyes roll back in my skull. She's pulling my soul out through my dick and eagerly swallowing. It takes minutes for me to regain clarity. Even then, my vision still swims. I blink at the spots and focus on a solid fact.

"My teeth are numb," I mutter.

Paisley eases me out of her mouth, which is much easier after I came my brains out. Her tongue pokes out to swipe at a droplet clinging to my tip. "Fucking delectable."

My heart kicks into a gallop as she reuses my description

of her taste. I'm a goner for this woman. "What am I going to do with you?"

She taps her swollen lips. "Marry me? Oh, wait." Her smart-ass glances at the rock on her finger. "You already did that."

"Damn, you're incredible." I lift her against me, cinching us in a hug that's long overdue.

"Heard that before." Her voice is muffled as she rubs my back. She shifts to prop her chin on my sternum, gaze searching mine. "What were you going to say before I made you shut me up?"

The lingering effects of the best blowjob in history loosen my lips. "You give me peace, Twinkles. This unfamiliar sense of…" I pause and thump at the pang in my chest. "Rightness. Like I'm finally complete. I hope you'll stay with me much longer than tonight."

"Maybe," she evades. "I'll definitely use you as a pillow after all this sex you've promised."

"Better get to it."

After turning off the shower, I grab two of the robes hanging on a nearby hook. I hold one out and Paisley shrugs on the bulky material. The large size hangs loose on her small frame, but it's good enough to trap warmth. Once mine is fastened around my waist, I scoop her off her feet.

She loops her arms around my neck and relaxes in my hold. "I'll never want to walk again if you keep carrying me."

"Just treating you like the priceless cargo you are."

"It's official. I can get used to this." She nuzzles into me before I drop her on the bed.

"Stay," I command when her stomach grumbles. "I'll get you food."

"Such service." She props herself up. "Don't you need dinner?"

My chuckle is famished as I lick my chops, gaze feasting at the spot between her legs. "Don't worry about me, wife. I'm going to eat you until you're ready for me to fill you up. Over and over."

Paisley's mouth pops open, forming a small circle. "That sounds… acceptable."

"Be warned," I rasp while backing out of the room. "I'm starving, and I won't stop until you beg me."

CHAPTER TWENTY-SIX

Paisley

"We've got it made, sister." Bianca raises her soda to mine.

I stretch from the comfort of my camping chair to tap her can. "Impromptu trips to barrel jackpots are the best. This one has poles too."

"Bonus!" She pumps her fist. "We're gonna bring home some big money."

We're parked at the Shetland County fairgrounds, waiting for our next turn to ride. The sun is shining. Our cooler is packed to last us all day. A gentle breeze chills us under the autumn heat. Four horses are tied to the trailer. Manure and dirt hang heavy in the air. It's a core memory in the making.

"Haven't done this since Mom was alive." Bianca's wide smile fades, hidden in the shadows of grief.

"How are you doing?" It's been too long since I've asked.

"Depends on the day." She sniffles and drops her gaze. "I just miss her."

"Constantly," I murmur. A familiar ache stabs at my chest, reflecting my own sorrow. "You'll always have her close. She's weaved in the best parts of you."

Her nod is fast. "Right."

"It fucking sucks that she's gone," I blurt. The foul word blasts through the heavy weight of despair.

My friend hiccups a laugh and bats at a lone tear. "Gosh, it really fucking does. She was totally fine until she wasn't. I'll never get over that."

My arm loops around her shoulders for moral support. "Is there anything I can do?"

Bianca leans into me, our chairs tipping inward. "You're already doing it."

The knot in my throat doubles. "I'm glad we have each other."

"Couldn't manage without you, babes." She straightens, swiping at her wet lashes.

"And now we're related."

"In name only." Her eyes roll to the cloudless sky before she sobers again. "Has Brody talked about our mom?"

My shoulders shrug deeper into the folding chair. "There have been a few moments where he's brought her up but I didn't want to pry."

"You're probably the only one who can."

I choke on a snort. "Yeah, right."

Bianca squints across the crowded arena grounds, but is focused on the past. "He's different after you started butting heads. Happier. More carefree. I haven't seen him like this since before he got a big boy job at the company. You're changing him, Lee."

"We bring out the worst in each other," I mutter.

"That's not true. Not anymore." Her smile returns. "I think you're really good together. You should give him an actual chance to win you over."

Which reminds me of when her brother asked for the same thing, and why I agreed. "Want to hear something strange?"

"Always."

"While we were on our not-honeymoon, Brody asked me to stay after I found out about some of his lies. He thought an extra night would change my mind."

"Uh-huh, yep." She rolls her wrist. "And then what?"

"While I was deciding what to do, the sky opened up and the sun poked through. Those streaks of light spoke to me. I felt this... presence. Like a message from above." Heat rushes up my neck and I hide from her stunned expression. "It sounds loopy when I say it out loud."

"What? No way." Her slack jaw snaps shut, a thick swallow bobbing her throat. "Gosh, that gets me emotional just hearing it. Mom wants you to love him."

I blink at the sting in my eyes while she fans her watery ones. "Do you actually think so?"

"How can you not?"

The toe of my boot draws circles in the grass. "I dunno, but Brody kind of suggested that your mom brought us together."

Bianca sighs, clasping her palms over her chest. "See? Meant to be."

"He'd had entirely too much champagne at the time."

"Truth serum."

My lips twist to one side. "Our marriage is for his

convenience. Whatever is forming between us was built on deception."

She swats at the excuses. "Meh, it's fine. Do you like him?"

"Maybe." The flutters in my belly betray my feigned nonchalance. "He's semi-sweet when he wants to be."

"Mhmm, I bet. Did you make nice after he kicked us out of The Paddock?"

"That's asking for entirely too much information, sister."

Speaking of too much, a dull ache throbs from my inner muscles whenever I move. The reminder of just how *nice* we made it constantly replays his kinky demands that I eagerly followed. That man ignited flames in my body while bending me to his will. It released this sensual craving that I didn't comprehend previously. I rub at my wrist while a blush blazes across my cheeks, getting me feverish despite the cool wind. Need clenches my belly and taunts me for assuming I could escape his clutches.

Bianca shudders at whatever evidence is painted on my face. "No wonder you were walking funny this morning. But it doesn't explain why you rushed out of the house like your ass was on fire."

I squirm again, spreading another burst of soreness. "We agreed to one night and he didn't let a second go to waste."

She slaps a hand over her eyes. "Don't mind me while I picture you with Riley Green instead of my brother."

"Brody is better," I muse. "Especially in a pair of gray sweats."

"Good grief, don't tell him that. His head will never fit through the barn door again."

Laughter shakes through me. "You're the one who thinks we're meant to be."

"Um, duh. My best friend married my much older brother after he conned her into the arrangement, and now the heavens are blessing your union with vigorous consummation."

I bob my head, digging her summary. "Sounds like a book I'd read."

"Based on your true story starring Riley Green." She wags her brows.

"Fine, let's turn the tables." I'm more than willing to get evicted from the hot seat. "Have you and Colton messed around?"

"He wishes," Bianca is quick to grumble. Her blush tells a different tale.

I poke her in the ribs. "Did you shag him silly?"

"Absolutely not. He's the worst. Ever. I swear his sole purpose is to aggravate me. We're better off as enemies."

"That's vaguely familiar," I ponder. "You might be in trouble, Bee."

"Pretty sure it's the other way around." Her attention snags on something across the field. "That mother trucker. Are we not allowed to have a moment's peace?"

I jolt from her harsh tone, turning to see what's causing the upset. Brody is stalking toward us at a fast clip. Surprise freezes me in place as I take in the state of his appearance. Shirt untucked and jeans half shoved in the tops of his boots, he looks like he got dressed in a hurry. There's no sign of his hat or tightly leashed composure. This isn't the broody billionaire who steps foot off the compound.

His gaze is a frantic beast stolen from the wild and

trapped behind bars with no escape. My pulse leaps when that crazed look burns into me. Am I the cage that confines him? Or the key to unlock the chains?

Without taking my eyes off my husband, I mumble to his sister beside me. "More carefree, huh?"

"Trust me, it's a vast improvement." Bianca doesn't sound the least bit concerned as her brother storms at us like a cyclone.

I lift my brows at his hasty incoming. "What are—?"

The rest of that question becomes a whoosh of shock when he hauls me off the seat in an urgent upheaval. I'm crushed against him and his wall of muscle before the breath returns to my lungs. He inhales my sputter when our mouths collide in a punishing kiss. Thunder pounds in my ears from the thrashing in his chest. A muffled groan parts his lips over mine. Manic hands roam over my body, squeezing too tight. I become lax against him, waving a white flag.

Brody pulls away at my surrender. Our foreheads touch while his gaze searches mine. Tense silence consumes us, his ragged exhales puffing against my face. I'm stunned again when his eyes pinch shut like he's trying to unsee an uncertain horror.

"You're okay." The relief in his voice clenches my heart.

I lift a palm to cradle his scruffy cheek. "Um, yeah? Why wouldn't I be?"

"What if something happened to you?" Anguish drips from his guttural tone.

It's like a punch to my heart. I think of his mom, and how she collapsed suddenly. But that was a rare occurrence. The scar still leaves a haunting mark on those left behind to pick up the pieces. Maybe that's not what's causing his drastic reaction, but I should've considered the possibility.

"I'm okay," I reassure again.

He nods against me, but then his expression steels into unbridled fury. His fingers clutch at the nape of my neck as if tempted to throttle me. "What were you thinking?"

My empathy leaps into the backseat, whistling like she took the wheel prematurely. I rear my head but don't get far with his grip on my nape. "Excuse you?"

"Why did you leave without telling me where you're going?"

"Listen, old man." The name is used on purpose and he stiffens in recognition. I struggle until he releases me to stand on my own feet. "You're not actually the boss of me. I don't answer to you. If I want to go somewhere, I'm going to go. Besides, I left you a note."

Green anger gleams in his gaze. "That scrap of paper said nothing other than you were grateful for the endless orgasms and you'd see me later."

"Nasty." Bianca gags from her front row seat to our shit show.

That has Brody swinging his glare to her. "And you didn't answer my calls."

She blinks innocently. "How does it feel?"

"Real shitty. You took my wife and didn't have the decency to pick up the phone. I've been going out of my mind." He rips at his hair, disheveling the mess even more.

"First of all," his sister cuts into his mental breakdown. "Paisley drove. It was her idea. Screw you and your assumption I snatched her from you very much. Second, we're grown women capable of taking care of ourselves."

"That doesn't mean you disappear without a trace!" he shouts.

My friend inspects her manicure, not bothered by his tone. "Oh, please. You found us safe and sound. Who ratted us out?"

"Nobody in particular. The entire town is in my pocket."

I cluck my tongue. "We've got nowhere to hide, sis."

Which takes a slight edge off Brody's scowl. "That's true. Once I got my shit together, I realized several horses were gone. Your trailer and truck too. It was a process of elimination after that."

"Left entirely too many clues," Bianca mutters.

Brody's wrath narrows on her before swinging to me. That blistering ferocity snuffs out, collapsing in defeat. A wounded noise rips from him as he gathers me back in his arms. He pulls until our chests are flush. Only then does the tension loosen from his muscles. I wrap myself around him, understanding he needs the comfort of my touch. The pained rumble that spills from him guts me. His face dips into the crook of my neck where he breathes me in.

"Please don't do that again," Brody rasps.

My nose buries in his hair, drawing in woodsy spice and an irrational attitude adjustment. "I didn't think you'd care."

"How can you say that?"

"Well, this"—I straighten slightly to gesture at him—"is extremely unexpected."

"*This* is what happens when you've wrecked me beyond repair. I've become unhinged and it's your fault."

The audacity behind his blame steels my spine. "No way, husband."

He nods against me. "This is your consequence. The

only option is to accept it." He cinches me in an unforgiving hold.

I don't bother trying to free myself, but he's not getting out of this either. "I'm not responsible for you acting like a man possessed."

"You are, wife. Only you."

"Totally meant to be," Bianca chimes in.

"Whatever," I lament.

Brody's unwavering stare burns into mine. "How can I convince you?"

"Just take it easy." I pat his chest. "We're barely married beyond name only."

"Am I coming on too strong?"

My fingers lift a pinch of space. "A little, and all of a sudden."

Not that I mind, but I'm not about to fall at his feet. Mama didn't raise me to be weak. Just too much sparkle and the right amount of sass to wrangle this fella.

His grunt echoes my thoughts. "Can't help it, Twinkles. Once I got a taste—"

"La-la-la-la," Bianca blurts and starts singing "Worst Way" by Riley Green.

I laugh at her antics before addressing the grump towering over me. "Okay, I'll compromise and give you a heads-up about my plans. I probably would've texted this morning but—"

"That reminds me. This is yours." A new iPhone is pressed into my palm. "Just arrived. I've already put myself at the top of your favorites."

"Shocking," I laugh. "I'm still not in love with the fact that you bought this for me."

His expression hardens. "You're not paying me back, wife."

"But it's not my money."

"It is, and you'll get used to spending it."

"I'll help," Bianca volunteers.

"Problem solved." He tugs on my belt loop, the flirty move melting me against him. "But before you go on a shopping spree, allow me to make up for this rude interruption."

My smile is effortless. "And how might you do that?"

"Go on a date with me."

"When?"

"Right now," he blurts.

"Show isn't over, husband." I blindly swat at the competition behind me.

"Then I'll wait until you're done."

I stare at him, suspicion narrowing my eyes into a squint. "Why aren't you at the office? Shouldn't you be worrying about making your next billion now that you're in charge?"

"Didn't I already tell you? Owning Benson Farmstead isn't all that matters." Brody clutches my chin between his thumb and forefinger, tilting until our lips meet. "Work can wait. My wife cannot."

CHAPTER TWENTY-SEVEN

Brody

Paisley peruses a rack of shirts, humming absently. "I thought Bianca was going to help me spend your money."

"Changed my mind." I'm shamelessly staring at her while she shimmies to the upbeat song playing in the store. "I'd much rather do the job myself."

Especially after witnessing a nonstop slew of men slobber over her at the fairgrounds. They should've applied to be rodeo clowns considering their cheesy performance. Paisley's obvious indifference is the only reason their kneecaps are intact. When she flashed her wedding ring and proudly pointed at me, I smirked at them like a smug jackass who has everything he wants. If they only knew the threat of bodily harm that was hidden behind the expression.

"Doing okay over there, husband?" Paisley's voice clears the haze of violence from my vision. "You're looking a tad… tense."

I stretch my arms along the back of this uncomfortable sofa. "Are you offering to sit on my face to take the edge off?"

Her complexion reddens into the shade of a tomato. "You did not just say that."

"Need me to repeat myself?"

"No," she rushes to silence me. "And I'm not doing that here."

I lick my lips, getting half hard when she tracks the motion. "Who's going to see, Twinkles?"

"Is that what makes this a hot date?" She gestures around the vacant shop.

"Go look in a mirror and find your answer."

Her blush reignites and she ducks her chin. "You'd love to corner me in a dressing room."

The thought drills a hot spike of arousal into me. "Take your pick. I'll be right behind you."

"Stay where you are. You've already chased everyone away. Again." She sounds disgruntled, but her smile reveals the truth.

My gaze feasts on her. "Don't want to share your attention more than I already do."

And I made that perfectly clear when we stepped inside Cowgirl Charm. The sales-clerk was very willing to close the boutique to give us exclusive access and privacy. After locking the doors, she made herself scarce. It's just the two of us, and Paisley is in her element.

Except she hasn't picked a single thing in the hour we've been here. Her browsing is enthusiastic until she looks at the price. I watch as she grabs a pair of studded jeans, but then flinches at the cost. She moves on and the process repeats.

Little does she realize, I'm keeping track of every glittery thing she admires. And to think I first called her Twinkles as an insult. I snort at the long line of my mistakes where Paisley is concerned. This woman dazzles me with her sparkle—inside and out.

"It's not that bad." My wife pouts at the sequin dress she's holding up. That bottom lip sucks in once she peeks at the tag. "You're right. It's too much."

Just for that comment, she's getting two in each color.

I sit forward, propping my elbows on my knees. "Should we go somewhere else? I'll take you wherever you want to go. Just name it."

"You're becoming quite a smooth talker."

"Does that make you happy?"

She hesitates before nodding. "But you make me happy when you're surly and dirty too."

"Since when?" My mouth is a firm line, but I'm beaming on the inside.

Paisley gestures wildly at our surroundings. "I usually avoid this store because it's too expensive, but you rented it out so I can shop in peace without feeling judged."

My ass is off the cushion in the next second. "Who makes you feel that way?"

She laughs a twinkly tune. "As if I'm going to tell you and your grumpy side. But see?" A pink polished nail points at her wide grin. "Happy."

Another burst of need jets through my veins, pumping me with desires only she can fulfill. I rumble while taking a meaningful step toward her. If she's not ready to leave, I'll drag her behind the curtain for a quickie.

My wife notices the change in me and visibly squirms. "Uh-oh. I've awoken the fiend."

And he's famished. "Are you done here, wife?"

A longing look drifts over the so-called country couture before a sigh slumps her shoulders. "I think I've had my fill. We can go."

"Right after I pay."

The clerk magically reappears as if summoned. "Allow me to assist with that. I'm Monica, by the way. Please let me know if you need anything else while I collect your selection. I'll get a total for you shortly."

She begins gathering the clothes and accessories Paisley quietly admired. There must be a camera somewhere or Monica is too good at her job. My wife gawks at the other woman grabbing several pairs of jeans. Shirts and dresses are next.

Her baby blues widen exponentially as the stacks on the counter grow taller. "What's happening?"

The clerk doesn't pause while explaining, "Mr. Benson gave me explicit instructions to collect the garments you're interested in."

Paisley's jaw drops again. "But this is your entire selection in my size."

Monica's smile is professional. "And we're grateful for your business."

My wife sputters and begins arguing. The other woman doesn't listen, choosing to wisely follow my orders. While those two are preoccupied, my attention wanders out the front window.

I freeze when my gaze lands on Uncle Jimmy across the street. He's talking to a very recognizable loan shark with a reputation more crooked than Main Street. What's worse is the connection this man has to certain unlawful individuals in our community. Unease slithers through me, replacing the comfort my wife provides.

She rests a gentle hand on my arm as if hearing the knots clenching my gut. "Is that your uncle?"

I bob my head while expletives play on a soundless loop.

Paisley narrows her eyes at the sight. "Who is he talking to?"

"You don't want to know."

"Bad news?"

I cup her cheek, smoothing the worried furrow between her brows. "Don't worry about it. Dad will deal with him."

Wouldn't be the first time. Jimmy has an unfortunate tendency of sinking himself in hot water. It's precisely why he could never take ownership of Benson Farmstead. I still wasn't willing to take any chances, which turned out to be my best decision yet.

That's why I turn away from the unsavory scene playing out. Paisley follows my lead, allowing me to guide her to more favorable outcomes. Bags stuffed full of clothes line the floor.

"All set," Monica chirps from behind the register.

My wife attempts to block my path to completing the purchase. "I'm flattered, husband. Truly. But this is too much."

"Not possible. Hope it's becoming clear that I'll never get too much of you."

"Which is why you're showering me with a new wardrobe?"

"All the sparkles and rhinestones your heart desires,

Twinkles." I snatch her hand, lifting our linked fingers to kiss along her knuckles.

She exhales, swaying into my side. "This reminds me of when you bought every stem Sassy had in her shop. You paid off that bartender too. It's a very expensive habit."

My lips roam to her inner wrist, breathing in vanilla and sunshine. "I can afford it."

She rolls her eyes. "Okay, Edward Lewis."

I bristle under an intense explosion of jealousy. "Who the hell is that?"

My wife laughs as if my reaction is amusing. "It's the character Richard Gere plays in *Pretty Woman*."

"Never seen it," I grumble.

"That's a travesty I'll fix immediately. I've actually compared our relationship to theirs on a few occasions."

That narrows my eyes into a glare. "We're one of a kind, wife."

"Yes, of course." She runs a palm along the snaps of my shirt, soothing the feathers she's ruffled. "But our story is somewhat of a Cinderella retelling too."

"Very loosely," I concede begrudgingly.

"Only the main premise. Rags"—she stabs at her chest before pointing at the shopping bags and wiggling the bling on her finger—"to riches. That's what you're doing to me."

"Are you complaining?"

"Probably not enough." Paisley rolls her lips between her teeth. "You shouldn't spend so much money on me. This isn't..."

My stare bores into hers, daring her to claim we're not real. "Finish the sentence."

Her lashes flutter under the weight of my gaze. "This

isn't fake anymore, but it's very new. I feel weird accepting all of these clothes. It must've cost a small fortune."

Which prompts me to tap my phone to the machine. I don't bother glancing at the total and wave off the sales associate's offer for a receipt. Monica grins, dutifully waiting for us to move along. Her stare is unfocused as if she's mentally tallying her commission and trying not to faint.

"Somebody will stop by to collect the bags," I tell her before pressing a palm against my wife's lower back. "We're going to the next boutique. Bronco Bling is expecting us."

Paisley tries to slam on the brakes. "You're not buying me more stuff."

"We both know I can, and will." I dip until my lips brush her ear. "You'll be a good little wife and try everything on for me at home later."

She trembles against my demand. "Okay."

"And you can wear your favorite outfit tomorrow."

She quirks a brow. "Did you make plans for us?"

"I took the liberty of inviting our family over for dinner."

"Our family?" Her stride is slow while we approach the exit.

The early evening chill smacks my face as I open the door for us to leave. "Yes, as in both. Combined. The one big happy variety that we've become."

Paisley naturally cuddles against me to ward off the cold. "Uh-huh, and what's the occasion?"

"Figured it's high time we set the record straight and come clean. No more lies standing in our way."

"Really?" She smiles up at me, but then a thought seems to occur to her. "Would this include Gemma and Ryder?"

I nod. "Already spoke to them."

Her steps falter and my arm tightens around her waist. "What? When?"

"Earlier when I was looking for you."

Paisley's eyes round into saucers. "I haven't told them we got married. Last Gemma heard, you were pressuring me to fake date you."

"They didn't seem shocked by the news. I'm sure your parents talked to them."

She chews on her bottom lip. "I guess."

"Would you prefer to wait?" A bell jingles overhead when I lead us into the shop. Two associates hover nearby, but wait to be acknowledged. "Since you just accepted that this is real between us."

She glowers at my smug comment. "Are you actually asking me?"

My head dips in confirmation. "I'll cancel the chefs if you're not comfortable sitting everyone down yet."

Her eyes blow wide again. "What chefs?"

"The duo I hired. It's a husband-and-wife team, which is fitting. They've earned all sorts of prestigious awards for their food, including a James Beard and Best New Restaurant from *Food & Wine* magazine."

"I don't know what that is," she mumbles.

"It means their food is worthy of your palate. Have you heard of Two Spotted Cows and a Gray Duck? It's an upscale farm-to-table downtown." A grumble rises from my stomach in preparation.

"Oh!" Her gasp drowns out my hunger pangs. "They're viral on TikTok a lot. It looks really fancy."

My flat expression isn't surprised to discover where she

finds news on the latest hot spots. "Kate and Pat own that place. They'll be cooking for us, but only if you agree."

Paisley appears dumbfounded and it takes her several seconds to escape the daze. "How is that possible? Tomorrow is Saturday. Don't they need to be at their restaurant?"

"I made them an offer they couldn't refuse." After cradling her face between my palms, I swoop down to press our lips together.

Her cheeks heat under my touch. "Mhmm, I'm quite familiar with your persuasive tactics."

"Is that a yes?"

"Yes," she breathes against my mouth.

"The starter course will be served at six sharp."

"Do you assume I'll be late?"

"We might be if you don't get to browsing." I tip my head toward the eager employees.

She stiffens against me, just remembering where we are. Her gaze sweeps across the interior of Bronco Bling. "Oh, no. I'm done spending your money."

"You've barely begun, wife." I turn her to the nearest rack and lightly spank her into motion. "My credit card doesn't have a limit."

Paisley whirls back toward me. "Are you serious?"

"Try maxing it out and see."

My twinkly cowgirl is already shaking her head. "Nope, not happening. You've given me too much already."

"Have it your way." I sweep her into my arms before glancing at the sales-clerks. "We'll take one of everything in a size six. Send me a bill."

"Don't you dare. This will not end well for you," my wife mutters.

"Love when that sassy mouth comes out to play." I lean in and nip at her lips. "You're itching to get stuffed, huh?"

Her eyes glaze over, and she sags into my hold. "Yes, boss."

"That was quick." My cock jerks while I carry her to the truck.

"But accepting no limits won't be," Paisley quips.

My wife is determined to test me, and I'm feral for it. "We'll see how you feel after coming to your senses on my tongue or losing them underneath me."

CHAPTER TWENTY-EIGHT

Paisley

K ATE AND PAT—THE CHEFS FROM TWO SPOTTED Cows and a Gray Duck—wait at the head of the table while servers deliver the next course. Mouthwatering aromas waft from the plates, steam rising to tease my taste buds. Before we take a bite, the culinary pair will launch into an explanation of what's in this particular dish. I've learned this is customary during events such as a Benson dinner party hosted by my husband. There's an exclusive menu that they created just for tonight.

It's a rather impressive affair. We're dressed in our Saturday evening best. The men have their hats hanging on the backs of their chairs. Brody hasn't taken his eyes off me or the sequin dress I chose to wear. A thrill rushes through me whenever I catch his fiery stare.

Pat clears his throat once the final plate is set in front of my brother. "What you have in front of you is cider-braised, slow-roasted pork. We've included a salad that features farm-fresh ingredients. Apple, avocado, blue cheese, and radish tossed in a maple vinaigrette."

Several looks of confusion are exchanged between us, especially from my side of the family. We're unfamiliar with such an elaborate presentation. It sounds too fancy for us to eat, much like the three dishes before this.

Who knew caviar went into deviled eggs? Or how pumpkin complements beer cheese soup? Certainly not me. I'm still scratching my head about the hamachi crudo with pickled squash, but it sure was tasty. The confusion has been filling my belly with delicacies I can't afford.

At least until Kate takes her turn to speak.

"You'll notice one more item on your plate," she announces. "As an added indulgence, and a special surprise for Mrs. Benson, we've included a baked five-cheese macaroni with bechamel and toasted breadcrumbs."

I gasp and swing my gaze to Brody. "You asked them to make my favorite?"

"Even had them leave it off the menu to get this reaction." He cups my cheek before giving the couple responsible a cool grin, which is a big gesture coming from him.

"Thank you." My gratitude spreads my lips a bit higher.

The culinary experts bow in unison and disappear into the kitchen. Utensils instantly scrape fine china in a collective wave. Boisterous foodgasms erupt around us, but I'm distracted from digging in just yet.

Brody's palm glides along my thigh under the table. "You'll have to tell me if their version is better than mine."

"That doesn't seem like a fair comparison." Drool is about to spill from my lips just looking at the macaroni.

He squeezes me gently, drifting higher under my dress.

"Don't worry about hurting their feelings. Chefs are used to harsh criticism."

I laugh at this cocky cowboy. "I'll keep that in mind."

My adventurous spirit stabs at the salad first. It's zesty and packs a crisp punch. The dressing is rich but subtle. This is another exquisite mix of ingredients that I wouldn't have thought of myself. I eagerly dive in for more.

The prongs of my fork glide into the pork like it's melted butter. Countless flavors burst across my tongue in a savory wave. I barely trap a moan, my eyes sliding shut in pleasure.

The meat is tender and cooked perfectly. Whatever seasoning they used adds more depth, not that it's needed. My taste buds are dancing for joy.

And last, but certainly not least, I lick my lips while spearing several noodles for consumption. High expectations are stacked against this recreation of a classic, but it doesn't disappoint. An explosion of bold goodness and comfort fills me. The cheesy blend demands appreciation. Delicious bliss spreads from my mouth and I slump against the chair with a wistful sigh.

"Careful," my husband warns. "You're making me jealous of what's sliding down your throat."

I choke on my next forkful. "It's very thick and creamy. You should try it."

"I'd rather watch you eat." His voice is wolfish, jaws ready to snap me in half.

"That's a little creepy." But I blush and focus on my plate before bursting into flames.

Brody rushes through the process of trying a bite of each thing. "Satisfied?"

Desire pools and I gulp. "Far from it."

His gaze is riveted on the pasta sliding past my lips. "What's the verdict?"

"This might be the best meal I've ever had." My gaze cuts to him, catching his conflicted expression. "But I prefer your recipe for the mac and cheese."

He chuckles and our families pause their gluttony. "If you recall, there's nothing soft about me. No need to spare my feelings."

"Your ego might be a bit gooey 'round the edges," I reply. "Especially when trying to get my approval."

His fingers roam between my thighs. "Do you need a reminder of who gets off on praise?"

I clap my knees together, trapping his attempt to rattle me. "Nope. Completely unnecessary."

My husband sits back, his heated stare devouring me whole. His hand moves to a more respectful position considering our company. "That's my good little wife."

"Babes," Bianca murmurs from the corner of her lips.

My body jolts as if shocked by her gentle whisper beside me. "Um, yeah?"

She examines me for several seconds. "I don't want to know what you did to my brother to get us this food, but bravo."

I flush from head to toe, fighting the urge to squirm under Brody's smolder while his sister talks to me. "Thanks, I guess."

"If the portions were any bigger, you'd have to roll me out of here." Dad pats his belly.

A chorus of agreement circles our full group.

Once the plates are cleared, we're informed that dessert will be served shortly. I glance at Brody while my pulse kicks. This seems like an opportune moment to shatter the illusion. Brody tilts his head, allowing me to do the honors. Such a gentleman.

I clasp his hand, linking our fingers in solidarity. "There's something we wanted to talk to you about."

"You're pregnant!" Mom claps in celebratory fashion.

An indignant puff escapes me when I pinch the bridge of my nose. "Not this again."

She pouts. "Does that mean there's no baby?"

"No baby," I confirm. "And there probably won't be."

A sharp grunt from my left has me glancing at Brody. His brows are drawn tight to match his frown. I'm not sure why, but an image of this broody billionaire changing a dirty diaper pops into my mind. It's adorable, and too endearing to resist. I roll my lips between my teeth to trap a laugh.

"Um, okay. Maybe we'll have babies eventually," I amend.

The noise that rumbles from him in response is pleased.

My mom is satisfied with that revision as well. She smiles while twirling her wrist. "What do you have to tell us?"

"Well… uh," I stall and fidget with the tablecloth. "We have a confession."

"It's mostly mine to make," Brody pipes in. His grip on my palm tightens while I gladly hand over the reins. "I needed a wife in order to secure ownership of Benson Farmstead. There was a very recent and bogus contractual obligation put in place before the company could be officially mine."

Dennis clucks his tongue. "Just did what needed to be done."

"And I followed by example," Brody says gruffly. "I convinced Paisley to marry me using… unconventional methods."

Bianca snorts. "Mhmm, and that's just the half of it. He had Colton steal my phone so I couldn't stop him."

He gives her a stern glare. "Thanks, sis."

"Just doing my part." Her smile is gratified.

My dad's stare pins Brody with violent intentions. "What kind of unconventional methods?"

"It wasn't anything bad," I rush to explain. "Well, it was bad, but not that bad."

"Blackmail mostly," my darling husband clarifies. "And I was never going to actually sell Echo."

"Ah," Dennis breathes. "That explains a lot."

Mom appears puzzled. "Paisley wouldn't agree to do something that she wasn't comfortable doing. I'm sure she would've told us if she felt forced into it."

My siblings exchange a glance and I glare at them to keep quiet. Those two have gotten me into a lot of trouble when I've spared them from it.

"I didn't want to disappoint you." My focus shifts between all three parents seated across from me.

Dad silently chews on that for a moment. "You don't love him?"

"I didn't at the time," I mumble.

"But now?" Mom is sitting forward, eager for another modification to this scene.

I gnaw on my inner cheek, sliding a glance to Brody. "Maybe?"

His smirk has me ready to throw caution to the wind. "We've come a long way, Twinkles."

"Pretty quickly," I murmur in return.

"This is super romantic," Gemma croons.

Ryder pulls a face. "The grub is worth sitting through it."

"For what it's worth, I'm glad he buckled me in barbwire." I hold up my ring, which sparkles in the dim lighting. "Our relationship is real and I'm happy."

My husband presses a kiss to my inner wrist, which earns him a unified sigh from the peanut gallery. "You gave me more chances than I deserved."

"It's turning out to be better than the best bad decision I'll ever make." I wink and blow him a kiss.

"Okay, enough of that. Dad?" Bianca turns the spotlight on Dennis. "Don't you have anything else to say?"

He shrugs, scratching at the whiskers on his chin. "Not sure what all the fuss is about. They're crazy 'bout each other. I just gave Brody a nudge in the right direction."

"More like a shove," my husband corrects.

"Okay, fine," the old man concedes. "This might be my fault. I put too much pressure on you."

Brody's scoff smothers the excuse. "That's not the issue, and it never has been."

Dennis exhales a wry chuckle. "I selfishly wanted to see you settled, but my intentions were good. Besides, arrangements like this used to be common practice."

"In ancient history," Bianca huffs.

He waves that away. "Doesn't matter how it started. It's about what you do with the opportunity. Walking away is easy. Sticking around for the fight takes effort. From what I can see"—he points his fork between us—"it's worked out just fine."

And the rest of our meal follows that theme. Dessert is served soon after our parents give us their blessing. Again. We gobble the cranberry upside-down cake like heathens.

An orange glaze and maple whipped cream were the literal icing on top.

When we're about to burst, hugs and warm wishes are exchanged before calling it a night. I hug my parents and siblings, sending them home with plenty of leftovers. Dennis wanders off in the direction of the backyard while Bianca saunters to her prospective personal space of the mansion.

"This might be a silly question," I ponder while Brody escorts me back to the dining room. "Do we have to do the dishes?"

He grunts and shakes his head. "But I'm going to do you on top of them."

"What's that now?"

"Dinner was great, but food is just bland sustenance. I barely taste it. You're the only thing my appetite craves."

That's how I find myself hoisted onto the table in front of his chair. Warmth washes over me when Brody unbuckles his jeans before sitting down. His cock juts upright in obvious excitement. My stomach clenches, still hungry even after that incredible feast.

"Take off your underwear," my husband commands.

"Bossy." I immediately settle into the role while removing the scrap of lace from underneath my dress.

He grabs the discarded bundle from my grip, bringing it to his nose and inhaling deep. "Fuck, you smell like sugar."

I gawk at the filthy act while his eyes burn into mine. "That's dirty, husband."

"You love it," he rasps. "Now lie down and spread your legs."

I do as I'm told, thankful that the place settings have been taken away. My feet slip before gaining a grip on the arms of his chair. Brody flips the hem of my skirt to put me on full display. His voice is rough with the next demand.

"Wider." A rumble spills from him when I allow my thighs to split apart.

Cool air tingles my slick flesh and I shiver. The solid wood beneath me is cold too. That keeps me from spontaneously combusting as fire rushes through my veins. I peek at Brody, admiring the way his forearm flexes while he strokes himself. He's rolled up his sleeves to reveal his ink and ropey veins. The sight fills me with need, eager for release.

My husband doesn't make me wait long. "Feed me your pussy while I fuck my fist."

There's no hesitation from me. I scoot my butt to the edge until I'm holding myself aloft for his taking. My elbows ache from bracing in this position like a serving tray. Brody ducks forward, hooking my knees over his shoulders. His palms cradle my ass and allow me to relax.

A long exhale blows against my parted heat. "Are you wet for me?"

"Yes," I whimper.

His tongue swipes through my center and I jerk from the stimulation. A low groan vibrates my clit. I cry out, curling my fingers over the end of the table to stay grounded.

"Already close," he observes.

It's not a surprise that he can tell. Our relationship might be in the learning phase, but we don't require training wheels for this journey. Natural attraction and chemistry blaze between us. My body speaks to his in a language that's been fluent from the start.

I grind forward when his tongue spears into me. My tentative motions fill me with him in a jerky loop until he licks to my clit. Hard suction pulls the promise of relief closer. My soft mewls beg for more.

His mouth doesn't relent the pressure on my arousal, but there's subtle movements elsewhere. I bobble slightly as he adjusts his grasp, shifting my weight to balance on one hand. Lust fondles me while I imagine his other palm wrapped around his shaft.

"Pinch your nipples," he growls into my sex.

Green desire swirls in his stare as he watches me comply. I scramble to rip my breasts free from the cups of my bra. A sharp sting radiates outward and I repeat the clamping motion. My empty core clenches in silent demand. I'm almost there.

Rapid lashes against my clit douse me in flames and pleasure. My mind swims while I launch over the peak. Spasms attack my limbs, quaking me against the table.

As the convulsions are thrashing through me, Brody stands and guides my legs around his hips. One thrust shoves him inside of me to the hilt. I scream against the added pressure when he bellows his release. Heat consumes me, muscles contracting for every drop of him. We ride the high wrapped together as one. His arms clutch me tighter against him, rapid breathing jostling us in an uneven tempo.

"And that"—he exhales against my throat—"is how we'll end our dinner parties from now on."

My body goes lax in his capable grip. "Won't hear an argument from me."

Brody pulls away slightly to catch my bleary gaze. Green clashes with blue. "Can I carry you to bed?"

I laugh and kick my feet. "As if you even need to ask, husband."

CHAPTER TWENTY-NINE

Brody

PAISLEY MAKES ANOTHER PASS IN FRONT OF MY office door. Her hands are fidgety as if she's juggling something hot. I've given up trying to concentrate on anything other than counting her laps. This is the eleventh sweep she's done. The next will be her last.

"Twinkles," I holler.

She pokes her head inside. "Hi."

The expense reports on my desk are completely forgotten once she's fully in view. Her usual cowgirl attire flatters her curves. It pleases me beyond comprehension to see her in clothes I bought. I love to provide for her, and plan to do so at every available opportunity.

My chair squeaks as I stand to get a better look. "Why are you pacing?"

"I wanted to… um, ask you something." Her nerves fuel mine.

My gut tenses as I motion for her to come closer. "Out with it."

She pauses about halfway and rocks in her boots. "Are you busy?"

"Yes"—I hold up a palm when she begins backing away—"but I'm never too busy for you."

"I thought we could go somewhere, like on a trail ride. It's a beautiful day to be outside. Together." She gulps and wrings her fingers again. "And then we can talk."

"About what?" Consider my suspicion piqued.

"Us? You? Me? The weather?" She laughs, and the tune is a bit breathless.

I narrow my eyes at the missing pieces. That doesn't stop me from telling her, "Okay."

Paisley blinks. "Okay?"

"I love spending time with you, wifey." After shutting down my computer, I saunter to where she's stalled. "Especially for no reason other than to get to know each other better."

"Same."

I gather her hand in mine, leading us to the nearest exit. We step into the sunshine and I tip my head to the sky. She was right about the temperature. Late September can be finicky, but this afternoon is mild. It feels damn good to take advantage before the snow flies.

I have this woman beside me to thank for that.

"One horse? Or two?" My wife squints up at me as we approach the barn.

My fingers clamp against hers. "I wouldn't mind going double with you."

She grabs a halter off a hook near the hitching posts. "Ritzy, Maverick, or Echo?"

"Doesn't make a difference to me. Whichever you choose." But my eyes drift to the buckskin mare.

Paisley's smile is warmer than the rays above while she heads straight for my mom's cherished steed. "Should we go bareback?"

My gaze is glued to her ass as she slips through the fence. "Don't we always?"

Her bottom lip is trapped between her teeth when she glances at me hanging off the boards. "I suppose."

Hinges creak as I open the gate for her to bring Echo out of the pen. "We don't need a saddle. This one will give us a gentle ride."

"Which is actually true, unlike you." Whatever tension she was carrying earlier drifts away with a throaty laugh.

"You're the one always begging for me to go harder, wife."

Her lashes flutter, a blush coloring her cheeks. "Maybe you know me too well already."

"Gonna dig a little deeper. Giddy up."

That prompts her to fling the lead rope over the mare's neck. A quick knot attaches the loose end to the other side of her halter, creating makeshift reins. My brows rise at her confidence in our mount.

"No bridle either?"

"We're throwing caution to the wind." Paisley tosses her head to let a gust thread through her blonde waves.

And her reckless spirit spurs mine, not that there's anything to worry about.

My palm smooths along Echo's golden coat. She might be a barrel racing champion, but she's also trained to be safe and reliable. That's why Mom treated her like a third child. This buckskin can do no wrong.

I ditch my hat so I'm not constantly thumping Paisley with the brim. While using Echo's wither as a handhold, I swing astride the mare's back in a practiced motion. My ass scoots backward to make room for my wife.

Paisley chomps on her bottom lip. "You make everything look sexy, cocky cowboy."

My brows waggle and I extend an arm toward her. "Need a boost?"

"No," she huffs. But her boots remain planted on the ground.

Without hesitation, I lean over and grip the waistband clinging to her rear. A strong tug hauls her up in front of me. Paisley fumbles and squirms before securing her seat. The huff she releases wants to smack me.

"Good quality jeans. Worth every penny." I wedge a palm into her rhinestone pocket and get a grip.

"No limits," my wife mutters while nudging Echo forward.

She lets me hold her like that while steering the mare toward the path between the pastures. I'm tempted to slip in my other hand for additional support. But in truth, it would only serve to cup a butt cheek.

The strain already pinching in my arm demands that I switch position, revealing it's not comfortable for either of us. Instead, my fingers wrap around her hip and pull her tighter against me. We sway in tandem to Echo's slow gait.

"What should we talk about?" My hands wander along her thighs, roaming higher to circle her middle.

Paisley twists slightly to catch my gaze. "Ask me anything. I'm an open book."

Laughter presses my chest flush against her. "Oh, we're playing that game."

"Figured it was time."

"Gonna take turns?" We've been traveling along a two-way street lately, but I fucked up enough to know this could still be one-sided.

But my wife is too forgiving. "It's only fair, husband."

I nuzzle into the crook of her neck, scratching her with my stubble. "What's your favorite pizza topping?"

Her hum is conflicted. "I only get one?"

"Those are the rules."

"Since when do we have those?"

My insatiable hunger for her races upward to palm her breast. "Only when necessary."

She gasps when I squeeze slightly. "Pepperoni."

"Mine too." I glide my fingers down to reclaim a more modest hold on her. We don't have many restrictions, but screwing around on horseback is just plain dumb.

Paisley relaxes into my embrace, trusting Echo to walk straight ahead. "If you could go anywhere in the world, where would you go?"

"Wherever you are."

She exhales a twinkly tune. "What a line."

"Doesn't make it less true." I press a kiss to her slender throat. "If you could go back, would you stay away from me?"

"No," she says without delay.

"You're happy?"

"That's two." Her elbow bumps into my stomach. "Cheater."

A harsh rumble rolls off me to reject the notion. "Never. You're the only one for me, wife."

"Do you love me?" Paisley's voice is soft, the breeze almost carrying away the uncertain tone.

"Yes," I exhale beside her ear.

She shivers and reclines against me. "Since when?"

"Now who isn't playing by the rules?" But my scold is a flimsy barb. "Our honeymoon. There was magic in that cabin."

"The hot tub and boat weren't too shabby either. I could tell something was happening."

That acknowledgement has me tightening my grip. "You felt it?"

Her nod bumps into me. "My heart was warming up to you, but then I found out you'd lied. Again."

I flinch. "Have I redeemed myself?"

"Mostly."

My gut lurches. "Does that mean you love me too?"

Paisley tilts sideways to stamp her mouth onto mine. "Yes."

There's a clench in my chest before the pressure releases. It's like a key turning into a lock to grant entry. I instantly feel lighter. The warm sensation that I've recently tied to comfort begins spreading through me. If I only listened sooner, we could've established this bond at the beginning. But we're here now.

My arms form an unbreakable cinch around her. "Damn, Twinkles. I needed to hear that. It's the most valuable thing anyone has ever said to me."

"I've never been in love before," she admits. "There's a decade and countless experiences separating us. That doesn't mean I'm foolish or take this step lightly. Please don't break my heart, husband."

The request carves a singular priority into the depths of my soul. "This is a first for me too. I'll never give you reason to doubt me again. You're all that matters to me. Now and forever. I want you to depend on me, and trust me completely."

"I already do. You can rely on me too. I'm here for you, whatever you need." Her hand settles over mine.

A drum bangs against my sternum and I inhale a deep breath. "That means a lot. I don't have many people in my inner circle. You're very important to me, wife."

Paisley doesn't respond, at least not right away. A heaviness settles between us. I flex against the forceful friction, angry that it's intruding. That jittery energy returns and she toys with the lead rope in her grip.

"If you ever want to talk about your mom, I'm a really great listener. No pressure," she rushes to add.

And that urgent clarification is my fault. Guilt sits heavy in my gut like a stone. Sunshine still bathes us, but there's a chill in the air. It's not fair for me to expect her to dive tits first when I'm still holding back.

This conversation is long overdue.

"Let's get off over there." I point to the large willow swaying in the breeze.

She guides us in that direction without question. Once we've stopped, I slide off Echo's rump before grabbing my wife. Her dedication shadows me while I tie the horse to a fence post.

A burst of wind kicks fallen leaves across our boots. I settle at the tree's base with the trunk supporting my back. Paisley folds herself onto the ground next to me, but she isn't close enough. My arm curls around her and pulls until she's pressed into my side.

Words gather before scurrying away like bad choices. The air changes, sweeping in a somber mood. There's a ball forming in my throat just from poking at this wound.

A throbbing pushes at the base of my skull and I clench my eyes shut. "I'm not good at this shit, which shouldn't be shocking."

Paisley lifts her gaze to search mine. "You don't have to—"

My kiss steals her voice. "I'm sorry for how I treated you at the funeral."

"Don't apologize about that," she blurts. "I shouldn't have approached you. We were strangers, and I stuck my nose into your grief."

I caress the velvet of her cheek with a bent knuckle. "You were trying to offer condolences. I was just too damn stubborn to accept it. Mom was probably ashamed of me at that point already."

"No, she could never be disappointed in you."

My snort is hollow. "Ever the optimist, Twinkles. I admire that. You've given me reason to believe in selfless compassion."

Her expression brightens. "Really?"

"And every other good quality a person can possess. That's you, wrapped in sparkle and glitter."

Paisley sighs and drapes herself halfway on top of me. "I'll make a romantic out of you yet, husband."

"Don't doubt it for a second." Shit, I'm already a sap for this woman. "In case you didn't notice, I don't open up easily. I've never expressed myself with a wide range of feelings. Until you."

"That semi-sweet side might be earning its full potential," she croons.

"You bring out these visceral reactions. I don't need to bottle it up when you're here." My next exhale is a loud stream. "Ever since my mom died, there's this hole inside of me that just gapes open. I buried myself in work, pushing to make more money. Anything to ignore the pain. It worked in keeping me numb. But what kind of life is that? I have my dad to thank for snapping me out of it. Without his contractual obligation, I would've ignored the greatest gift practically dropped at my feet."

"Don't let Bianca hear you give him all the credit. She put me directly in your path to begin with," Paisley reminds.

"Both of them had an equal influence," I amend.

"And we're grateful."

"Pure sunshine, wife." I drop a kiss on her forehead. "We didn't know each other at the funeral, but I knew your connection to my mom. There was this… animosity building inside of me against you. I was jealous of your relationship with her. Such an effortless attachment that thrives on emotional support. Loyal and fierce and irreplaceable. It's similar to what she shared with Bianca, but I can't hate my sister for it."

"But you could resent me." The pain in her voice cuts me deep.

"Unfairly so," I murmur. "Mom would talk about you,

and I'd tune her out. Fuck, that makes me feel like such an asshole now."

"It's okay." Paisley lifts a palm to cradle my clenched jaw. "We found our way."

The ache in my chest softens into a dull pang. My gaze shifts to the sky as my pulse soars. "I feel her presence a lot."

Paisley focus follows mine. "I do too."

"Yeah?"

"Especially since we've gotten together. I think she approves." She blinks rapidly, shuttering unshed tears.

I hold her left hand in mine, our rings clinking together. "It's the barbwire."

Her nail traces along a strand of my tattoo. "We're buckled and bound and beloved."

A sting burns across the bridge of my nose. "If only she were here to see it."

Another strong gust whips across the open field and my wife shivers. "Maybe she is."

Comfortable silence descends like a warm blanket. I'd originally thought this emotional overload would lead to us making love. That no longer feels right in this moment. A better alternative surfaces, settling deep in my bones.

"Can I just"—I gulp around the lump in my throat and crush her impossibly closer—"hold you for a little while?"

Paisley sniffles while snuggling into me. "I'd love nothing more."

CHAPTER THIRTY

Paisley

"Pssst." That insistent noise tries to barge into my fantasy again.

I swat at the pest before rolling over to get pulled under again. It's such a vivid dream. Brody was just about to—

"Paisley." The low whisper breathes against my ear. "Wake up."

I fling upright off the pillows, the blanket falling to expose my nakedness. "Whuh?"

Bianca slaps a palm over her eyes. "Good grief. Put some clothes on and meet me downstairs. Hurry."

Muscles still snoozing, I tumble out of bed in a disheveled heap. The sheets are tangled around my ankles. That reminds me of how they got there. I sigh, arching in a lazy stretch. But then I remember Bianca's impatience.

Grumbles trip from me as I force myself off the floor. My movements are sluggish while I get dressed. Brody is already gone, most likely holed up in his office. Some mornings, he's still snoring beneath me. Others, like this one, give me the grace to lumber around without disturbing him. A glance in the mirror is a mistake. My fingers begin working on untangling blonde snarls while I make small strides in the right direction.

The instant my hand grips the knob, the door is wrenched open. I pitch forward directly into Bianca. My friend shoves me upright and spins us around. It's all a blur as she hustles me along the hallway.

Drowsiness sits heavy on my eyelids. "I thought you said—"

"No time. Let's go." She grabs my arm and hauls me down the stairs.

"Jeez, Bee. What's the rush?"

"I need you to go somewhere with me." There's a restless urgency in her tone while she shoves me out the door.

My left boot is barely on and I hop across the porch. "Sure, of course."

"But you can't tell Brody. Not until we get back."

I slam on the brakes. "That's a no-go, sis. We're in a really good place now. I won't jeopardize that by running off again."

"This is really important, and we need to go." She motions for me to get moving. "Right now."

Her insistence raises a red flag, flapping in the early breeze. That's when I take notice of the scene she's set. There's a truck idling in the driveway. She's backing toward it, beckoning me to follow. A gooseneck trailer is hitched to the bed. Prickles spread across the back of my neck.

I pin her with a stern stare, hands parked on my hips. "What's going on?"

Tears collect in her unblinking eyes. "I'll explain on the way. There's only so much I can share."

"Are you in trouble?"

"No." But she drops her gaze.

I approach her slowly, gathering her hands in mine. "Spill, Bee. Or I'm not going."

She's wringing her hands to the point that her knuckles are white. "I'm afraid you'll tell Brody, and I was given explicit instructions not to do that."

My stomach sinks to the concrete. "You're freaking me out."

"I'm freaking out! Please," she begs. "Just do this for me. Brody will forgive you."

"I'd rather not give him a reason for needing to," I argue.

Her lips wobble before she traps the bottom one between her teeth. "Text him that we're leaving. Be super vague."

"He'll want to know where we're going."

"Good thing you don't know. That means it's not lying when you can't tell him."

But I still hesitate. "I don't like this."

"Too bad." She opens the passenger side door and sweeps her arm. "Get in."

My knees lock. "I need more information first."

"If you care about Echo, you'll get. In. The. Truck."

A switch is flipped and I instantly respond. I stumble forward after her punctuated demand. My hands tremble as I fling myself onto the seat and buckle up. Bianca does the same, speeding through the motions. Tense silence smothers us while she slams on the gas.

The farmstead becomes a fading dot behind us.

"Echo has been taken," she whispers after several minutes.

My heart lurches. "Taken?"

Her nod is a bobble. "Stolen. Held for ransom. Horse-napped."

I stare out the window but don't see the passing landscape. "Who took her?"

"That's what we're going to find out."

"Holy shit." I grab my phone, thumb poised to request backup.

Bianca blindly smacks it out of my hand. "No."

"But—"

"I won't let them hurt her. Brody isn't allowed to know or they'll do just that."

This is beginning to sound entirely too familiar but in a much more extreme context. "We're supposed to go alone?"

"Yes."

Pulse squeezing my throat, I try to find logic. "This seems… scary."

"The guy who called earlier assured me that there's nothing to fear unless I don't follow their directions."

My blank stare whips toward her. "And you believe him?"

"What's the alternative?"

I rake trembling fingers through my hair, no longer caring about the tangles. "How did this happen?"

"Uncle Jimmy handed her over to them to pay off a debt."

"You better be joking."

"I'm just repeating what I was told," she exhales roughly. Her hands tighten on the wheel. "My uncle is in cahoots with these nincompoops. He's fallen off the wagon again. Worse than before. Dad is going to lose his shit when he finds out."

"What if we don't get the chance to tell him?" This must be related to the bad news Jimmy was talking to the other day.

"They're not going to hurt us. Aren't you listening?"

"You can't be that gullible, Bee." One glance at her bleak expression confirms otherwise. "This is just like the gummy bears."

Bianca's posture slumps. "This creep has my mom's horse. What else was I supposed to do?"

"Tell Brody," I cry. "He'd burn their shady operation to the ground."

She shakes her head, eyes on the road. "I couldn't risk it. He sounded serious, like he won't hesitate to inflict harm for fun."

"And we're driving straight into his trap."

Her gulp is audible and she turns up the radio. "Don't assume the worst."

But as civilization evaporates into rural fields, it's obvious we're in trouble. The address appears to be in the middle of a wooded area. It looks abandoned or undeveloped. There's nobody out here to help even if we yelled. My blood pressure is ready to blow as we crawl along a gravel path.

"There!" Bianca points at a lone building straight ahead.

"I have such a bad feeling about this."

Her hand sneaks along the center console to clutch mine. "We'll be okay."

As she parks, I send a text to Brody. It's basic and bland, but will hopefully soothe his feathers that are certainly ruffled by now. I'd call him if it were up to me. Bianca seems convinced that would end poorly. Unease slithers down my spine and I can only hope we escape this situation unscathed.

Bianca cuts the engine when a man appears in the doorway of the steel structure. His stature suggests we don't delay. A sideways glance reveals that my friend is eager to get this over with. I follow her bold lead, hopping out into the morning chill.

"You made the right choice, Bianca Benson." The guy uncrosses his arms and steps into the sunlight.

It's difficult to stifle a gasp. One glance and I can tell he's bad news, like the type I cross the street to avoid. But this threatening presence is looming directly in front of us.

He's older, probably in his sixties. Age doesn't appear to have slowed him down. Muscles bulge under his Western shirt. There might be a few weapons packed in the mix too.

His expression is flat to match the dead stare in his eyes. It's unsettling in the worst way. I shiver from that hollow glare even though it's not aimed at me. He ignores me completely, focusing entirely on Bianca. It's obvious I'm just here for her sake.

Almost on cue, she shuffles closer to me while addressing him. "Where's Echo?"

He lifts his chin to where the mare is getting loaded in our trailer. "This won't take long. I just needed to get your attention."

"By stealing my horse?"

"Jimmy owed me money. I have something we need to discuss. Opportunity fell in my lap."

"Okay, so…?" My friend rolls her wrist, in possession of some large lady balls for trying to speed this process along.

Without looking at me, the man passes along the message that whatever he has to say is private.

Bianca's smile is the fakest thing I've seen since our spray tans last winter. "Will you go check on Echo while I finish this… friendly chat?"

Uncertainty has me glancing from her to the scary dude and back again. "Are you sure?"

She nods. "I'm fine. Echo needs you more than me."

Which convinces me to do as she says while constantly glancing over my shoulder. My friend stays in my sight as I approach the trailer. Frantic whinnying shrieks from inside. Rapid pawing soon follows. A cramp tightens my gut as I hurry to calm her nerves. She's probably terrified after getting snatched.

I unhook the latch, pulling the thick door open. More hysterical neighs greet me. The upset rattles the metal surrounding us. She's in the front stall and mostly concealed behind the dividers. Routine motions make quick work of getting to her.

"Hey, pretty girl. I've got you." But just as I'm about to pet Echo's neck, she swings her head at me.

And everything goes black.

CHAPTER THIRTY-ONE

Brody

DAD STARES STRAIGHT AHEAD WHILE A FAMILIAR vehicle approaches the gate. "Think they'll come clean?"

"One will," I assure. "The other is more your problem than mine."

We're standing at the bend in the driveway when the women pull in. Paisley's eyes are wide on mine through the windshield. My sister is making a point to look anywhere else.

"You got this?" Dad gestures at the mess that just arrived on our doorstep.

I grunt. "Only one way to find out."

He claps a palm to my shoulder. "Proud of you, son. Your mother would be too."

I clench my eyes shut and give him a nod. "Thanks. That's… nice to hear."

"Nice to hear," my dad echoes on a chuckle. "That wife of yours will make a fine fella outta you yet."

"Wouldn't go that far." But if that's how Paisley wants me, I'll bend to do her bidding.

"You're a good man." Dad smiles before his expressions sobers. "Gonna track down Jimmy and get this sorted."

I was there when he got his call earlier to apologize, but my uncle hung up before we got any valuable information. "Let me know what I can do."

"Enjoy being young, and mostly carefree. It's a fleeting gift." And with that, he ambles off in his bow-legged stride.

Bianca runs into the house before I can grill her. My wife slinks toward me like there's molasses stuck to her soles. She flashes a sugary grin meant to butter me up. I'm about to fall for it until I get a look at her cheek. My knees almost buckle at the sight.

But I'll be no use to her then. I straighten to my full height, ready to raise hell. "What happened?"

She lifts a palm to where there's a dark bruise already forming. "Just a little mishap. Probably looks worse than it is. Didn't stop to ask for ice. Bianca scooped me up and we got the fuck out of Dodge."

"Who did this?" My tone is deceptively quiet.

"She feels really bad, or so I'm told."

Every muscle in my body flexes for a fight. "Don't bull-shit me. Give. Me. His. Name."

"Not he. She," my wife reiterates. "Echo moved too quickly when I approached her in the trailer. Her head swung at me and knocked me out cold. Should've known better considering her agitated state."

My glare narrows on her mottled skin. "Who took her?"

"Some guy." Paisley shudders, going a bit pale.

I pinch the bridge of my nose. "What's his name, wife?"

"He didn't bother introducing himself. Probably doesn't have to," she mumbles absently.

My molars grind. It's more than we got from Jimmy, but there's not much to go on. The list of suspects is short regardless. Only a few are dumb enough to cross me in this town.

Bianca reappears with a bag of frozen peas clutched in her hand. Her motions are stilted while she unloads Echo. The mare whinnies once her hooves touch grass. A chorus of neighs from the herd welcome her home.

"There's something about that horse," I ponder as Bianca approaches with the buckskin. "Seems to get herself wrapped up in drama."

A crease forms between Paisley's brows while she gingerly probes at the shiner marring her cheek. "That's not Echo's fault."

"Still," I grunt. "Maybe it's time I actually got rid of her."

Paisley whirls on me, blue fury sparkling in her eyes. "That's not funny."

"You should take her off my hands."

"What?" Her voice is barely a whisper.

"We want you to have her, sis." Bianca passes the lead rope and peas to my wife.

The mare is quick to flank her as if they're already a team. Paisley's palm trembles when she rubs along the buckskin's nose. She ignores the frozen vegetables completely. Indecision hangs thick in the air like incoming rain.

"I can't accept her." The rejection is weak while she presses the makeshift ice pack to her injury.

"She's meant to be yours," I insist. "Mom would want you to have her."

"No," Paisley blubbers. "That's too much."

"We already decided," Bianca cuts in. "That's why her disappearance was extra upsetting."

"You've talked about this?" Awe is bright in her features.

My sister grins, but the expression wobbles. "It's not like she's going anywhere. I can take her for a spin whenever I want."

Paisley's eyes are glassy. "Really?"

"Well, yeah. But I'm about to have my hands full," Bianca mumbles.

I freeze on the spot. "What's that supposed to mean?"

"You'll find out. Eventually," she evades. "Love what you've done to your room, by the way. Pink is definitely your color. Tah-tah!"

My glare watches her flee the scene. "Bianca is hiding something."

"That's her story to tell," Paisley whispers.

"What do you know?"

"Not much, but I promised." Her shrug is cagey.

"Is she in danger?"

"Ummm…" My wife squints into the distance, choosing to leave me hanging.

"The fuck?"

"She's probably fine."

"Gonna get to the bottom of this." I'm about to stalk after my sister when Paisley's arm hooks mine.

"Hey, old man. Calm down."

I bristle at the name. "Not the time, wife."

"It is. Your sister needs space. If she wants help, I'm sure she'll ask." Her measured reasoning deflates my agitation.

But only slightly. My body is still strung tight. "I don't like this."

"That's exactly what I said, but we made it out okay." She shifts the peas on her face.

"I can't believe that you went with her."

"Wasn't going to until she told me that Echo was at stake. Couldn't let them hurt her." Paisley sways into the horse who nuzzles her in return.

"Your text was shit." Just three short statements that gave me nothing but a crumb of relief.

My wife winces. "That was on purpose. You weren't allowed to know where we were going."

"Why not?"

"The creepy dude gave Bianca specific directions to follow. At least I'm assuming it was him," she says absently.

"What does he look like?"

"I've already said too much." She buttons her lips.

"Too much," I grumble. "You'll never let me forget it."

"Probably not." Paisley sidles closer, fluttering her lashes at me. "But I love you."

"Say it again."

"I." Her lips peck mine. "Love." Another kiss. "You." She slips me some tongue on the last one.

I groan into her mouth. "Fuck, I can't stay mad at you."

My wife pulls away, searching my expression. "Were you actually upset?"

"Nah, but I can pretend to be." My palm molds to her ass and yanks her against me.

Paisley flattens herself on my chest. "And why would I want that?"

"I'll make you beg for mercy," I rasp into her ear.

She mewls and sags into my grasp. "What else, boss?"

"Eat you for every meal."

Her whimper spurs me on. "More."

"Spend the rest of my life making passionate love to you," I breathe against her parted lips. "And then you'll never forget this is real."

Our noses bump when she nods. "Nothing fake between us ever again."

"We'll fix a bunch of shit around the farm. Chase cattle and chickens. Have a couple kids to expand the family." My palm wanders to her flat stomach that I can picture growing round. "Keep convincing you that I'd be lost without your twinkle. Those sparkles will brighten my darkest days."

"And then we'll ride off into the sunset."

"Bareback on one horse," I add.

Her gaze is bleary when she blinks up at me. "I'm very happy that you coerced me into marrying you, husband."

"Best damn decision I never planned to make." My thumb traces the shape of her upturned jaw. "You're stuck with me forever, wife."

Paisley leans into my touch. "No regrets."

"Or limits."

"And so much more than in name only."

"Everything," I rasp before sealing our fate in a kiss.

EPILOGUE

Paisley

Eight months later…

I FEEL BRODY APPROACH ME FROM BEHIND. IT'S AN instinctual awareness that thrums through my body whenever he's close. My lashes flutter shut while I soak in the comfort of his presence, just like a warm hug.

"Mind if I steal my wife for a moment?" His gravelly tone is a shot of hot arousal.

I bite my inner cheek to rein in the urge to squirm. A knowing grin instantly appears on my cousin's lips. Cassidy's husband Drake wears a smirk to match. Gemma and Ryder exchange a glance. The conclusions they're jumping to are less subtle than Lynn Ellen Paige. I brace for embarrassment when my cousin smiles brightly.

"Give yourself more credit, stud. I'm sure it'll take longer than that." Cassidy's wink is aimed at me. "Although, your boobs are boner-inducing in that sweetheart neckline,

Lee. Might only last a few pumps drooling over those voluptuous cans."

I choke on a sip of champagne, shooting her a glare. "Did you seriously just say that?"

"Women spend a fortune to get cleavage like that." She points a manicured nail at my chest.

"And theirs still pale in comparison," my husband rasps.

"Good grief," I mumble and fan at the flames on my face.

"She's right, by the way." Brody's voice drops lower, drifting across my neck to incinerate me completely. "But I'll do my best to make it worth your while."

"Um, what?" The heat is getting to me.

"I'm trying to be discreet," is his response. "Don't want to draw too much attention to our disappearance."

"We'll create a distraction if people start to wonder," Gemma offers.

"Only if it involves that redhead at the bar." My brother wags his brows. "She can cause a disruption under me all night long."

The bubbly I've been drinking is about to make a reappearance. "Oh. My. Gosh. What is happening?"

"We're taking a walk." And then Brody whisks me away from the group.

"Where are we going?"

"Somewhere private." His gaze is locked straight ahead.

Our pace is brisk, impatience tugging me along. My heels make rapid clicks against the wood floor. It's old and original, much like the rest of this building. The owners of Two Spotted Cows and a Gray Duck wanted to restore as much natural charm as possible. Sunlight streams into the restaurant through large bay windows to showcase their success in that endeavor. Stained glass and brick walls speak of days long gone, but it's still modern to fit the posh vibe.

The chatter of our guests fades as we turn a corner and disappear behind an ornate cast iron divider. This leads to the foyer where we met Kate and Pat before thoroughly devouring our tasting menu. There's a much more intimate dining space at the end of the corridor on our left. That's precisely where my husband is taking us.

"Wait." Laughter sputters from me in a disbelieving trail. "You actually want to—?"

"Yes. Badly. It's all I can think about, which is really inconvenient while we're surrounded by family and friends." Shadows swallow us, but antique sconces expose the unmistakable hunger in his gaze.

"I thought you were just messing with them." My focus slides backward into the empty hall.

Brody's fingers clench against the base of my spine. "I'd never joke about something this critical, wife."

The temperature is cool but a fiery rush burns through me. "We can't sneak off, husband. It's our wedding reception."

"Which is exactly why we're doing this." He opens the door, which isn't locked until we're inside.

Low lighting casts the small space in a cozy invitation. I feel that allure beckoning to my husband from between my legs. He's turned me into a fiend.

But there's still hesitation squaring my shoulders. "They'll notice we're gone."

"Better make it quick then." His eyes gleam. "I need to fuck you in that dress, and it can't wait another second. It wasn't an option the first time. Or at least not one that seemed doable. That missed opportunity has haunted me, and I won't let it slip by again."

I'm backing myself into the far corner while he's talking. The round table between us might as well be a taunt. My chest rises and falls rapidly, heaving faster when he begins to stalk forward.

Static energy sparks between us. We aren't touching yet but I feel his intentions between my legs. That throb pulses a frantic beat while I watch him approach.

Brody becomes an imposing force that towers over me. A muscular arm braces on the wall over my head. The backs of his fingers on the other hand brush along my cheek in a gentle caress. That tender touch hitches my breath before I melt into him.

"Have I told you how beautiful you are?" His smolder burns into me with the heat of an inferno.

"Yes, and thank you," I manage to whisper.

"Gonna repeat myself." He dips to drift his lips over mine. "You're so beautiful, wife. Inside and out. The rare kind of beauty that radiates from you and makes me want to deserve your sparkle. Sometimes I don't believe you're real."

I lift a palm to trace the buttons of his dress shirt, up to the undone collar, and then to the heat of his skin. "This is very real, husband."

He shifts closer, allowing me to feel more of him. "What would I do without you?"

The vulnerable edge in his tone shocks me. This isn't what I expected when we came in here, but he loves to keep me guessing.

"You'll never have to find out," I murmur. "We're forever."

My thumb drifts along his jaw. The usual scruff is barely

there now, groomed for the occasion. I want the coarse rasp from the stubble to burn my sensitive flesh.

As if listening, Brody swoops down to bury his face in the crook of my neck. He maps the slope of my throat with his nose. I go boneless in his hold, allowing him to have his way with me. His loud inhale vibrates through me. Something about him smelling me is extremely sexy.

"Mine," he breathes into my skin.

"Yours."

"I've changed my mind."

A shiver pairs with the furrow that creases my brow. "About what?"

"I don't want to fuck you in this dress."

My arousal falters, the warmth dropping to a mild simmer. I laugh to avoid pouting. "Um, okay."

His smirk is a distraction, catching me off guard. "I want to make love to you instead."

"Oh," I sigh.

"But we have to make it fast."

Lust rekindles in my veins and I snap into action. "Are you hard for me, boss?"

"Always."

My gaze lowers to the bulge straining against the seams. "Will you show me?"

"Be a good little wife and do it yourself."

I don't hesitate. Routine and desire compel me to move quickly. My swift motions unbuckle his belt and pants, reaching inside tented cotton for his dick. He's hard and eager in my palm as I give a trial stroke. A grunt puffs from him when I squeeze his shaft.

Brody's hands hover over the bell shape that flares out

from my hips. I lift a leg to wrap around him. That doesn't work with what I'm wearing. He tries to hike up the bottom half of my dress, but the bulk doesn't get past my knees. The mountain of fabric is like a shield against him. He grinds out several foul words while attempting to flatten the fluff again. It rebounds almost instantly.

A fierce scowl scolds my dress. "Why is there so much of it?"

"Too much?" I giggle.

Determination flashes in his gaze. "Never."

"It's a ballgown style. Extra poof and material for structural integrity."

"Won't let it stop me."

And he doesn't. Somehow, the multiple layers of tulle and satin get bundled at my waist to give him access. After he hoists me up against the wall, I'm able to cinch my legs around him. Fingers slide under the elastic of my thong to find me wet and ready. He tugs the scrap of silk to the side before wedging his hips between mine. A tremble writhes through me when his tip nudges at my opening.

Brody pushes into me slowly, forcing me to accept all nine inches in one stroke. My exhale is stilted as I try to relax against the pressure. I should be used to taking his girth by now, but there's still a dull ache whenever he enters me. There's no getting accustomed to a man like Brody Benson. He'll keep me guessing until we're wrinkled and gray.

Our eyes lock in a lover's embrace. There's so much emotion swimming in his bottomless depths. At this moment, he's letting it pour out for me to see. Only me. That gets my body thrumming for more of his. My hands grip onto his shoulders for balance while his hold me against him. Brody's next thrust manages to shove him impossibly deeper. We're joined as one.

"Love you, wife."

"And I love you, husband."

Brody rumples the designer couture beyond repair just to kiss me. Our mouths fuse while his need fuels mine. Heat builds and expands. We move together to chase a fast release.

His tongue slides along my bottom lip. "You look stunning, Mrs. Benson. Lace and luxury looped around your hips. Should've done this much sooner."

"Took a while to plan." Not to mention waiting until everyone could safely attend.

"But we're here now." He punctuates that meaning with a flex of his hip.

I arch against the onslaught, a mewl spilling from me. "Yes, we are."

Brody slips in and out at a leisurely pace. "I have a surprise for you when we're done."

My vision is getting hazy. "Another one?"

"Gonna keep 'em coming."

Tingles erupt from my core. "Not sure I can handle more."

"We're going on our honeymoon."

"Again?"

"The first one didn't count," he rasps into my throat.

I stretch my neck to grant him more room to roam. "Where are you taking me this time?"

"You'll find out soon. We leave at midnight."

And then we're done talking. I'm pinned against the

unforgiving surface behind me by his steely demands. Each glide drags against the clench of my inner muscles. The friction builds until I'm burning with the need for relief. He feels my frantic urgency and shifts his hold. I jolt against him when his thumb finds my clit. His downward palm flattens against my center, fingers split apart to frame where he's spearing into me. That added stimulation is what pushes me over the peak.

A soundless scream rips from me while I convulse against him. Contractions clamp him in a vise, demanding he follows me. His steady tempo fumbles before turning into a pounding rhythm. I'm lost to the spasms of pleasure as he rushes to come along. A final stroke gets him there.

He tenses and lets go. His bellow is muffled against my chest while I cling onto him through the quakes. We ride the orgasmic bliss in silence. Only our uneven breaths dare to break the quiet.

At least until voices carry from the hallway.

Brody lifts his head off me, sweat slicking his brow. "Guess they found us."

My smile is lopsided and sated. "Or they got lost trying."

He presses our foreheads together. "I'll get rid of 'em."

"Eh, don't bother." I hook my arms around his neck. "It's our wedding reception, and we're celebrating."

The next night...

My stare doesn't leave Paisley while she gawks at the penthouse suite. She spins in a slow circle, admiring every

detail of the spacious room. Her appreciation doubles once she catches sight of the enormous bed and shower. It reaches triple status when she gawks at the best view of Broadway Street money can buy. I mentally pat myself on the back for bringing us to Nashville.

"And there's a hot tub," I tell her while striding to the leather sectional that occupies entirely too much real estate. "It's on the rooftop."

"That's a thing?" Her wide eyes fling to the vaulted ceiling.

Warmth spreads through me. Damn, she's adorable. I'll never get tired of witnessing the shock bloom across her features. That's something I gave her. Pride expands my chest and I find myself grinning. If I spend the rest of my days putting that expression on her face, I'll be fulfilled.

"Husband?"

It's only then I realize Paisley has been talking to me. "Hmm?"

"Did you hear me?"

I walk toward her, wrapping my arms around her waist from behind. She's quick to sag against me. My face lowers into the dip between her neck and shoulder. Sunshine and vanilla greet me when I inhale.

"Apologies, wife," I murmur against her fragrant skin. "I was just thinking about how much I love to surprise you."

A contented hum breezes from her. "Is that so?"

"Along with many other things."

She spins in my hold, our gazes colliding. "Such as?"

"How much I love you in general. Now, what were you saying?"

Paisley parks her chin on my sternum, excitement shining in her baby blues. "Let's go in the jacuzzi."

I release her from my hold and step back. "On one condition."

"Which is?" She bites her bottom lip as I begin unbuttoning my Western shirt.

"You have to wear this and nothing else." I pinch the front of my white undershirt.

"Is this some fantasy?"

"Big time. Ever since the cabin." I strip off both top layers and begin undoing my jeans.

After removing her tank top and bra, my wife accepts the tee and tugs it over her head. The hem nearly touches her knees, almost bringing me to mine at the sight. Then she goes and shucks her silky thong, flinging it at me.

I catch the scrap in one hand while ditching my pants. Her panties get tucked in the pocket. She won't be needing any on this trip if I do my job right.

Once we're ready, I yank open the patio door and usher her outside. The summer evening offers a slight chill compared to the heat of the day. Paisley cuddles into my side as I guide her up the short staircase. Our private section of the roof spreads out in front of us.

My wife ignores the intimate layout, heading straight for the lofted whirlpool. It's built into a small deck that grants us an even better view of the busy street below. Steam rises off the surface when we remove the cover. I get the jets going while Paisley steps onto the wood ledge. She moans while sinking into the bubbling water, causing me to falter with the controls.

My mostly naked ass is quick to follow her into the

warmth. I relax into the corner seat until the froth touches my chin. "Damn, that's good."

"Mhmm." Paisley stays where she is, which is opposite of me.

"If you think you're sitting all the way over there, think again."

She rolls her eyes but scoots to where I'm sprawled out. Before she can try cozying up beside me, I haul her onto my lap. A squeak escapes her, but then she molds into a straddled position astride me. Just the way I planned.

The white fabric clings to her skin, exposing her pebbled nipples. I thumb at the points and she jerks against me. The heat rushing through me has nothing to do with the whirlpool. My cock jerks in the confines of my boxers, begging for escape.

Paisley's lips part to say something but she stops. Head tipped to one side, concentration strains her features. "Do you hear that?"

I do, but that would spoil it. "Traffic?"

"It sounds like…" Her voice trails off as she listens closer. "The Rhett Taylor Band."

"Interesting," I muse.

Paisley gasps. "It's totally their song. They're my favorite."

"Did you know they own a bar down there?" I point at the country chaos below us.

"Yeah, but it's just their album name. I'm sure they rarely step foot in Booze and Bad Decisions."

My palms coast along her outer thighs, slipping under my shirt that she's wearing. "Wanna bet?"

Her eyes narrow. "What do you know?"

"They're performing live right now," I reveal.

Her jaw drops. "For real?"

"And they're putting on a private concert for us tomorrow night."

"Shut the front door!"

I chuckle, the jovial noise grinding her into me. "Found out you like them and made it happen. The fact their home base is Nashville felt like a sign. Unlike Riley Green, which was who my sister suggested."

"Forget Riley. I get to meet Rhett, Aiden, Nick, and Lyle. Will their wives be there too?"

"Probably."

She looks star-struck from the thought alone. "There are romance novels based on them. Heather M. Orgeron wrote them to feed our fantasies. All of the guys are pierced and tattooed and very well hung. *Pour Judgment* is a personal obsession."

"Maybe we shouldn't meet the band," I grumble.

"Too late," she quips. "You already spilled the beans. I'm gobbling them up."

My molars grind. "Not helping, wife."

"Fine, I'll chill." Paisley sighs, slumping against me. "There's actually something I wanted to talk to you about."

My heart lurches. "Good or bad?"

"I think it's good, depending on how you feel."

My grip on her tightens. "Tell me."

"Well, uh…" My wife drops her gaze. "I have a doctor's appointment in two weeks."

I grip her chin to reunite our eye contact. "For what?"

"Just an annual exam, but I was thinking I could remove my birth control implant."

I go still and stare at her. This gorgeous woman who

found the patience to deal with me. My pulse thunders while I try to gather enough composure to respond.

"Say something," she whispers.

I lunge to soothe her concern, crushing our mouths together. "Yes."

Paisley blinks at me. "Really?"

"There's little else I want more than getting my baby in your belly. I wasn't sure how long you wanted to wait. You're still really young."

"Not that young," she argues.

"Younger than me and kids change things. Wasn't sure you were ready. I sure as shit didn't want to pressure you."

"You're not." She confirms that with a gentle kiss.

The outlook of our future settles deep in my gut. That uplifting visual clogs my throat. To make matters worse, moisture collects in my eyes. Fuck, I'm going to cry about us trying for a baby. How far the mighty have fallen. Damn glad for it too.

At least until my wife notices.

Her keen focus studies my unraveling grip on my emotions. "What's wrong?"

"Not a thing." I scrub at my eyes.

"Are you—?"

I tip my face to the sky, hiding the evidence. "No, it's the chlorine."

She cups my cheeks, forcing me to reveal my glassy eyes. "You wanna be a daddy?"

I sniffle, gulping at the pressure squeezing me. "Only if you're the mommy."

Paisley rests her forehead on mine and exhales. "That sounds like domestic paradise."

"Our parents will be thrilled," I chuckle.

She nods against me. "We'll never hear the end of it."

Temptation sets my hands into motion along her body again. "How about we start practicing the best positions?"

"Now?"

I cinch my arms tight around her, holding my everything against me. "Never a better time, Twinkles."

That's the end, but I have a free bonus scene or two from *Buckled in Barbwire* HERE.

I also included a little something from the next book. If you're curious about Bianca's private conversation with that strange man after Paisley walks off, turn the page…

BIANCA

The stranger looming in front of me is like a moldy sack of expired produce. I can tell he's rotten from the inside out. His creepy focus watches Paisley walk away before flicking that empty gaze back to me.

"Do you know who I am, Bianca?"

My hip cocks to the side, feigning nonchalance. There's no reason to expose the tremble in my fingers.

"Other than the guy who accepts stolen horses as payment?" I glance at the sky, avoiding his creepy focus. "Not a clue."

The man's flat expression remains devoid of any emotion. "I can see why he likes you."

Meanwhile, he expects a response from me. Too bad. I lift my brows, unwilling to eagerly grab for the carrot.

"Gonna need a favor," he drawls.

"And I'm gonna need to get gone before you ask." I kick it in reverse, keeping him in my sights.

A muscle jumps in his clenched jaw. "I'd wait if I were you."

My boots pause in the gravel. "Why would I?"

"I'd hate to make your life difficult."

"More threats? How innovative." Not sure where this bold attitude is coming from, but I hope it sticks around.

"Just need you to pass along a message. That's all," he states.

"Why don't you do it yourself?"

"He won't listen to me, but I have a feeling you'll get a different result."

"Not sure how that's possible." Any acquaintance of this man's is now an enemy of mine. "My son is quite taken with you."

"I also find that extremely hard to believe."

Something unsettling glints in his eyes. "Colton hasn't mentioned me?"

That blow almost tips me sideways. "Colton is your son?"

"Indeed. We're estranged but I'm hoping to fix that. With your help." That last part isn't a request.

"What do you want him to know?" I hate that my voice shakes.

"The family business needs him. Daddy wants him to come home."

My lips part on a disturbed breath. But then, by some miracle, a loud commotion distracts me from the disturbing news he just threw at me. I whip around to my trailer before he can drop another bomb.

"This conversation isn't over," he bellows.

I don't spare him a backward glance. "It is for me."

Does this get you excited? I sure hope so!
Saddled in Secrets is coming later this year. You can pre-order the e-book HERE.

In the mood for another country romance? Cassidy (Paisley's cousin) has her own book. Take a peek at this excerpt from *Headed for Home*.

Cassidy

Someone knocks into my shoulder, sending my phone flying into the air. The thrill of my saucy read fades with my terror at the unknown fate of my beloved device. But the person who rammed into me snatches the soaring object out of midair.

"Caught it." The masculine voice beams with pride.

I launch to my feet and whirl around to confront him, but immediately freeze. He seems just as shocked to be facing the distant past. Memories resurface while we continue our staring contest. The boy from my teenage fantasies has grown into a man so far out of my league I can't believe he's standing in this crowded coffee shop with me.

Our reunion was bound to happen eventually. It's just probability. There's a few thousand people in this community but it's still small compared to most. Thanks to the very active rumor mill, it's common knowledge that the former professional baseball player resides in Knox Creek. Drake Granger is a name frequently spouted around town, especially by beautiful bombshells in their early twenties with the freedom to dream big. Me on the other hand? I didn't dare to hope that our paths would cross again. Yet here we are.

"Cassidy Brooks," Drake breathes. His expression sobers suddenly. "Is it still Brooks?"

Whatever he says doesn't register. I'm too busy sipping

on the erotic elixir of his voice. The gravelly tone is a promise to provide endless pleasure. A whimper trickles from my parted lips. I blame the lingering effects of the scene I was reading. Or maybe it's his eyes.

Their bottomless shade is the type of blue I could swim in until I forgot my own name. Staring feels mandatory—and is most likely encouraged—which leads me to his full lips surrounded by dark stubble. I lower my gaze to his sculpted muscles barely concealed by a t-shirt, and immediately regret it. Now my fingers practically beg to stroke over those defined edges. And don't even get me started on the colorful tattoos that decorate both of his arms.

Drake looks like he just stepped off the set of a photo shoot advertising seduction while I'm not certain I combed my hair this morning. The wild mane could stop traffic. It's not like I anticipated him literally bumping into me. I inhale deeply, which is another mistake. He smells like the sex I've always dreamed of having.

Holy horse shit, hornball. Get ahold of yourself. He's just a guy.

My reaction is purely based on the fact that I spend most of my days surrounded by farm animals and children. Not to mention the few men I interact with regularly are more weathered than an antique saddle. It's humbling to admit I haven't kept the company of an attractive male since… I can't even remember when I stopped counting.

Drake clears his throat to knock me from that lost cause. An awkward minute has undoubtedly ticked by while I shamefully ogled him. Based on the curve of his smirk, he doesn't seem to mind the attention.

It's only then I recall he had said something that

resembled a question. Maybe. One fact sticks out in the lustful fog my brain has become.

"You remember me?"

The notion is more presumptuous than I'd ever give myself credit for. I haven't seen Drake since we were teenagers. Not only that but he went on to become a famous athlete who's undoubtedly met more people than I can count.

His gaze heats on mine. "As if I'd ever forget my first kiss."

I feel my eyes bulge. "We were just kids."

"Doesn't make it any less meaningful." Drake's blatant interest roves over me. "So?"

"Buttons," I reply automatically.

"What?" His laugh is rich and bolder than the coffee aroma wafting around the cafe.

My cheeks get warm while fellow Bean Me Up patrons send us curious glances. "It's just this silly retort my grandma used to toss out whenever someone used 'so' as a full sentence." I chew on my bottom lip at his look of confusion. "Because you sew buttons on stuff…"

"Ah." He nods.

My face flames hotter. "Told you it was silly."

"I like it." Drake's shrug is carefree. "But what I'd like more is to know if your last name is still Brooks."

"Is that your not-so-subtle way of asking if I'm married?"

"Can you blame me? You look…" His throat works hard to finish the statement. "Better than faded memories."

"Should I take that as a compliment?"

His eyes remain glued on my curvy waist. "Definitely. Why didn't we ever date?"

I squint at him. "Probably because you transferred to Edina before ninth grade."

"Great decision for baseball," he muses. "Not so great for us."

"As if you have any regrets."

He's quiet for a pregnant pause. "Would you believe me if I said I think about you often?"

Flutters erupt in my stomach, but I can't allow myself to get swept away in a long-lost fantasy. "Probably not."

"It's true, Cassidy…"

"Brooks," I relent. "Never been married."

"Me either." Drake's voice is smoother than churned butter.

Keep reading *Headed for Home* today!

How about another enemies to lover romance? I have several to choose from, but enjoy this snippet from *Gent* where a grumpy mechanic butts heads with the sunshine baker who is new in town.

As I push through the double doors, it's like entering a different world. This place typically turns into a dance club on the weekends, but tonight is something else entirely.

What the hell did I get myself into?

On the brightly lit stage, the band belts out a popular country song, and the sound is deafening. Apparently, this show is drawing people in from several towns over. Bodies are packed in the dark room, so many it's impossible to count. Thick smoke and fog coat the air, which makes visibility even harder. I rub the sting from my eyes before pushing toward the bar.

Out of nowhere, a tornado of blonde hair and flailing limbs crashes into me. I reach out to hold her steady as she stumbles again.

"Shit. You okay?" I yell over the racket.

She wobbles in my grip before standing upright and spinning around. Ice floods my veins and everything around us slams to a stop.

Raven.

Fuck. What are the chances?

Pretty damn good considering the size of this town and my shitty luck. Regardless, this seems like a far-fetched stretch. I yank my hands off her smooth skin as if the touch suddenly burns. Another curse flies past my lips as I get a look at her outfit… or lack thereof. The sorry excuse for a dress is just a scrap of red material, a bright signal for trouble. My gut clenches as I glare into her glassy eyes.

"You hounding me, Princess?" I growl in her ear.

"Why do you insist on calling me that?" Raven jerks away, only to topple back into me.

"How much have you had to drink?" Not sure why I'm asking—she's obviously had plenty.

Raven holds up her thumb and pointer finger, indicating only a pinch. She squints at me and tilts her head. "Crazy running into you here. This place is packed."

I roll my eyes. "Yeah, real great. Where are your friends?"

"Why do you care?"

"Because you're alone in a massive crowd. Don't know where you're from, but girls around here tend to travel in packs." And for some stupid reason I don't want her wandering into the wrong hands.

Raven jabs my chest several times. "I'm from here now. And you better get used to it."

I grab her wrist and yank her closer. "Didn't you learn not to poke the bear?"

Her unfocused gaze morphs into blue flames, threatening to incinerate me. "Oooh, big scary furball. I've heard all about you. There's nothing to be afraid of."

I'm sure she's heard all sorts of shit, most of it bull. The urge to shake some sense into her rattles through me. Raven needs to stay the hell away from me. Yet I don't let her go.

She peers down at my grip on her arm. I'm about to snarl something nasty about her getting dirty until she swipes along my torn-up knuckles. The tentative touch is an electric surge to my system.

"What happened to your hand?"

"Fighting."

"With who?"

"Myself."

Raven's focus jumps to my face. "You're hurt. Why'd you do that?"

"Better than breaking someone's nose."

She smirks. "I don't believe you'd actually harm anyone."

I bark out a sharp laugh. "Well, you're dead wrong."

"Does attacking others make you feel better, then?"

Red flickers on the edge of my vision. "You shouldn't test me, Princess."

"Why's that?"

"Because I'm not a nice guy. I won't hesitate to wreck you. That's what gets me off."

She squeaks, "On purpose?"

Frustration is coiling tight, strangling any patience I have remaining. "And I won't be there in the morning to put you back together."

Keep reading *Gent* today!

ACKNOWLEDGEMENTS

Well, hey there. Thanks for reading *Buckled in Barbwire*. It means more than I'll ever be able to explain. I'm able to keep living this author dream thanks to you choosing my book out of the endless options available. I'm crossing my fingers that you loved Paisley and Brody. This is my first cowboy romance, which is long overdue considering I'm a born and raised cowgirl. There will be many more to come if I get my way. Yeehaw!

A huge thanks to my husband for giving me endless inspiration for my broody heroes. He's the grump to my sunshine. My better half. The reason my hopeless romantic heart gallops to a giddy beat. I couldn't do this without him and our sweet kiddos. Love you!

To my work wife for always being there. Whether it's sending me nonsense Reels or telling me this is my best book yet, Heather is my ride or die. Don't eat the gummy bears!

I also need to send warm hugs to Shain, Kate, Allison, Renee, Jackie, and Jodie for all you do. This author gig is a lonely business, but I'm blessed with incredible friends. You make me smile when I need it most.

Thanks to Alex with Infinite Well for editing my words to make them sparkle. Leticia's Editing Service is a must for cleaning up after me and my lingering typos. I appreciate you always squeezing me in!

I need to give a huge shoutout to Kate and Pat. They're an actual married couple who own a restaurant. (It's not actually called Two Spotted Cow and a Gray Duck but never say never!) The dinner party scene wouldn't have been as professionally polished without their advice. That menu was actually custom made just for this book, and I'm ready to eat!

Major thanks to Candi Kane PR for always rockin' the promo for my books. Your services and friendship are invaluable. I appreciate you so much!

The beautiful interiors of my books are thanks to Stacey and Champagne Book Design. She always wows me and makes each one unique. You're stuck with me!

All the love to Harloe's Hotties—my reader group. These are my people. My safe space. The reason I'm excited to write books. Why I push myself to be better. Thank you! Your support is a priceless gift and I'm eternally grateful. Same goes for my review crew, influencers, bookstagrammers, betas, and YOU for picking up this book. You're all the reason I get to continue doing this job. Keep reading for me!

Cheers to book baby number twenty-three. If you loved Buckled in Barbwire, and want to do me a small favor,

please consider leaving a review. Even one sentence helps
new readers find my books.

Thanks for everything, and until next time.
Happy trails!
xx
Harloe

ABOUT THE AUTHOR

Harloe Rae is a *USA Today* & Amazon Top 5 best-selling author. Her passion for writing and reading has taken on a whole new meaning. Each day is an unforgettable adventure.

She's a Minnesota gal with a serious addiction to romance. There's nothing quite like an epic happily ever after. When she's not buried in the writing cave, Harloe can be found hanging with her hubby and kiddos. If the weather permits, she loves being lakeside or out in the country with her horses.

Broody heroes are Harloe's favorite to write. Her romances are swoony and emotional with plenty of heat. All of her books are available on Amazon and Kindle Unlimited.

Stay in the know by subscribing to her newsletter at
bit.ly/HarloesList

Join her reader group, Harloe's Hotties, at
www.facebook.com/groups/harloehotties

Check out her site at www.harloerae.com